Dangerous Hearts

Oleta Smitham

Contents

Chapter 1

What the heck is true love? I was curled up on my couch, shivering but too lazy to get up to get a blanket that was literally inches away from where I was laying. I had been so sure that I knew what true love was. Then again, I had always been good at tricking myself. The tears had stopped flowing a couple hours ago and at the moment, to an outsider, it wouldn't have shown that I had even been crying if not for the pile of empty tissue boxes and toilet paper rolls beside me. Of course, for the first few hours my parents had tried to console me but after more than two hours of relentless sobbing, they got up and left.

At the moment, I was bitterly wondering what that other girl had over me. I definitely wasn't the prettiest and maybe I wasn't the smartest but I was still more than the other girl. What was it about me that had five guys and one dog fleeing? That''s right, one dog. My own dog – Peter – had actually run away. My dog that I had lovingly fed and walked for almost 8 years of my life. I'd even taken it with me during my Spring Break! I really loved that dog, I thought bitterly, tears pricking the edges of my eyes. My eyes flick to my cable box, wincing when I realized that it was already 12AM. Reluctantly, I rolled off of the couch and stood up. My shoulders slumped forward and my hair swished forwards, hitting me with the stench of sweat and tears. I briefly contemplate showering but when my feet take me past my bathroom I decide against it. I lazily push open my bedroom door and grimace when I realize that I had pictures of us hung up all over my room. Instead of tearing them down, I felt anger sweeping through my body. Anger at myself for falling so hard. Anger at him for dumping me the way he did. Anger at me for crying, anger at me for throwing away every-hecking-thing for him, anger at me for being angry at me.

What had happened to the strong girl that everyone was afraid of? What happened to the girl that boys drooled over? What happened to the girl that everyone wanted to be? I had been in the top 5% of my class, had been president of the student council, had been apart of the movement to create a co-ed football team. I had been. I was a has-been. The realization crashed over me like Wildwood waves, pulling me out in the ocean that was soon to be my sadness. Slowly, I shuffled towards my bed, picking up the covers and laying in a fetal position underneath them. I felt tears rolling down my cheeks and maybe the conscious part of me was sad, but the other part of me was numb.

I had changed so much. And for what? For a 6 month relationship that had me crying over some boy that didn't love me back? That never loved me back? I roll onto my other side, pressing my face into the pillow and taking in several deep breaths. People can tell me that it's impossible for me to get over a break up overnight, no matter how strong I am. I was determined to get over him overnight and move on with my life. That very same hour, I had pulled myself out of bed and into the shower. I shaved my legs, tweezed my eyebrows and took care of myself. I changed into a pair of shorts and a hoodie and made my way back to my room with a garbage bag in one hand. I proceeded to pull down every picture that I had of us and put it into the bag. I cleaned my room for the first time in 3 months and made my bed. I walk towards my vanity and take the towel off of my head, letting my damp hair fall to my waist. It was already starting to dry, meaning that it was starting to turn into the curls that he had hated so much. I was going to be fine, right?

Turns out, I wasn't going to be fine. The minute I saw him, a lump formed in my throat and I could feel my face crumpling. To make matters worse, I had stopped in the middle of a crowded hallway, causing a ruckus and bringing his attention to me. I could see a flicker of remorse but it was gone as soon as Lacey, his new girlfriend, came around and wrapped an arm around his waist. Her long, straight blonde hair was shoulder length and styled to perfection. She was slimmer than nearly 75% of the school and she was also shorter than me. I had always been jealous of Lacey but at the same time, I had gotten along with her fine. Even now, even as she covered his mouth with her own, I found no reason to hate her. My shoulders slump forward and I take a deep breath, praying that my cheeks hadn't gotten blotchy and red from nearly crying. Mechanically, I lift both my feet and take awkward steps around the two of them. I'm incredibly awkward with the way I move, considering the fact that I had one foot over the rest of the kids my age. I kept my eyes on the floor but I could still feel everyone's stare at my lowered head. We had been nominated for

Cutest Couple and even Prom King and Queen. I wasn't exactly wildly popular but I was still well-known.

I turn on instinct and push my classroom door open, trying to ignore the heat of the stares from the kids in my classroom. I shuffle to the back of the room and plop myself down on a seat that I wouldn't have normally sat in. When I looked up, I saw several heads turn around and whispers started up subsequently.

"Heard he dumped her for Lacey."

"Heard that she cheated on him...what a whore."

"Alice told me that she wanted to get married to him and run away to Paris or something."

"Someone said that she's a heroin addict – that's why he broke up with her."

Instantly, the tears evaporate and I sit up taller and clear my throat. The whispers stop and I can see several peoples' necks getting red. My eyes meet with the Ms. Grie, whose eyes were crinkled with sympathy. I held back the impulse to huff and sat back in my seat. The door opens and everyone's head swivels toward it. It was always extremely funny when Andrew walked into a room. Someone always gasped or blushed and some girls I knew even fainted. Ms. Grie's cheeks flush pink and I snort loudly. Andrew's gaze flickered towards me and his eyebrows come together, crinkling. "What are you doing in my seat?" He asks calmly, one eyebrow raising slowly. I feel blood rushing to my face and spreading towards the tip of my ears. I wince, embarrassed that I was blushing at all. "I'm sitting." I say, praying to every kind of god that my voice wouldn't crack. His eyebrow is now back in position and I find myself admiring the beauty of his face.

He has that 50s kind of gang member hairstyle, coiffed and perfect. The girls all doted on him and I heard that someone had made him a fan blog. His eyes were the clearest blue in our county and long, thick eyelashes framed them. He had the smoothest skin of anyone around and his lips were perfectly pouted. Totally kissable. His jawline was defined and manly. When I finally realize that I'm staring at him, I snap back to reality and notice that his lips had curved up into a smirk. Of course, today I had decided to bum it and wear a hoodie and jeans with my hair up in a ponytail. He comes closer to me and I realize that he was probably expecting me to get up and scurry across the room. I stayed put, but I could still feel the heat rush back into my face.

Ms. Grie clears her throat and I remember that we were in a classroom. Everyone had their heads turned toward us but I genuinely didn't give a flying fuck. "That break up certainly made you grow some balls there!" Someone yells proudly. I shrug and Andrew slides into the chair next to mines, his face stoic. The lesson starts and by the end, the tension had lessened. The bell rings and I get up quickly – too quickly. I trip over the leg of my chair and find myself thisclose to smacking my head on the edge of the lab table. A warm hand wraps around my stomach seconds before I smack my head and I feel heat rushing towards where his arm was. He sets me upright and turned towards him, and I can see a smirk on his face. I realized that I had to look up to see his entire face and I realized that he was actually freakishly tall...like me. "If you wanted my attention, you could've just asked for it, you know." He winks and lets go of my waist, throwing a wicked grin over his shoulder as he walked out the door.

I stand there awkwardly, my cheeks still heated. The students beginning to fill the room stared at me quizzically and I awkwardly cleared my throat and finished packing up my things. I keep my eyes on the floor as I scurry out of the room, thanking whoever programmed my schedule that I had lunch this period. I mindlessly round a corner and grimace at the sound of giggles and bodies slamming against locker doors fill the empty hallway. I look up, my lips already pursed but the sight of the two culprits had tears filling my eyes. "Lacey," the familiar voice breathes huskily. I watch as Lacey kisses the neck that used to bend to kiss me. She has her tanned arms wrapped around his waist and she pulls back, smiling up at him goofily. Remember when you guys looked like that? A voice inside of me whispers, which initiates a wave of sadness that washes through my body. He smiles at her, all teeth, and I wince, remembering being in that exact position just two weeks ago. He leans down pressing a kiss against her still-smiling lips.

A warm hand wraps around my wrist and pulls me to the side of the hallway that blocked my view of Lacey and my ex-boyfriend. Belatedly, I realize that there were tears rolling down my face and I quickly swipe at them, embarrassed. "That's kind of perverted," a familiar husky voice says, snapping me out of my reverie. "watching them like that." My eyes raise and land on a figure with broad shoulders and beautiful light brown coiffed hair. My cheeks flame and I open and close my mouth awkwardly, unable to speak to the god that was in front of me. "Are you okay?" Andrew says softly, searching my face with his clear blue eyes. I shrug casually, "Why wouldn't I be?" His eyebrow raises, "You weren't crying just now?" I shrug again and mutter, "Yeah, sometimes my eyes water like crazy. It be like that." The side of his lip hitches up and he stands there, staring at me. "'It be like that.'" He says, sounding like he was trying to hold back a chuckle. Boldly, I raise both of my eyebrows and purse my lips. "Yeah, it does be like that sometimes." He takes a step towards me and slings a heavy arm over my shoulders. "You're going to be alright." I sigh, "Yeah, that's what they all say."

The rest of the week is uneventful and I find myself driving home in a daze everyday after school. Everyday, the sound of their kisses echoing through the empty hallway reverberates in my mind, and bile still rises in my throat at the thought of Lacey's arms wrapped around him. What had I done wrong? I had been at every one of his games, had never flaked on one of his dates, had bought him presents for his birthday and Christmas. I laugh bitterly. That's what I was; dependable. I'd always be dependable – even when I didn't mean to be, or even want to be, I was there and in return, I got empty buckets of ice cream and a ridiculous credit card bill from going on frozen yogurt runs at 2AM. But since when was being dependable a bad thing? Last I heard, someone was always complaining about how no one was ever there for them and here I was, always there. I'd been there for him through everything and -

Stop. The more I thought about him and everything I had done for him, the angrier I got and I'm not an angry person. Anger left me feeling disgusting – like a humid 90 degree day. I often embraced being sad or even numb more than I did with anger. I hated the way that it had me acting; I never thought straight. I wasn't practical, and more than once, he had said that I looked really ugly when I was mad. Memories of us flit through my mind, each memory leaving me more and more disgusted with myself and that relationship. I remember all the times that he had called me ugly, stupid or annoying. I was sort of kind of in an abusive relationship when I was with him, and maybe that's dramatic, but deciding that it was an abusive relationship had me realizing how grateful I was that it was over. And it'd taken a week for me to realize.

CHAPTER 2

I roll over onto my back, reaching for my phone and dialed the number that I hadn't dialed for a week. "Tessa?" I ask, surprised that she had picked up. Tessa is perpetually partying; even when we had sleepovers with our other friends, she was partying. To be honest, this brought us even closer. I tended to attract people that weren't dependable. In all my friendships, I'd always be the rock that you could lean on in a storm. "Lena, what a surprise!" She says sarcastically with a laugh at the end. I wince, "I'm sorry, Tess. It was a hard -" "I heard about Lacey. You know, Lena, I'd always said that he was a bad guy - from the first time that he had," Tessa pauses, fumbling for a less obscene word, "fucked you over, I'd told you that he was a bad guy. Anyways, what's up? Make it fast, too, I have an insane hangover." Hesitantly, I answer her, "I kind of wanted to go to a party -" Tessa cuts me off by emitting a high-pitched squeal. "I'm seriously so glad that you called - you know that guy, right? Like 6 feet, broad shoulders, with the hair? You know how he never, ever is spotted partying? Elena says that he's coming down to Broderick's tonight," "Tessa..." "and Broderick's parties are radical. We're totally going. I was so totally afraid of going alone," "No you weren't." "I totally was! Pick me up?" I sigh and hang up, regretting my decision to ask Tessa about a party.

Tessa's house is pitch black - mostly because her parents are almost always out of town. I honk my horn and her door immediately opens. Tessa, like Lacey, is blessed with stick-straight blonde hair and an insanely skinny body. Tonight, she's wearing a black dress that dips all the way to the small of her back and strappy teal sandals. She skips down her driveway and by the time she's in my passenger seat she looks like she's about to explode with energy. "Are you excited? I'm pretty excited, A, because that total hottie, Andrew, is going to be there and, B, because you're finally coming to party with me - we're going to get totally wasted..." Tessa spends the next 10 minutes chattering mindlessly about how excited she was and I found myself already tired by the time I pulled into Broderick's driveway.

Loud. I think, annoyed. Tessa is practically shaking from excitement and she begins to briskly walk towards his house, leaving me behind. When she reaches the door, she turns around and flashes me a bright smile before opening the door and walking in. I sigh, cursing the muggy weather. I pull at the maxi dress that I had pulled on earlier that night in an attempt to cover my skin. I had also curled my hair so that it fell down my back gracefully instead of in a messy tangle.

"Hey! You! Take a drink!" I look up, wincing at the sight of a completely wasted boy trying to pass me a cup. "You're totally hot - wait, aren't you Stephen's ex? You know, like, he used to have pictures of you in hissssss locker." He slurs, his eyes comically wide.

"You're like really hot and I'm n - not drunk of anything, so, it's not beer-goggles." He chuckles, and maybe if he was sober I could've considered it hot, but he was basically just blowing his rancid breath into my face. "Take the drink - maybe you'll stop being as frigid as Stephen said you are if you take a drink." I calmly shake my head, "I don't drink." The boy snorts and steps closer, stumbling over his own feet. "Just take the drink," he says, "it's totally great." My lips press together in a thin line and I feel my face twisting with annoyance. "I don't drink." He steps closer and I step back, fear causing goosebumps to rise on my skin. I was outside, alone with a drunk boy, and the only people around were completely smashed. He pushes his face closer to mine and I flinch, "Take the fucking drink!" He growls, angry. I wince and push at him, angry. "Fuck you!" I say, slapping him across the face, ignoring the sting and instead focusing on the fact that his face with clouding up with rage. "You're a fucking bitch - no wonder Stephen broke up with you," He sneers, spittle coming out of his mouth. "yeah, and it fucking makes sense that he cheated on you with Lacey. She's a better romp in bed anyways." He shoves me, my shoulder making bitter contact with the rough tree bark.

Tears prick at the edges of my eyes, and with shaking hands, I wipe them away. Of course, like a regular teenaged girl, rejection coursed through my body and left the bitter taste of "not-good-enough" and "never-gonna-be-enough" in my mouth. And then I straighten up, angry. He had cheated on me and he broke up with me to be with some girl that I had spent so long trying to get along with. And, now, I'm finally realizing that I need to move on. No more skulking and moping.

I step away from the tree, my hands shaking and my eyes fall on the familiar broad-shouldered boy that had stopped me from falling earlier that day. He turns his head as if he knew that I was staring and our eyes met. His face is expressionless and I don't think he recognized me - at least I didn't think he recognized me until he started walking in my direction. Should I run? Was I supposed to stand there or meet him halfway? What if he's not even coming in my way? I was really, truly rusty. At least with Stephen I knew exactly what he was going to do when he was going to do it and maybe it's because he's a stranger but Andrew...

Is right in front of me.

"Hey. Lena, right?"

I stare at him, my mouth opening and closing. I shift on my feet awkwardly, not sure what to say. "You can just wave if I'm too stunningly handsome for you to reply back." He says, smirking. My mouth snaps shut and I wave at him awkwardly. "So what are you doing out here?" I shake my head and my shoulders rise and fall awkwardly. "You're really not gonna talk?" "I don't know what to say." I say curtly. "Do you want to go in?" I shake my head no. "I drove somewhere here tonight and I should stay but I'm sure she'll find a ride home." I say, laughing bitterly. Andrew's face still has that impossibly attractive smirk pasted on his face. "So what do you want to do?"

That night, Andrew and I drove around the not-so-sunny state of New York, the top of his car down. With the wind rustling his hair and messing it up, I had to admit that he looked just as normal as the rest of us. Maybe that's who he is; an insanely hot boy that had more secrets than the American government that was just normal and just wanted to be normal.

"So, Lena. Is that your full name?" He asks, his eyes still on the road. "No, it's actually Elena. But I like Lena better." "I don't. I think Elena is...it suits you." I blink. No one thought that Elena suited me. They said that it was too proper, too prissy and too cold. I'd always preferred Lena because that was a name that my parents didn't call me. One of the only names that that they didn't call me. "It's...cold but warm and beautiful at the same time." He says honestly, still not looking at me. I turn to look at him and note that his jaw is clenched. "You don't even know me."

He chuckles and finally turns towards me, his eyes dropping onto my lips.

And, I'd managed to drag him into the lake with me and we almost skinny dipped - we would've had I not pushed him in fully clothed.

After that night with him, things had changed between us. If we were a TV show, they'd call it an undeniable sexual connection. Reviewers would say that we had great chemistry and that our sexual tension was off the charts. Or maybe it was a one sided thing. I may be 'sizzling' to others but to me, I was just plain.

We hadn't had a conversation since we'd driven around New York together. I'd resorted to watching him in class and lately, he'd been different - not that much different but I'd started to notice the little things that changed. Like, for example, the fact that he was usually in a trance when I saw him in class. He'd sit there and while Ms. Grie called attendance, it'd take me nudging him for him to actually raise his hand. And he also had gotten more clumsy. I had thought that I was the only person that was able to trip over air but, after seeing Andrew stumble several times on the way out of the classroom, I quickly learned that I'm not. Besides that, I noticed that he was coming into class early and looking ruffled. He was suddenly the first student to show up and the one that looked like they needed at least four more hours of sleep.

"What are you looking at?"

I choke on my own breath and my knee jerks, banging against the underside of my desk and attracting the attention of at least half of my class. I cough awkwardly and avert my attention to my notebook, which was blank.

"I asked you a question." Andrew whispers, which, if I might add, shouldn't even count as a whisper because it was mostly just the rumble of his voice. "Uh," I start awkwardly, my eyes still on my notebook, "I wasn't looking at you, if that's what you think - I was just...the window..."

"Is on that side of the room, not my side." "R - Right. I was just looking for the window." I look up to find him watching me, his perfect eyebrow raised and traces of his usual smirk on his lips. He chuckles quietly before turning back to the front of the room, his right hand picking up his pen to write notes.

On the way out of the class, I notice that Andrew isn't stumbling and that he knows exactly what he was going to do. Somewhere deep down inside of me, I knew that he had fixed whatever was going on with him and, for some reason, that gave me just a little bit of peace.

I sigh, dropping my keys on the kitchen counter and snatching up the usual note that was placed on the refrigerator door. Occasionally, I'd feel pangs of anger when I realized that my parents had gone off on cruises without me and left me at home alone with 50 dollars and my own savings to feed myself for two weeks while they were gone. I crumple up the note and pad towards my garbage can, which had me releasing a groan when I realized that it was filled to the very brim. Sighing, I bend down and pick up the garbage can and hip-bump the front door; just in time to see someone hoisting themselves over my backyard's fence.

I drop my garbage can with a thump and his head snaps up and his eyes meet with mines. My blood runs cold at the sight of his face covered with dirt, sweat and blood - again. My eyes trail down his body and linger at the sight of his leg, which had blood running down the jean side.

"Holy fucking sh -"

Andrew limp-jogs towards me, his eyes wide, shaking his head feverishly. He wraps an arm around my waist and uses his other hand to push the door open behind me and push the both of us into my house. I feel something running down my leg and the heat rushes to my cheeks because at that moment, I thought that I had peed on myself. I look down and realize that no, I hadn't pee on myself. It was more like Andrew had blood that had started to drip onto my leg and was now running down my leg and onto my white socks. "What the fuck?" I ask, fully aware that his arm was pressed again my back and that my entire leg was between his. He sighs and I note that his skin had paled. I wrapped an arm around his shoulder and turned so that we were now side by side. "I need you to help me out. I'm going to sit you on the chair and clean out your cut. And then I'm going to clean that cut above your eyebrow, okay?" I pause, my other hand shaking. "And then you're going to tell me what happened to you." He opens his mouth to protest but I laugh sardonically, "You're really going to argue with me after getting blood all over my clean backyard patio and my leg?" He doesn't reply, instead opting to shrug and clench his jaw. "Just - just please. No hospital."

"You don't have to press so damn hard!" He says, barely audible through his clenched teeth. I shrug. "Well, I mean, you can get an infection and then you'll end up at the hospital. Is that what you want?" I ask, my eyebrows raised. Andrew sits back, his jaw clenched. Sighing, I lean over and pull out a pad of gauze. "Here." He stares at me dumbly, his jaw still clenched. "Clenching your teeth means you're grinding them and that's not good. So take the fucking gauze." As he reaches for the gauze, I quickly stand up and jab my hydrogen peroxide drowned cotton ball onto the cut on his forehead and he hisses, almost hitting me in the stomach instinctively. I lean down and pick up a bandaid.

"So tell me how you managed to get hurt twice in one week." He takes a deep breath and looks at me apprehensively. "I was free-running with my friends and I tripped over someone's skateboard." He grumbles. I straighten up, "So you're telling me that you were running because you tripped on someone's skateboard? And that's why when I saw you, you ran to me and shoved me into my house - because you tripped on someone's skateboard?"

Andrew doesn't speak and I notice that his eyes had shuttered at the mention of him running towards my house. The room is filled with silence and if not for the fact that I knew that Andrew was lying to me, it probably would've been a comfortable silence. I stand up and shrug, turning around to put away the first aid kit. "I can't tell you." I turn around and meet his eyes, eyebrows raised. "You can't or you won't? There's a difference." But, again, his jaw is set and he's not talking to me, back to the usual brooding Andrew that most girls knew and obsessed over. I purse my lips and sigh,

"Just - Well, if you're in trouble, I would really like to know. It'd be nice to know that I'm not nursing a murderer..." I trail off, throwing Andrew a pointed look. He doesn't reply, his face still turned away from mines.

My eyes drop to his lips, perfect and pink and then his jawline, which was even more perfect from the side and I literally felt my mouth start to water. "See something you like?" He asks, smirking. I laugh nervously, "Something I like? What?" He chuckles and then flinches. The room settles into an awkward silence and I cough.

"Maybe you should be getting home now," I start, motioning (albeit awkwardly) to my back door. "Yeah, but I was wondering..." He starts, trailing off. I turn towards him and search his face. "Can you walk?" "It's just a cut but my house is really far -" "Where do you live?" "The Heights."

The room falls into silence again but this time, the silence is lined with the furious beating of my heart. The Heights usually iced over the blood in anyone's veins. With a reputation of gang violence, multiple instances of robberies and kidnapping, driving through the Heights at night will never, ever be a good idea - if not because of the gang violence it'll be because someone will come and steal your car while you're driving it. I didn't question why Andrew lived in the Heights - almost every other person I knew lived in the Heights.

The housing is cheap, which is pretty much expected because of how insanely dangerous it is there. My blood didn't stop pumping because Andrew had told me that he lived in the Heights, it was because I was wondering if he had any associations with the gangs there. I had caught him - twice - with blood running down the side of his face. I had found him twice, with wounds that would've been deadly if they weren't looked after. He had just jumped into my backyard with fear in his eyes that would alarm even Karl Marx.

"Do you -" I break the silence hesitantly, my eyes unable to meet his.

"No."

"But are you -"

"No." He bites out harshly, as if offended.

"But you -"

"No. I'm not and I didn't and I will never again. I'm not going to steal anything from your house. I just want to stay the night. Even you know that driving in the Heights this late would mean rape and I can't protect you," He says, his words cold and low. "if someone shoots at you on your way out." I stare at him, searching his eyes, searching for any traces of him lying. I sigh, "You can sleep in the guest bedroom - after you shower. I washed those sheets last week." "Thank you." He says, his voice noticeably soft.

CHAPTER 3

The next morning, Andrew pads out of the guest room, which is across from my room, at the exact same time as me. To say that I was just embarrassed is an understatement. My hair was tangled and fell to my back and I could bet my entire house that it was also extremely frizzy. I was wearing a ratty t-shirt and shorts and, on my feet, faded Hello Kitty slippers. And Andrew? He was tall enough that he was able to touch the top of the door if he wanted, but short enough that he didn't hit his head on the way out. And he was shirtless. I bit the inside of my cheek, trying my hardest not to squeal. Instead, I said the one thing that I didn't ever think I'd say. "Put a shirt on." I say awkwardly, trying to look everywhere but his stupid abs. He chuckles, a low, husky sound that caused shivers to run through my small frame. "Don't pretend that you don't like the way I look!" He yells after me, and I could tell that he was grinning, like usual. "I don't!" I yelled back, lying feebly.

"So what's for breakfast?" He asks casually. I'm digging through my fridge and sighing, "Well, seeing as I only have Cap N' Crunch,

Cocoa Puffs and milk, looks like we're having a cold breakfast this morning." I pass him a bowl and the cereal boxes and he sits down - still shirtless, by the way - and begins to make his breakfast. He sits back, "Where are your parents?" He asks casually, picking up his spoon and stirring his cereal around. I shrug, "I don't know. Mumbai, by now, I think." He looks up at me, eyebrows raised. "Why are they in Mumbai?" "They're on a cruise." "So they just leave you alone? At home?" I shift in my seat, uncomfortable. "Enough about my parents; what about yours?" A shadow crosses onto Andrew's face suddenly and looks down at his bowl before picking up his spoon. "Well, my parents are dead." My spoon drops into my bowl with a clatter as I awkwardly laugh and Andrew looks up, his lips pressed into a thin line. "I don't want any sympathy."

"Just - you said it so..."

"Bluntly? Casually? Carelessly? Heartlessly?"

I nod, "If my parents died..."

"You'd be a sobbing mess. Who's to say that I wasn't?"

I smirk at the thought of Andrew crying because the notion of someone his size crying was actually hilarious to me. "Well, did you?"

"Do I look like the kind of person to cry?"

I laugh, "That's a good point. So who do you live with now?"

"I live alone." "What?" I ask, incredulous. "You live alone? In the Heights?" Andrew continues eating but shrugs, as if living in the Heights alone was an everyday thing.

"You don't just live in the Heights - and you sure as hell don't live in the Heights alone!" I say, practically shrieking. "Why do you care?" "Well -" But I couldn't explain why I cared. It definitely wasn't because he was flaming, smoking, burning hot and it wasn't because he turned out to be a good guy after all. "Mother Theresa." I say quietly, trying to look everywhere but his angelic face. "Mother Theresa?" He repeats, confused. "Yes. When I was little, my teacher started calling me Mother Theresa because I helped everyone. Someone told me that I gave some girl my lunch because she was hungry and her mom didn't pack any for her. My mom yells at me sometimes because I give too much. At least that's what she says. She doesn't understand, though. I have to help. It's an obligation to myself. So, tell me. How are you keeping yourself safe in the Heights?" "My father had a good reputation. People know me and they stay away. It's nothing crazy." "Hmm." I say, dropping the subject. No one in the Heights just has a 'good reputation' - everyone there has that kind of 'kill, steal, lie or be killed, stolen from or lied to' mentality. There was no way that Andrew was getting by just because his father had a 'good reputation'. But I let it drop because along with my Mother Theresa complex, I also had killer instincts and I could tell that Andrew didn't want to talk about his living arrangements.

"So, do you have a girlfriend?" I try to ask casually, trying my best to look disinterested. I feel Andrew's gaze fall onto the top of my head and I literally have to repeat 'don't look up' in my head in order to restrain myself from meeting his eyes. "No..." He asks, a smirk clear in his voice. "Why do you care?" I cough awkwardly to hide the smile that was slowly finding its way onto my face. "I don't. Just a casual question. I don't care." He chuckles, "Yeah? So why are you so red?" My ears started to burn, "Uh, what? I'm not..." But just as I started to deny how red I supposedly was, my eyes fell onto my spoon and winced at the fact that I was bright red. "You're not what?" Andrew asks teasingly, grinning. "N - Not red. I'm still not red.

This happens when I'm...when I'm hungry." I say lamely, internally cursing my pride for not letting me admit that I was wrong.

"Is that -"

"What a whore -"

"What does she have that I don't?"

"It's only been a month."

"Looks like a one night stand."

Andrew walks beside me, his face stoic, his movements stiff. He doesn't say anything, but I know that he can hear what they're saying. Suddenly, he slings his arm around my shoulders and pulls me closer to him, letting me bask in his warmth. I stiffen, but Andrew bends down and says simply, "I don't like that they're calling you a whore." I relax but just for a few seconds, because then I catch sight of the person that I definitely didn't want to see right now. His jaw drops and Andrew squeezes my shoulder ever-so-slightly. "So you're with this...guy now?" Stephen says, his voice disbelieving. I don't reply but Andrew does. "Yes." He says, his voice cold. Stephen's lip curls with disgust and I flinch at the sight of him. You used to kiss those lips, a voice whispers. But now they're kissing Lacey's lips. Stephen studies my face and when my eyes meet his, I can see regret flickering through his eyes.

"Don't look at my girlfriend like that." Andrew snaps coldly before pulling me away. "Jesus," he whispers, "that guy is a complete douche bag." I don't say anything, part of me excited that I was in Andrew's arms and the other part of me still mourning for my lost relationship. "Why did you do that?" I ask quietly. When Andrew doesn't answer, I look up and I realize that his jaw was clenched and he wasn't paying attention to me. I follow his line of vision and realize that he's looking at someone at the end of the hallway.

His hand clenches tightly on my shoulder and I try not to show him that his grip was putting me in pain. "Andrew?" I ask timidly, looking up at him. He blinks and drops his arm from my shoulders and turns towards me, a smirk on his lips but the usual mischievous glint in his eyes gone. "Are you okay?" "Yes. Why wouldn't I be?" He says, repeating exactly what I had said when he had pulled me away from Lacey and Stephen's make out session. "You seem...I don't have a word, but you're crinkling." I say, still watching him. He hesitates, as if looking for a good reason, and then says, "Yeah, I'm confused because I just realized how big of a douche that guy was. Wondering what a beautiful girl like you is doing with that a dirtbag like him. D - Don't take it the wrong way or anything - you and I are just friends." I frown, "I wasn't going to take it the wrong way anyways." I decide to drop the subject because I knew that he was probably only going to lie.

With Stephen, everyone knew me as "Stephen's Girl" and that had always bothered me and I never knew why. After all, I was his girlfriend. The title was an expected thing - but I definitely didn't appreciate it. Maybe it was my subconscious telling me that I actually didn't like Stephen at all and I was just one of those girls that had to convince herself that she liked her own boyfriend. And maybe I wouldn't even be thinking about this if not for the fact that people around the school had started to call me Andrew's girl - and I wasn't even fazed by the new name. I didn't know what was different this time around, but I knew that I liked it. I knew that I liked be called his girl because then other girls knew that I was his girl. Maybe I was glad that the attention was off of me for once and instead on Andrew or maybe because I was glad that girls looked at me with the respect and admiration that I used to have from them. Or maybe, a voice whispered in the back of my mind, you like being called Andrew's Girl because you like him. And even though I usually battled with this insistent voice and told me that I didn't - or couldn't - like Andrew, deep down in my gut I knew that I had started to develop feelings for him sometime between the first time that I had found him injured and the time that I had found him in my backyard.

"How do you know Andrew?"

I groan aloud, cursing everything for my horrible luck. "I didn't know that I knew him." I say frostily, my eyebrows raised. Lacey feigns surprise and throws me a blinding smile. "Well, Stephen said that he saw you and Andrew together and that Andrew said that you're his girlfriend," Lacey leans in conspiratorially, "so how did you guys meet?" Subconsciously, my eyes narrow and I feel my lips twist into a frown, wishing that Andrew hadn't fleed the scene after lying about what was wrong with him. "We met in class." I reply icily, hoping that my eyes were shooting her daggers. Her eyes widened for a split second before she purses her lips and leans even closer, "They say you're frigid, you know. If you're blaming me for your guys' break up, I really don't think you should. They call you heartless when your back is turned and even though you're 'smoking hot', your personality will never be enough." She turns to leave, flipping (basically flaunting) her hair but I pull her back by the wrist. I lean in close enough that my lips were inches away from her ears and say, "I didn't have sex with Stephen because he told me that he found a sores on his dick...and I was smart enough to know what that means." I let go of her wrist and step back, flashing her the sweetest smile that I could muster. "Might wanna get that checked out." I mock, winking at her.

Of course, Stephen actually didn't have Herpes or any STDs. I didn't sleep with him because I felt that I was obligated to and I had learned from my mother during the awkward birds and bees talk that sex should never become an obligation and if it was, something had gone wrong or it just was never right.

While walking away, a rough hand grabbed my arm and pulled me into an empty classroom and flush against the person's front. "You Andrew's girlfriend?" Timidly, I nod. "Do you know who I am? And more importantly, do you know who he is?" "Didn't Mommy teach you not to talk to strangers?" He says, his uncomfortably warm breath sliding beneath the collar of my shirt. "You don't even know him - that's how it always starts. They all think he's innocent; all of them. Little do they know, he's anything but. He's ruined lives without blinking an eye; he ruined mines without even giving me a second glance. I didn't deserve it," The assailant takes a second to gather himself, "but no one ever does. That's the thing! He doesn't care whose life he ruins, as long as he gets paid. You're probably just like him - conniving and heartless. I'd be doing the world a favor if I -" The assailant doesn't finish his sentence, instead opting to swiftly stab me in the side with his knife.

The world faded to black.

Chapter 4

I hear Andrew's worried voice before I actually see him. His footsteps approach me rapidly and I can tell he'd seen my assailant's unconscious body by the way he looked when he dropped to his knees in front me, his eyebrows scrunched together with worry. His usually clear blue eyes were clouded with poorly concealed rage and he leans forward, brushing my bangs out of my face with shaking hands. "I did this," he started, his voice hard. I shake my head but he plows on, his eyes dragging up and down my injured body. "they know about you - I should've been more careful. Damn it; I should've listened to Adam. I thought I had made it obvious that I don't -" He says, breaking off at the end of his sentence and dropping his hand from my face. "You're bleeding!" He says, leaning forward to grab my arm. I pull back and he interjects coldly, "Now is not the time to be heroic, Lena." I shake my head, taking in a shaky breath to try and cope with the pain wreaking havoc throughout my body. "My arm..." I say, trailing off. Andrew stares at me uncomprehendingly. "It's broken or something. He twisted it after I hit him in the knee." Andrew's eyebrows raise and the traces of a devilish smirk appears on his face. "What are we gonna do about the body?" I ask breathlessly.

"Adam will take care of it - hospital?" He asks, his voice laced with clear concern. "No, my arm was broken like two weeks ago. I know what to do -" "You're going to go to the hospital." He says, this time more firmly. Gently, he wraps an arm around my waist and pulls me up, eliciting an electric current to run up and down my body. "I don't think he just passed out like that, Lena. What did you do to him?" I smile sheepishly, "My dad taught me how to fight off a mugger and I figured the situation was close enough so I just hit him with the back of my head and I might have kicked his knee in." Andrew's lips curve up into a grin, "I like a woman that knows how to fight!" I roll my eyes and spear him with a withering glare, annoyed that he had managed to turn the conversation towards the one direction that I didn't want to talk about. "Aw, don't look at me like that, Lay." And now he was using nicknames? I shake my head, withholding a sigh. Our eyes meet and I find myself tingling in places that I didn't think I could tingle. Stephen had never had me feeling like this; I'd always just been comfortable with him. But Andrew? He had me feeling a whole spectrum of feelings and always at the same time. Andrew walks me around the body of the unconscious assailant and towards the door, chuckling when I stumbled.

"Lena?" My eyes drag away from Andrew's reluctantly and they meet with Stephen's, who stands just a couple feet away from us, his lips twisted up into a sick smile. Andrew's grip on me tightens and I wince visibly. Stephen comes closer but I note that he's far off enough that Andrew wouldn't be able to hurt him. What a pussy, I think, trying to suppress a laugh. "Did he hurt you?" Stephen's voice raises at the word 'hurt' and fear flashes across his face, an emotion that I was used to seeing on his face. "Because even though we're not together and you're probably feeling insecure, just know that you're worth something. Don't do this to yourself. Don't let him -"Andrew steps forward with me still in his arms and I shakily wrap my unbroken arm around his waist, trying to restrain him. His eyes drop down to me, and his eyes clear up. "I have to take her to the hospital, so if you'll excuse us..." He says, his voice trailing off menacingly. Stephen steps aside almost instantly and I notice that both of his hands had started to shake and he had paled considerably.

"So, what happened?" The doctor asks casually, throwing a glance at Andrew, who was standing outside. I sigh, "I took a trip into the Heights. It was a dumb idea but we'd gotten into a fight," I throw in a tired look towards Andrew for good measure, "and I wanted to show him that I really loved him so I went over to his house and, well, I got stuck in the crossfire, I guess." The doctor seemed to buy my story but he watched Andrew walk back into the room with a wary eye. "I'm going to prescribe her some medication and I also advise that you should take her home and watch her to make sure she doesn't break her stitches or hurt herself." The doctor walks over to Andrew and takes him by the elbow out of the room, leaning in close to Andrew's ear and speaking lowly. I strain to hear their conversation and quickly realize that they were speaking too low for me to comprehend anything that they were saying.

Suddenly, they both turn around and the doctor's eyes were softened towards me and Andrew's were shuttered. Andrew claps him on the back and the doctor sighs, turning to quickly embrace him before turning to walk out of the room. "Who is he?" I ask, curious. "He's my...friend." Andrew says gruffly, eyes not meeting with mines. He lies to you too much. "Really?" Andrew looks at me after hearing my accusatory tone, his eyes still closed off to me. "Yes." The room drops into a tension-filled silence. Sighing, I swing my legs over the side of the hospital bed and let my feet drop down onto the floor. In a flash, Andrew was by my side, an arm around my waist and the other steadying himself. "Don't lie to me, Andrew. You've been lying to me too much. Just -" "I haven't been lying." Again, I sigh. I'd been doing a lot of that around this boy; everything he did had me sighing happily or sighing frustratedly - there was truly no in-between for us.

"Where are your keys?" "Why do you need my keys?" I snap irritatedly. He blinks and stares at me, gape mouthed. "Well, the doctor did say that you need someone to watch you - and I'm going to be that person, seeing that your parents are in Malaysia or Mumbai or some crazy shit." I flush red with embarrassment, "Mailbox - Mom always says to put it under the mat but I think that's a stupid place to put it." "Yeah, and the mailbox isn't? Your mail man can find your key and open your door and rob you!" I shrug and say simply, "It hasn't happened yet." Andrew snorts and fishes the key out of the mailbox, staring at it in disbelief. "I can't believe you actually keep it in there."

"I can walk on my own!" I snap as Andrew makes a movement to hold me by the waist again. "Are you okay?" I spin around, gritting my teeth as the pain shot through my body. "Well, let's see. I went to school today after finding you in my backyard and got pulled into a classroom where some psycho threatened to ruin your life by killing me in school, by the way - SCHOOL! And then I got stabbed, twisted my arm and you're asking me if I'm okay?"

Andrew stares at me, shaking his head. "Good thing I have painkillers - heard that knocks you right out." I smack his incredibly large bicep and mutter a curse.

"What do you want for dinner?" "Just a second ago you were yelling at me and now you want to cook for me?"

I shrug, "I have to eat and seeing as you're hellbent on staying with me, I might as well cook for you too." Andrew shakes his head again, his expression a mixture of confusion and something else that I couldn't place. I shuffle towards my fridge, pulling out pasta sauce and potatoes and beef from the freezer.

"My mom used to make this when I was little - called it Ragu. She was never that creative - she basically named it after the sauce that she used. Basically, you make pasta sauce and then pour it into a pot and then cut up the beef to let it cook in the sauce. It kinda marinates it while it cooks in the sauce. Meanwhile, you can cut the potatoes and then you'll throw it in there when I bring the pot down to half heat. It's really simple." I ramble, secretly glad to have someone to talk to. I pass him 3 potatoes, a peeler and a knife, directing him towards the granite countertop.

"You know how to peel, right?" He scoffs dramatically, "What? Yeah, of course? Like this, right?" He puts the blade of the peeler on the potato and tries to scrape the potato skin off but to no avail. I snort, "Yeah, you keep doing that and we'll be waiting for dinner for another four years." I pull the peeler from his hands and show him the correct way to do it. He takes the potato back from me and I watch as he slowly peels off one slice of skin.

"Shit!" He mutters and I turn towards him, expecting to see him about to leap out the window and over my fence and back into the Heights. I turn the heat to a simmer and walk towards him, staring at the massacre at potatoes in front of him. Somehow, in an hour, he had only been able to peel two potatoes and cut up one. "What happened?" I ask curiously, looking at the counter for any traces of blood. "Nothing - I just remembered that I had to do something tonight." I blink and quickly take the knife from his hand. "Go ahead. I'll be fine. After I eat this dinner I'll probably just knock out. I don't think I can manage to hurt myself in this empty house." Andrew laughs derisively, "I wouldn't jinx myself like that, Lay. Is it okay if I leave?" I'm used to being home alone anyways. I nod quickly peeling and chopping the other potato as he stands next to me, indecisive. "Save me some dinner - I'll come back later tonight and check on you, is that okay?" "Take the key." I mumble, embarrassed that I actually wanted him to come back.

CHAPTER 5

Andrew's POV:

I smirked at her reddened cheeks, amused by how she kept on trying so hard to hide them from me. I pick up the keys from the living room table and yell goodbye, my smirk dropping as I remembered what I had to do. Living in the Heights was never going to be easy for me - despite my father's reputation, people still messed with me. More than once, my apartment had been broken into. Of course, no one dared to steal anything as soon as they figured out whose house they had broken into but it still aggravated me to see that my door was wide open.

"Andrew." I hear as soon as I push the door open. I sigh, "Adam, look, I know that you said -" "That you'd get her involved and that they're going to find her? You're in too fucking deep and you don't even know it." I shake my head, "There's nothing between us! She -" "Saved you twice and let you stay over at her house. Let me ask you this, Andrew, doesn't it hurt you to think that you're going to be the reason for her death?" Adam asks coldly, ignoring my flinch and plowing on; "Because that's what's gonna happen. They're never going to stop, Andrew. They'll kill her and then they'll continue to try to kill you." "They're not going to get to her!" I snap, angry. Adam opens his mouth and I shoot him a glare, knowing exactly what he was gonna say next. Resignation passes over his face and sits back on my couch. "You know, Lacey said that she saw you guys together and that you called her your girlfriend? Who is this girl, Andrew?" "Is it any of your business?" Adam's mouth opens and then snaps shut. "That's what I thought." "What are you doing tonight?" I shake my head, "I finished the job last week - I just came back to get a bag." Adam shakes his head, smiling sadly. "When will you stop lying to everyone that cares about you?"

"Why did you send someone after her?" I ask, my arm pressing tightly onto their trachea. The person shook their head furiously and I muttered a curse. "Don't make me do it - you know how I hate it when they scream." But he's still shaking his head and whimpering. I sigh. I really did hate doing this - it was always my least favorite job but business was business. I push him away from me, shaking my head. I lean forward, a snarl on my lips. "If I find out that even one more of your goons goes after her -" I say menacingly, my teeth clenched together. He stumbles backward, choking as the oxygen rushed back into his lungs. He shakes his head furiously, "No, I'd never. No one is ever gonna bother her again - don't worry about it, Mr. Wayne."

I didn't necessarily have to go chase this creep down but after threatening Lena's life, I knew that I had no choice. In the Heights, someone's position is determined by the fear factor that they have when someone says their name. I knew that my last name, Wayne, stopped the hearts of too many creeps in the Heights and I also knew that my father's name was something that sent even the most intimidating drug lords into cardiac arrest. Names are a big deal in the Heights and I was going to make sure that Lena's name was known so that if she ever made the mistake of coming to the Heights alone, just telling someone her name would cause someone to run away in fear. There's an undeniable sexual tension that runs between us. Even though I had to mentally grow up, it didn't mean that my body had grown up as well. Being around Lena made me feel aroused - something that Lacey couldn't ever do for me. I let my mind drift of to Lena's smiling face, thinking of all the dirty things that could happen between us...and then I hit myself in the face. What kind of person had I become? I was fantasizing about I girl that I swore is only my friend? She's only your friend, Andrew. Only your friend.

I push my way into her house and my heart begins to beat furiously - I couldn't stand the thought that someone had come to her and stolen her while I was gone.

Andrew -

This is your dinner. Heat it up for 2 minutes and there's soda in the fridge. See you tomorrow.

Lena xx

A smile stretches across my face at the sight of the dish on the table. I contemplate eating before checking on her but I push the thought away, instead turning towards the stairs to walk towards her room. "Lay?" I walk towards her bed and notice that she had rolled over at the sound of my voice and a goofy smile was now on her face. My lips twitch as she pulls herself up into a sitting position, groggily patting the spot next to her on her bed. "Come, we need to talk." I freeze, but sit next to her anyways, seeking her warmth in the air-conditioned room.

"I've been thinking," She starts awkwardly, her hand twitching in her lap. "ever since I've met you, I've been getting into a lot of...t hings." My mouth opens but she turns to me, her eyes surprisingly clear despite the fact that she had just woken up. "I've found you bleeding and injured. I've been confronted by rumors and psychos - and I'm not talking about the guy in the classroom - and being near you has gotten me stabbed in the side and I now have a twisted arm. And all through that," Her tone softens, "I still want to know you - as a person. Which is fucking crazy, if you ask Tessa, because even though you're super hot, I have a stab wound because of you. Jeez, what am I even thinking when I say this...but if you need help. I'll be there. But you need to tell me what's going on with you; please." I turn away from her hopeful face - a face hopeful that I would finally open up but I'm trying to conjure up reasons why I shouldn't.

"Andrew?" Her soft voice interrupts my train of thought and I turn back towards her and a look of apprehension flashes through her eyes.

"It would be better if you didn't know." I say darkly.

But she doesn't want to take 'no' for an answer - it figures, she's pretty head strong - instead plowing on with her speech.

"If you don't tell me, I'll tell everyone that you - that you...I'll think of something! But it'll be bad. So."

I chuckle at her weak threat and pat her on the thigh which brings her cheek to a pretty blush. "It's not something I can tell people."

Her eyes widen comically and her mouth opens but I sigh.

"I'm not an undercover agent..." Her mouth snaps shut and she blushes before opening her mouth again, her eyes lowered guiltily and her ears flaming. "And I'm not a stripper or a hooker or a pornstar."

Her cheeks flush even redder.

"I..."

She turns towards me, her eyes trained on my face. "You..." She says as I trail off, unsure.

"I'm...not who you think I am."

A small smile graces her lips and I wince at the sight of it.

"I knew that already," she says, still unsure. "what I don't know is who you are."

I open my mouth again but she beats me to the punch.

"And if you're going to lie then I don't think that I want to know who you are." She says, her gaze icy. My mouth shuts.

"So until you can tell me the truth, I don't want to hear anything about the person that you are. Until you can tell me why you showed up in my backyard bleeding, I don't want to know who you are."

My mouth drops open as she turns her back towards me and lays down, twitching at the pain in her stabbed side.

But it's not that I don't want to tell her - it's not that I wouldn't tell her. It's that I really can't tell her. How am I supposed to tell someone that I'm finally beginning to consider my friend that I'm a gangster? This isn't Grey's Anatomy or Arrow or one of those overrated Korean dramas - this is real life. If I tell her that I kill people to survive in the Heights, she'll turn around and never look back. A voice in my head whispered that she wasn't anything like Lacey - Lacey, who was now dating Stephen. Lacey, who had decided to skip town as soon as she found out the kind of person that I am. And, okay, maybe I didn't entirely expect her to stay and deal with my problems but I didn't expect her to never talk to me again. I didn't expect her to throw out a childhood of friendship and become some completely different person. But a voice whispers to me from the very back of my mind, a warning tone lacing the words. Tell her before it's too late, Andrew. She's going to run just like Lacey. Maybe if you had told Lace earlier...

"Andrew!" Lacey yells, a bright smile on her face as she pushes the door of my apartment in the Heights open. Even with the horrible reputation that the Heights had, Lacey had still trekked across the city to come see me while I was sick. "I brought you chicken so -" Her eyes fall on the gun on my coffee table and the decrepit couch and the grimy kitchen table. "Andrew?" She asks, her voice small.

My heart pounds and I can literally hear my blood rushing through my body. "Lace, I can explain." "Did you kill someone, Andrew?" I open my mouth, not sure whether or not I was could tell her that I was the son to the biggest gangster in the Heights. "Andrew!" She shrieks hysterically, her cheeks beginning to color. "I'm a Wayne." She pales and her bottom lip trembles. "You said -" "Lacey -" "You said that you're not a Wayne - you said..." She looks at the ground, and her shoulders begin to heave up and down. "I -" I begin, trying to find words to explain but I couldn't think. Lacey looks up, "We've been friends for 10 years, Andrew. Ten years - and in those 10 years you didn't think that it would be nice for me to know that you - that you're a Wayne?" She shakes her head, her face beginning to redden with fury. "Have you killed anyone, Wayne?" She says, her voice spitting out my last name like it was venom. I shake my head, unable to respond. "And I'm supposed to believe you? You're the liar here!" She yells. She throws the chicken soup at my couch and turns around, running out of my building.

I had ruined all the chances with my best friend and the girl that I had fallen in love with in one fell sweep. It was as if I had taken a bulldozer and bulldozed our relationship.

That was just two years ago - sophomore year of high school. Now, we don't talk and that's why it's surprising to see Lacey in front of me before first period. "How do you know Lena - and don't tell me some bullshit story about your fucking relationship because I know as well as anyone in the fucking Heights that you don't get involved with girls!" "Why do you care?" I say dryly, stepping around her fuming 5'1 stature. I hear her snarling and suddenly she's blocking my path again. "God - I leave you for two fucking years and you go and start dating her? Of all people, you chose Elena?" I wince at Lacey's wanton pronunciation of Lena's full name. "It's not Ey-Lee-Na. It's Uh-Lay-Na." I mutter, irritated. "Two years ago -" I cut off her off, dropping my eyes to meet with hers. "I've changed a lot in two years, Lacey - and so have you. Two years ago, you wouldn't have gone for a guy like that douchebag Stephen. Two years ago, you would've stood by side no matter what. Two years ago -" "I didn't know that you were one of those Waynes. Two years ago, I didn't know any better."

Lacey steps away from my glare, unfazed. "Don't glare at me, Andrew Wayne. Don't you dare. You act like you can scare me away - well, guess again!" I send her another withering glare, "I've scared you away before. Don't lie to yourself, Lacey. You were scared shitless that day." Lacey presses her lips into a thin line. "I was angry. I wasn't scared. I knew that you would never..." "Rob you? Rape you? Kill you?" I deadpan, still glaring. She nods, not acknowledging my tone. "I miss you, Andrew. And I don't like Elena - I don't approve of her. She's too...good. It's fucking unnatural. She's hiding something." "Just because she's not a coward or a home wrecker it doesn't make her a fake. If anything, you're the fake one." Lacey blinks at me and steps towards me, her face a mask of fury.

"For your information, I saved Stephen. I saved him. He didn't love her and he wasn't fucking happy - and we're together now and we love each other. You don't know the things that she'd done to him - standing him up for dates, ignoring his texts...flirting with other guys? Lena is a whore and you - and you - you're dating her?" I stare at her flatly. "Please tell me you're not jealous." Lacey reddens and her eyes widen. "J - Jealous? Me? What? I -" "You're jealous." I say dryly, staring at her blankly. "I'm not! I'm just being a good friend - that's all. A good friend." She says, sounding like she was trying to reassure herself of her own actions. I smirk and sling an arm around her shoulders. "If it makes you feel any better, I feel absolutely nothing for her." Lacey opens her mouth to say something but a sweet voice interrupts her.

"Andrew?" "Speak of the devil and she shall appear." Lacey mutters under her breath, her shoulders slumping forward. I turn around, turning Lacey with me and my eyes meet with Lena's dark blue ones. She watches us suspiciously and I can see a mysterious emotion flick across her face but I wasn't sure. I didn't think that I'd ever be sure around Lena. Lena's blue eyes shift to Lacey and they narrow slightly but she doesn't saying anything except a feeble 'hi' and an awkward wave.

"Stephen doesn't have sores on his...on his thing." Lacey blurts loudly. Lena blinks and then turns towards me, shrugging her shoulders. "I don't know what you're talking about. I've never seen his thing. I think I'm late for 1st period. I'll see you later." I stare after her while Lacey elbows me rudely and says, "You look like a lovesick puppy." I clear my throat and reluctantly pull my gaze away from Lena's direction. "Don't call me a puppy." Lacey snorts and leans into me, shooting me a wicked glance. "What, do you want to be called; a man-dog?" "No. I want to be called my name." I say, shooting her a cold look. "Don't get snippy with me just because you have a ridiculous crush on a little slut." "I don't have a crush on her." "Yeah? Well prove it."

Lacey presses her lips against mines and I find myself kissing her back after a few moments of shock. My eyes snap open just in time to see Lena rounding the corner, limping and wincing.

Chapter 6

Lena's POV

I wince in pain as I try to walk away from Lacey and Andrew with my head held high. I didn't know what hurt more – the fact that Lacey had her slimy face buried in Andrew's chest or the fact that my stab wound was causing pain to shoot up and down my side with every step I took. I knew that coming to school today wasn't a very bright idea but, of course, the stubborn side of me won over my logical side. And, before someone decides that I came to school to be with Andrew, I actually came because I've had perfect attendance since Kindergarten and I was stupid enough to think that a stab wound wasn't going to hinder my learning process.

Stephen steps out from a classroom, both his hair and shirt ruffled. His eyes widen when he shakes me and he pales considerably before stepping back, as if trying to escape my own widened glance. "Jesus fucking Christ – are you cheating on Lacey?" I blurt, anger starting to course through my veins. He shakes his head but I can tell that he's completely bullshitting. "Are you serious?" I ask, incredulous. "Maybe you cheated on me with Lacey and maybe that hurt my feelings. But in no way is it alright for you to do it to Lacey. She's a good person – god, you're such an asshole and -" I'm cut off my Stephen's sudden movement. I step back quickly, grimacing at the pain in my side. "Don't touch me. You're disgusting and unbelieva -" And then the door opens and a redhead that I didn't recognize stepped out, her hair messed up and her lipstick smudged.

I shake my head and turn on my heel – back towards the direction that Lacey and Andrew were. As I round the corner, I see something that I didn't think I would see. Granted, this doesn't really count as cheating because technically, Andrew and I weren't really dating. Their heads were bent down and their lips were locked and moving in perfect synchronization. I clear my throat awkwardly and Andrew jumps back, pushing Lacey away in the process. His clear blue eyes widened at the sight of me and his mouth drops open. Meanwhile, Lacey was off to the side, staring down the hallway as if she was in a daze. Shaking my head, I step closer to the pair, my shoulders slumped in resignation. "You and Stephen sure do have a knack of breaking up people's relationships and cheating on people." I mutter, my eyes averted from Andrew's now stoic face.

"I came back to tell you, Lacey, that I saw Stephen coming out of a classroom with some redhead. Her lipstick was smudged. I just wanted to tell you that he was cheating on you because it would've been nice if someone had told me, but it looks like you're good. I'm just gonna go to class." I finish awkwardly, my eyes still on the floor. I hear someone starting after me but the footsteps stop almost immediately.

"Lena."

"Lena."

"Elena."

"Lena?" Andrew hisses, irritation creeping into his tone. I don't look up, embarrassed to look at his face. I was sure that if he saw mine, he'd know right away that I was jealous that he had kissed Lacey instead of me. His hand drops on my shoulder and I wince away from it, angered by the feelings that his abnormally warm hand gave me. "Lena, look at me." I turn my head just slightly, mentally slapping myself for not being smart enough to have moved to a different seat.

And then I'm standing and we're outside of Ms. Grie's classroom, standing in the empty hall with my face in Andrew's large hands. "Lena, look, I'm sorry -" He starts uncomfortably. I shake my head rapidly. "No, there's nothing to be sorry for - we're not even in a real relationship. It was just a fake thing. And this is just a fake breakup. There's nothing else to it. We're better as friends anyways and Lacey is a very nice person. You guys will have a good relationship - well, she tends to home wreck and cheat but you know, if she really likes you, maybe she'll -" "Lena." "change." Andrew's hands drop from my face and an emotion that I can't discern flickers onto his face. "I don't want to fake breakup with you," He says, teasing. "you know how much I enjoyed our relationship!" I snort, "You just enjoyed my extra soft bed - and the food. And the free first aid. And electricity. And Wifi. You probably appreciated the Wifi the most." He looks down sheepishly, his broad shoulders slumped. "Maybe Lacey will find out what you're hiding from me!" I say jokingly. Andrew's head snaps up almost immediately and he blinks at me. "She already knows." He says flatly, his eyes meeting with my now rapidly blinking ones. "So if I wanted to know...all I had to do with make out with you in the middle of the hallway?"

Andrew frowns, "She didn't – we weren't making out – we were just..." My eyebrow raises as I stare at him skeptically. "You were licking each other's lips, then. Because that's what it looked like." He shifts uncomfortably on his feet, "W – Well -" A grin spreads onto my lips, watching as he stood there uncomfortably, trying to look everywhere but my face. I snickered to myself and turned around. "Maybe we should go back to class, Andy." "Don't call me that!" "I'll call you what I want – this is America." "Yeah? Well then I can just..." "You can what?" I ask, still walking, my back to him.

On the inside, I was full-out chuckling, surprised that Andrew could get flustered in any kind of way. But, then again, I guess I was in for a ton of surprises if Lacey is his type of girl. I guess since I'd met him, I'd assumed that his type was 5'9, dark hair, dark eyes, supermodel face, super mysterious and so sexy that being in her general vicinity was uncomfortable. I push the door to Ms. Grie's classroom open and her eyes fall on me, her mouth opens, as if ready to say something. But then her eyes flick to Andrew, who was probably doing his 'ominous towering' act behind me and she turned back to the chalkboard hurriedly, muttering something about gangs and drugs.

I take my seat and so does Andrew, his head turned towards the chalkboard and mine turned towards his. So maybe I did have a tiny crush on him. I was just like all the other girls in my school; we all liked Andrew. Maybe I'm different because he slept over in my house a couple times and I made him dinner. Maybe I'm different because we have full conversations and – I stop myself. I'd always been apt at trying to convince myself that a guy is good for me.

A guy that gets stabbed and probably shot at is never gonna be good for me. And, plus, he doesn't even like you. Not if there's a girl like Lacey going after him, anyways. "Stop staring at me." He says calmly, not looking at me. "I'm not looking at you!" "Yeah, you're not looking. You're staring." I gape at him, "Same difference!" "Ms. Bryon, why are you shouting back there?" "I -" "Don't let it happen again." She says shortly, turning back towards the board. Andrew snickers and I mutter a curse, newly irritated at Andrew and his stupidly attractive face.

"Oh, so you think I'm 'stupidly attractive'?" Did I seriously say that out loud just now? "Yes." That too? "Yes." "Ms. Bryon!" Ms. Grie says, exasperation clear in her voice. Andrew clears her throat and Ms. Grie blushes furiously before flicking her eyes over to Andrew. "Actually, I was the one talking." She clears her throat awkwardly and someone on the other side of the room snickers. "W – Well, don't do it again!" Andrew flashes her a quick grin and she blushes even redder and quickly tries to turn back to the board, accidentally tripping over the leg of her desk in the process.

I gape at him openly, not caring about how dumb I looked. "Stop staring." He drawls, still not looking at me. I sigh. "Stop sighing." I turn back to my notebook, now irritated. "Stop doing...that." I blink and mutter, "What? What am I doing now?" "I can you see...thinking." "You can see me thinking?" "Elena, just stop." Before I could retort, the bell rings obnoxiously and I hear Ms. Grie's anxious voice over the sound of scraping chairs and rustling papers. "Test! Tomorrow! All of Act 1 in Midsummer!" Andrew smoothly gets up from his seat, surprisingly already packed up. "Test?" I mutter, confused. "Yes, 'test' is something teachers give to their students to make sure they know the information." Andrew says to me in a condescending tone on the way of the classroom. I glare at his incredibly broad back. "'Test' is something teachers give to their students blahblahblah." I mock, irritated. For the life of me, I really couldn't understand why I had such an uncomfortably intense infatuation with him.

"Laaaaay-nah!" I wince at the sound of Tessa's shrill voice yelling my name from the other end of the hallway. I stop in my tracks, moving over towards the sides to avoid the oncoming traffic. "Lena!" She says, breathing heavily. I stare at her in awe, wondering why she looked so... "Are you wondering why I look like this? Honestly, Lena, maybe you should at least try to be discreet about what you're thinking. You're basically an open book." I sigh, "What happened, Tessa?" She stands up straighter, her hands on her hips. "Why didn't you tell me that you dated Andrew the Adonis?" "What?" "Lena, don't try to lie to me. All day, Lacey's been telling everyone that her and Stephen broke up because she wanted to steal Andrew away from you. And, if I do say so myself, it's kind of upsetting that you didn't tell me yourself. We're supposed to be, like, best friends..." "I never agreed to that." I deadpan, staring at her. "Agreed to what?" "To being your best friend." "People don't agree...it just happens." Tessa says slowly, sure to drag out every word as if I was mentally retarded. I stare at her, newly irritated. "We're not best friends." "But -" "You just want to meet Andrew." "You call him by his first name?" She squeals, her eyes sparkling with excitement. "Yes...What did you expect me to call him?" She blinks and mutters, "Well, actually, that makes sense. Wait - stop changing the subject. We're best friends - I held your hair that time you got so wasted that -" I step around her and start walking towards my next class but Tessa is still chattering, just like she usually does.

"Lena, are you ignoring me?"

"Honestly, you act as if you hate me."

"Are you mad because I didn't tell you about Lacey and Stephen?"

I whirl around, my eyebrows drawn together. "You knew?" Tessa scoffs, rolling her eyes. "Honestly, Lena. After all those dates he stood you up on and all those times that he 'forgot' to pick you up after school? How about the time he came out of that closet with his hair looking that way? Did you really believe him?" I gape at her, angry. "You should've told me!" "Should I have? Would you believe me? Be honest, Lena. Would you have?" My mouth snaps shut. "That's...true." I admit begrudgingly. "Anyways, it's been like 3 months. Get over it already." "I'm over it!" Tessa's green eyes narrow. "Yeah?" "Yes!" "Okay? So why aren't you trying to get Andrew back? If you were over Stephen then -" "That literally has nothing to do with anything." Tessa shakes her head forlornly, as if I had just killed her mom. "Yes, it does. You have a crush on him!" "The entire female population in our high school has a crush on him -" "That doesn't matter. You might have a chance with him! You can steal him away from Lacey the way that she stole Stephen away from you." "Tess -" "No. Don't say my name like that. You're going to do this. Stop letting people step all over you. You're going to go get Andrew." "I don't like him enough to invest all my time and energy..." "Sure you don't."

Usually, Tessa backed off after I snapped at her but this time, she kept on going and didn't seem like she was going to stop. "I don't like him!" I yell as she turns around and walks back to her classroom. She turns around and winks at me, "Sure."

"Who don't you like?"

My head snaps around and I glare at Stephen, whose standing there, his eyebrows furrowed. "Is it me? Do you not like me?" I'm still glaring, irritated at how idiotic his question was. "Are you serious? Was that a serious question?" His mouth drops open and snaps shut immediately as he guiltily shifts his eyes to the floor. "Yeah? Yeah, it was a serious question." I snort, still staring at him, disbelief probably coloring my features. "You broke up with me to go fall in love Lacey, who you cheated on me with – not to mention the fact that you also cheated on her. And now, you're trying to butt back into my life? Do you really not have anything else to do, Stevie?" He colors red, rage flooding into his features. "Don't – Don't call me that! You know I hate it!" I glower at him; "Yeah, I know you hate it. That's why I did it." Stephen's face twists into a frown and he glares at me. "You're a bitch, you know that?" My eyebrows furrow and my lips twist into a pout. "Aw, Stevie. That really, really, hurt my feelings." But Stephen doesn't detect my sarcasm, "Okay. So it's obvious that you don't like me. Please don't tell me that you were trying to convince Tessa that you're not crushing on Andrew." I blink at him, my eyebrows furrowing even more and my pout dropping into a frown. "What -" "You do the thing!" Stephen says, waving his hands uselessly around in the air. "What thing?" He shakes his head. "The thing! You hate making eye contact with people but yet, you do it with Andrew all the time. And, you're clumsy. And the other thing comes out – what is that thing again? Your complex. The one where you have to help everything – remember that time that you made me stop the car on my 100 dollar restaurant reservation so that you could take home that stray cat with a broken leg?" My mouth drops open, surprised that Stephen had managed to remember all of that. "I -" "You have a crush on him."

He steps forward, weariness clear on his face. Slowly, he slings an arm around my shoulder. "But, he's with Lacey. And we need to fix that." I'm shocked into silence, not sure how to answer. "I'm going to make him jealous." Stephen mutters, tightening his grip on my shoulders. "We're gonna tell everyone that we're back together."

"You're what?!" Tessa screams, her face clouding with anger. I shrug. "He asked me out. He bought me like 10 dozens of roses," "Lena, you hate roses." "and he fixed that part of my car that he crashed." "You know, when I said that you need to get a boyfriend and get back in the game again, I didn't mean to do it with Stephen. He's scum, Lena. He didn't even remember that you're allergic to roses!" I sigh. "Yes, I know. I heard you but you don't get it, Tessa. When you fall in love with someone, you'll understand." Tessa's face hardens. "I get it, believe me I do. I just don't get how you fell in love with – with that thing."

"Is it true?" I turn around, and our eyes meet. "What's true, Andrew?" He glares at me. "That you're back together with – with that idiot." "What idiot? Did you mean Stephen? My honey?" I ask, my voice saccharine sweet. Lena, what are you even doing? Why are you even trying to make a boy you don't like jealous? "Yes! No, not your honey. He's the guy that cheated on you, remember? The guy that decided that it'd be okay for him to just – to just discard you!" Andrew says, anger leaking into his words. One of my eyebrows raises on it's own accord and I suavely lean my back against the cafeteria table, smirking at him. "And why do you care?" His mouth drops open, and for once, he's at a loss for words. I sit up straight and turn back to my lunch. "Better go back to your girlfriend before she decides to go cheat on you." I say coldly, picking up my fork and jabbing at my grilled chicken. Inwardly, I pat myself on the back, proud of myself for keeping my cool.

"What the hell – what the hell was that?" Tessa asks, her voice quivering with excitement, the anger completely wiped from her voice. I shrug, smirking. "He's playing games with me." "Yeah? So is Stephen." I shrug. "At least Stephen's blatantly obvious with me." Tessa ignores me, forging on. "He was totally jealous – like, totally." I roll my eyes. "He doesn't like Stephen so he's just doing the big brother thing." Tessa snorts, "Yeah? I've never seen a big brother ever look at you the way that Andrew looks at you. He doesn't know it yet, but half the school can see it. He has a crazy big crush on you." "He doesn't." I snap, annoyed. "I can see it in your eyes - I can see that you totally want him to like you back." Tessa teases, casually picking up a spoonful of yogurt. I don't say anything, instead opting to turn back to my sandwich and biting my lip a little bit too forcefully. "Honestly, Lay. Half the girls and a couple teachers in this school would kill for Andrew to give them a second glance and you don't even care." Tessa says nonchalantly, rolling her eyes. "I care that you're talking about me liking Andrew when I don't!" I yell, irritated. Heads swivel towards the two of us, and I can feel a certain someone's blue eyes glaring into the nape of my neck.

My head swings around, my anger coursing through my veins. Mostly because I was too stubborn to believe that Tessa had seen through my facade and angry that Andrew probably didn't like me back. Simply put, the thought of being single with almost no friends and nowhere to go afterschool really began to hit me like a ton of rocks. I couldn't stand being alone - call it being needy, call it being clingy, but I really, truly couldn't handle it.

"If you don't like him then why are you staring at him?" Lacey's voice pierces through my thoughts, effectively spearing the metaphorical train engineer that was driving my train of thought. "I -" My mouth opens and closes, probably causing me to look like a fish. "Don't talk to her." Tessa's cold, silky voice speaks up from behind me and I flinch at her tone. But, I had to admit, when she wasn't drunk she was pretty good at having my back. "Excuse me?" Lacey says, her voice rising nervously, scared of my blonde friend. Personally, if I wasn't friends with Tessa, I'd probably be scared shitless by her too.

Naturally, we had made friends after I met her at a bonfire and held her hair while she vomited into the dark lake when all her 'best friends' had ditched her. Although Lacey and Andrew were sitting at a basically empty table just a couple feet away from us, seeing them together had my heart aching. I wince internally, my head beginning to hurt at the thought of me beginning to get even slightly jealous at the sight of those two together.

"She said not to talk to me," I say, my voice low. "or are you also ditz alongside being a home wrecker?" Lacey gapes at me, twin splotches of red forming on her cheeks. "I -" "You?" I mock, my voice cold and dry. At this point, the entire cafeteria is completely silent. My chair scrapes against the cheap linoleum as I get up, my back ramrod straight, my chin raised in the air. Belatedly, Tessa gets up too, her chair also scraping against the floor. Still, this whole time, I can feel Andrew's eyes on the back of my neck but I remind myself that he's a liar and also an asshole. Anger surges up in me again and I attempt to push it down again, hating the dirty feeling it left in my body.

As soon as Tessa and I are outside of the cafeteria, her arm is slung around my shoulders and I can feel her eyes on me. "You're angry!" She notes, surprise coloring her voice. I shrug, irritated. "I -" "You?" "I'm angry." I concede, my shoulders slumping. "But I don't like him - I just...Lacey just angers me. I - I hate her." Tessa's arm slides off of my shoulder and her jaw drops. "Whoa, Lena. That's the first time I've ever heard you use the 'H' word. This must be serious." I sigh. "I don't hate her but she just gets me so angry - I didn't know it was possible for someone to get me that angry." I mutter. But Tessa doesn't say anything in response, which genuinely surprises me because she almost always has a response. I turn towards her, just a little curious, and find myself looking at someone who had a devious smile and a vicious glimmer in her eyes. I was prepared to nag her, but at the sight of her expression, all the words had died on my lips - and they had fought such a valiant battle. "You're not angry, Lay! You're jealous! You're jealous that Andrew and Lacey are together. It's jealousy!" Tessa exclaims excitedly, her hands waving around in circles in the air.

"Tessa -" And then the bell signifying that the lunch period was over rings and Tessa is sprinting down the hall, running away from me and the words of denial that had been ready to break out.

"Elena?" A gruff voice snaps me out of my focused glare on Tessa's sprinting, pixie-like figure and I turn around, unamused. "Andrew." I say curtly, reminding myself that I had absolutely no reason to be annoyed with him. "Elena, I'm sorry. I shouldn't have - I shouldn't have said all of that in the cafeteria. If Stephen makes you happy then I'm okay. But," Of course there's a but. "he's no-good.

Nothing good comes out of being around him and you should know that by now." I nod, sighing. "I'm regretting forgiving him." I say truthfully, shrugging. Andrew's face softens. "So why did you?" I open my mouth to answer but it snaps shut almost immediately. "And why do you care?" "You're my friend." He says quickly, his eyes sincere. My stomach drops and I shift on my feet awkwardly. "I -"

"Andrew!" The two of us turn around and Andrew's face hardens immediately. "Adam, what are you doing here? In public? Out of the Heights?" But Adam completely disregards Andrew and turns to me, his brown eyes flashing with lust. Of course, just like Andrew, Adam is actually fascinatingly beautiful - not as handsome as Andrew, but definitely on the same level. His eyebrow raises and a calculating mask lifts onto his face - this all happens in a matter of seconds. He smiles wide and his eyes glitter with goofiness. "Are you Lacey? Oh man, Andrew's been talking all about you!" I shift on my feet again, and I can feel my heart wrench. So Andrew talked about Lacey a lot? "I - well, I'm not. I'm Lena." I say, offering a hand. Adam's eyes shutter and he turns to Andrew, whose eyes are stone cold. "My, my, I didn't know that public school means that Andrew has beautiful women surrounding him all the time. If I knew that I wouldn't have turned down his offer to sign me up!" Adam chortles, clapping Andrew on the back. "Ha, ha." I laugh awkwardly, not sure what to do with myself. "I'm just gonna...go." I say, noticing that the two boys weren't showing any kind of attention to me.

I didn't know why it bothered me so much that Andrew talked more about Lacey than he did about me (if he talked about me at all) but it bothered me more than I wished it would. I was irritated, that's for sure. Once again, I wasn't good enough. How many times can this happen to me? How many times can I grow a ridiculous crush on someone - only to be crushed myself? Funny, how everything I had built to protect myself against this kind of monumental destruction on my heart had taken so long to build and only a couple sentences to break down. And then I realize something that fills me with absolute mortification. I'm easy. My crushes are easy to form because I'm easy. I form crushes easily.

Who is Adam? The question leads me to other, forgotten files in my mind; it leads me to questions such as; "Who is Andrew?" "Why does he keep on showing up hurt?" And then suddenly, all the hurt that came with realizing that Andrew is more interested in Lacey than he is in me is squashed because I remember that I'm supposed to be angry at that asshole. I don't know who he is - he could be some psycho and I mostly didn't even care. I remember that Lacey had known before I did and then another question flits into my mind; "What the hell is Andrew's last name?"

Funny, how I'd tended to his wounds and let him have a place to stay but I never even found out his last name. Upon further inspection, I found out that even Tessa didn't know his last name. Surprisingly, nobody I knew did. Maybe I was going crazy; maybe I had finally succumbed to the insanity that Andrew was shrouded in. Maybe - but probably not. There was something important about Andrew's last name and I was going to figure it out.

"Why is it even important?" Tessa asks, irritation creeping into her voice after she realizes that I hadn't been paying an ounce of attention to her. "His name is going to tell me something about him that I need to know. Names are important!" I exclaim, combating her annoyance with my urgent tone. Tessa sighs. "For a girl that says she doesn't like Andrew at all, you seem to be all over his business lately." Truthfully, I'd admitted to myself that my relationship with Andrew was more or less one sided; I was the only one crushing in this crush. But, like always, I deny Tessa's words and slump back in my chair. "Who do you think would know? And before you say the obvious, I know Lacey knows." Tessa sits back in here chair as well, while absentmindedly twisting a strand of hair around her finger. "Well, there's that guy. Adam, right?" I nod, but glower at the thought of having to be in the same area as him. "Maybe we should rule him out…" Tessa says after catching a glimpse of my face. I bite my lip; curiosity had killed the cat, but satisfaction brought it back. After a couple more minutes of silence, Tessa turns towards me, her eyes wide, lips parted. "I have an idea; why don't we just ask Andrew?" "Because I don't want to do it again." "Just do it. And bat your eyelashes while you're at it. No one can resist you after you bat your eyelashes."

For the next couple of days, I try to find a way to talk to Andrew while he was alone. It would've been an easier feat if he actually came back to my house after the day Lacey confronted me in the cafeteria, but he never did. Funny how things can change in just a couple minutes. Lots of things in my life had started to go funny. It became funny how suddenly, Tessa, a girl who I'd never ever gave a second thought to, had suddenly become my rock. Tessa, who vomited all over the place the first time we had met each other, was now responsible and often brought over movies and tubs of ice cream on Friday nights so that we could both wallow in self-pity over the both of us being pretty much single. Of course after Stephen had proposed that we get back together to get Andrew angry, he had decided to go off and cheat on me and that was basically the end of that. After that, I'd resorted to spending my time exclusively with Tessa who had taken it upon herself to try to get me to admit that I had started developing a crush on Andrew.

Alas, along with being friends with Tessa came the fine print of drinking with her when she got a little too lonely. Clearly, that's something that needed to be stopped, but the two of us usually preferred to drown our sorrows together. That night, Tessa hadn't come over, instead opting to stay home because she had caught a stomach virus. And that left me at home, alone on a Friday night with nothing to do but drive around. Maybe if Mom and Dad were home, you'd be doing something with them. But, if anyone is keeping track out there, Mom and Dad had a penchant for leaving me at home alone to go out on cruises and stupid vacations, which puts them on the list of 'People that Could Care Less about Lena'. I guess you could say that I should be grateful for their perpetual absence because that night, I'd decided to drive around.

A battered body staggers out into the middle of the street and I hit the brakes, grateful to whoever had invented the seat belt. The person staggers to the driver's window, which I belatedly realized was my window, and I noisily tried to find the button to roll my window up - mostly because I had driven dangerously close to the Heights and it was also conveniently 11PM. "Wait - before you drive out of here, hear me out." My jaw drops at the sound of the person's voice and I look up, my eyes meeting with none other than Adam's. "Get in the car!" I whisper urgently, quickly unlocking the door. "Where do you need to go? Why did you run out like that? God, I thought driving bloodied people around was going to stop after Andrew. Who are you, anyways? And, also, do you know what Andrew's last name is?" I spit out in a flurry while putting my car into drive and U-turning illegally. "Take me somewhere safe. No hospital." Adam finally answers, deciding to avoid the rest of my questions. I sigh, the feeling of deja-vu cramping up what little room I had in my beetle. "This is somewhat familiar." I mutter, rolling my eyes as I pull into my driveway. I unlock the car door and pull my keys out of the ignition, quickly running over to Adam's side of the car to sling an arm around his waist.

"Let's go. Honestly, it looks like you cut your leg open on something so I'm just gonna disinfect it - but if you cut it on metal then I'm forcing you to go to the hospital for a tetanus shot." I warn, pushing the door of my house open. Adam doesn't speak but I hear his grunt of agreement before he begins to lope towards my kitchen table. "Do you do this a lot?" He asks, his eyebrow raised as I grab the basket full of disinfectants and gauze from the supply closet. "I was expecting Andrew to come showing up again needing urgent care...and I tend to look after anyone - anything, really - that I find wounded. It's a problem." I admit, while ripping gauze and pouring a generous amount of peroxide on it. Adam stays silent while I dab the disinfectant onto his wound, occasionally letting out a hiss of pain every now and then. "The good news is that your cut is shallow. The bad news is that I don't have bandaids big enough to cover it." He shrugs and sits back in his chair and I can feel his intimidating gaze on me as I bent over to pick up the basket. "I could understand, you know." He says finally, smirking. "Understand what?" I ask casually, sitting in the chair opposite of Adam. "I understand why Andrew protects you the way he does." I blink, "He doesn't protect me - he bullies me." Adam's lips twitch. "But you like him anyways." I open my mouth to deny the statement but Adam's piercing glance warns me to do otherwise. "I do like him." I admit reluctantly. "He has Lacey, though. I think they're good for each other." He snorts, shocking me into silence. "Lacey is not good for Drew. He's just a baby - no matter how often he says he isn't. She's too selfish; they'd never work out." The room falls silent and I look up. "I guess you live in the Heights too. Stay the night. Andrew left some clothing in the guest room." Adam nods. "If you can, just drop me off at your school. I'll take Andrew's car home." The rest of the night passes without incident and Adam proves to be much, much more charming and a better conversationalist than Andrew. Still, I found myself wondering what he was doing and I found myself wondering if he was safe in the Heights, alone.

Damn. My head is so far over my heels someone could probably sign me up as a gymnast. I could be the next Gabby Douglas.

"Stop thinking about him." Adam says dryly, not looking up from his phone. "I'm not!" I snap. "You like him. It's a natural thing. Don't worry about it." Adam teases, still not looking up. "Why does everyone say that? I don't even like him. It's just a crush!" I blurt, pounding on my steering wheel with each word. "Oh? You have a crush then? What is this, 2nd grade? Who even has crushes anymore?" He says, finally looking up and smirking at me. I shoot him a quick glare before I pull out my ID and swipe so that the gates open for me to get into the student parking lot. "Get out of my car." Adam turns towards me, still grinning. "It would be good for him to like you. You're good. Strong, independent, kind, sweet, intelligent, witty and pretty hot, if I say so myself. He needs you. I really hate this word but you're mature. I want you guys together," Adam admits seriously. "but now is not the time. I don't recommend it. He's going through a hard time and it's not a good idea for you guys to be together right now." I open my mouth to reply to him but I'm too late because he's already sliding out of the car. Quickly, I reach for my backpack and sling it over my shoulder, simultaneously pushing open my car door. "Adam!" I shriek, surprised that he had managed to cover so much space after just a few seconds. I run after him, careful to avoid couples making out before first period and the teachers that usually handed out tardy passes for no reason.

As soon as I make it past the double doors, I'm running smack into a familiar broad chest. "Lena? Why are you running?" Andrew asks, pushing me back with his hands to look at me. "Adam..." I say, trailing off, trying to catch sight of the brown-haired boy. "What, he's here?" Andrew asks, incredulous. I sigh. "Yes, he's here. I was driving and I found him so I brought him home and -" "You brought him home?" Andrew interrupts, an emotion that looked suspiciously like jealousy flitting through his eyes. "Yeah. He was bleeding all over the road, Andrew. What was I supposed to do?" Andrew opens his mouth as if he had an answer but quickly snaps it shut, suddenly pensive. "Do you do that a lot? Do you just bring suspicious looking boys home with you?" He asks, eyebrows raised. "Only if they're bleeding boys!" I counter, realizing just how dumb that sounds as the words slipped out of my mouth.

Andrew mutters something and grabs my arm, pulling me to the other side of the hallway. "Elena, listen. Don't do that anymore. You can't just pick up strays and bring to your house - especially boys. It's dangerous, and frankly, it's dumb. Before you start blurting out a bunch of stupid excuses, just listen to me. You're my friend," The word friend drives a metaphorical knife through my gut and I finally realized why the friend zone was such a painful place for everyone. "and I care about you. I don't want to come to school one day and find out one day that you're -" "What's your last name?" I blurt. Andrew's face changes almost immediately, his face clouding up dangerously. "Why do you want to know?" He snips, clearly irritated. I hesitate. "I'm your friend...but I don't know your last name. That's kind of weird, don't you think?" "Wayne." He mutters, not looking at me. "Wayne?" I whisper, fear piercing through my heart. I smack his arm. "What, like Bruce Wayne?" I tease, trying to skirt around the fact that the boy I was completely infatuated with is a Wayne. Andrew looks up, staring at me curiously. "No...not Bruce Wayne. I'm a Wayne. The scary one. From the Heights."

CHAPTER 7

3 MONTHS LATER

"Shut up, Andrew. No one cares about your opinion." Tessa groans, throwing a handful of M&Ms at Andrew's unnaturally beautiful face.

"All I said was that I wanted to watch Finding Nemo!" Andrew whines, sitting back on the couch, pouting.

I roll my eyes and pick up the tray of hot chocolate and shuffle towards the couch where my two friends were sitting. "Elena, honestly. Why do you even deal with her? She's abusive and abrasive and mean and - and -"

"He's just grumpy because Lacey doesn't reply to his text messages anymore." Tessa says simply, a grin in her voice.

"I'm not grumpy!" Andrew snaps, still pouting.

I roll my eyes, "Shut up, Andrew. You're totally grumpy." I set the tray on the table and turn to him, shooting him a look. "Tessa is going through a hard time and you said you'd come over and help me cheer her up so no, we're not gonna watch Finding Nemo, we're gonna watch She's the Man." Andrew grumbles irritatedly and slouches even more in his seat.

In all honesty, getting close to Andrew meant getting closer to Lacey and I found that they had a pretty strong relationship - I guess 10 years of friendship does that - and they were practically always together. It hurt at first but then again, I'd always been good at suppressing my feelings while they festered inside of me. We were nearing their 5 month anniversary and Andrew was starting to get anxious about something everyday, often looking at things that weren't really there and generally just jumpier than usual. Being a Wayne hadn't really influenced our friendship at all; in fact, I found myself more interested in him and my complex had started to grow even larger around him. As for Tessa, she had started spiralling out of control. She started mystery dating some guy she had met in school and they had broken up, which is why she's on my couch, where half a year ago I was sobbing in a fetal position after Stephen had broken up with me.

"She texted me back!" Andrew yelps, sitting up quickly. I glance at him just in time to see his face falling and his shoulders slumping.

Andrew nudges me and points at Tessa who had somehow managed to knock out after 15 minutes into the movie. "Elena, I need you to drive me to the Heights. Lacey said she's home. At my house. Mine. In the Heights." He stammers, shock clear in his voice.

I lean forward and grab my car keys, slipping into my super warm pair of Uggs (I'm a white girl, don't judge) and pushing the door open. "Come on, if Tessa wakes up and finds out I'm not here she's gonna freak."

Having a Mother Theresa complex couldn't possibly be bad, they think. How could it ever be bad? Having my complex lead me to drive Andrew all the way into the Heights where I was leered at after driving the gates and witnessed someone getting shot while I was trying to park. Somehow, I ended up inside Andrew's decrepit apartment, sitting on his lumpy couch beside Adam while they - and by 'they' I mean Lacey and Andrew - had a shouting match.

"You brought her? Are you serious? What is this, a party? What part of URGENT, DON'T BRING ANYONE did you not understand?" She yells, getting redder with each word.

"Obviously, he didn't understand the 'don't bring anyone' part." I mutter.

"What's wrong with bringing Elena? Lacey, what's even going on?" Andrew says calmly, his eyebrows furrowed.

"Elena this, Elena that. It's always Elena, Elena, Elena. Everyday, Andrew. What happened to, 'How was your day, babe?' or 'What happened, babe?'" She screams, her arms flailing around.

Adam elbows me and I lean towards him. "She's jealous!" He whispers, chuckling slightly at the end.

Andrew's jaw drops. "Lace..."

"Don't 'Lace' me!" She shrieks, getting even redder.

Adam snickers, "She's probably starting to tire from having to commit to just one guy. It's really getting to her. You should've seen their fight last week."

Internally, I'm relishing at the thought that the two of them fought a lot. For some reason, that made me feel pretty happy.

"Andrew, all I ask is that you just - you just!" She says, grasping for words that she couldn't find.

Andrew stares at her, his face stony. "What do you want, Lacey? Because, lately, you've been wanting an awful lot and I haven't been able to keep up." He says, his tone suddenly tired.

Suddenly, the tension in the room drops to a more personal level and looking at the bickering couple stopped being enjoyable and leaned more towards uncomfortable. I force my eyes away from the two of them and begin dropping on things like the dirty kitchen table and the grimy walls. I could tell that this place was barely lived in even though Adam claimed that he was here every night. It was pretty dirty - not the kind of dirty that attracted cockroaches and the like but just...grimy. A fine layer of dust covered everything in the room and grease covered everything in the kitchen.

"I don't know, Andrew. I don't know what I want. Aren't you supposed to know?" Lacey whines, stomping her foot. I look over at the two of them just in time to see Andrew staring at her with a 'What-the-fuck' look on his face.

"Lacey...how would I know what you want?" Andrew says slowly, as if he was talking to an infant.

"I - I just...you always know what Lena wants," She says, still calling me 'Lina'. "and everytime she's upset you bring her a pint of Haagen Daaz's Coffee ice cream and She's the Man. But when I'm upset, you bring me The Notebook and milkshakes. I want you to know." She whimpers, her eyes beginning to fill with tears.

I sit up straighter in my chair and grab Adam's arm. I lean over and whisper, "Let's go for a walk. A long walk."

Andrew's head snaps over to us and he nods at something on the kitchen table that I had been trying to ignore.

Adam rolls his eyes, "Yeah, yeah. Of course, Andy."

"Don't call me that."

"Yeah, whatever, Andy."

"The problem with the two of them is that, well, Lacey is needy. She needs him all the time and frankly, Andrew doesn't have time for that. She's not independent. All she has is him and it's not healthy." Adam says, sighing. "He shouldn't be with her but at the same time, he makes her incredibly happy. Like glowing happy. Awkward to be in the same room happy. But they're not gonna work out - they're better off as friends. Just friends. As his best friend, however, I admit that if she makes him happy right now then it's -"

He's cut off by a crash from an alleyway that was less than a feet away from us. Gunshots start firing and I'm standing, shocked. Guns weren't a thing that were a daily fixture in my life. In fact, when my parents were home, they liked to pretend that guns didn't even exist. Being shot in my neighborhood literally never happened - you never got shot because no one owned a gun. As a matter of fact, I didn't even know what a gun was until literally last year. Adam is standing in front of me immediately, his shoulders seeming even broader as he stands up straighter while he flicks off the safety on his gun.

"We're with Wayne." He growls, his voice low and, for lack of a better adjective, dark.

"Yeah? A lot of people are with Wayne now." The voice sneers, coming closer to us with every word. "Funny, how I haven't heard about any deaths caused by a Wayne for a while now."

I step forward and grasp onto Adam's shirt in fear, suddenly afraid.

"Wait, is that a...girl? I didn't know that you had a plaything now, Adam."

"She's not mine." Adam says simply. I hear a click and rapid footsteps and then something cracking as Adam swings his right arm.

"She's Wayne's. I highly recommend that you run whenever you hear the name 'Lena' because Wayne is always two feet behind her. I assume you're new to the game because you didn't go running as soon as I said his name. Next time you're dead." Adam steps forward easily, even with my hands attached to his shirt and I look down to see him stepping on the guy's wrist, breaking it and picking up the gun. "You're one of Maloney's, then?" He says, his voice now taking on a peculiar edge. The guy whimpers and Adam snorts.

"Adam, who is Maloney?" I ask hesitantly, completely aware of how angry he still was. I'm still gripping onto the back of his shirt, my heart still beating furiously. You would be if you had just encountered an almost shoot out.

"Collin Maloney - 19 years old. He wasn't always bad, in fact, he was basically the epitome of purity back when the Heights wasn't fucking crazy. Apparently, one of the Waynes shot down the entire Maloney family one night and ever since then, Collin has been going after us. Well, not really me, but mostly Andrew." Adam spits out reluctantly, his face twisting into anger.

"'Collin' isn't really a scary name..." I muse, chuckling at the end.

"That's why we call him Maloney. He might not be as scary as his goons; they've been running rampant through the Heights ever since he got them together. They think they're the Robin Hoods and we're the Sheriffs." Adam mutters, pushing the door to Andrew's apartment open.

"We met a Maloney Man." Adam says as soon as we see Andrew.

"Where's Lacey?" I say after a painful pause. Andrew looks over me and my stomach drops. "Andrew..." I trail off, unsure of what to say.

He shakes his head and sits up straighter, his jaw clenched. "I don't want to talk about it. You met a Maloney Man? Does he know her name?" Andrew asks, eyebrows furrowed.

"He knows her name is Lena. No last names, Andy. That was the rule, right?" Adam responds quickly.

"His name kind of reminds me of that kid from Stuart Little; kinda dorky. Maybe lovable." I say, snickering.

"Don't let the name fool you, Lena. He's far from innocent. He has the blood of half of my family on his hands." Andrew says, his entire face serious.

Andrew's POV:

After Adam and Elena tried to leave the apartment inconspicuously, Lacey's voice began to raise and she was shrieking.

"Elena this, Elena that. You only care about Elena! And you've changed, Andrew. You're different - you're not the guy that I knew two years ago!"

"Of course I'm not! It's been two years, Lace! Years! People change! We've changed. You've changed."

The realization that everything between us was suddenly different hit me like a ton of bricks. I hadn't realized it at first; the elation of having Lacey under my arm for these past five months while she committed to me was blinding. Now? I saw it. Before, Lacey wasn't jealous ever. Before, The Notebook and milkshakes helped her get through a tough day. And now? I didn't know her that well anymore. Small realizations like that had started breaking the foundation of our relationship. Lacey and I got together because of our long history with each other and now that all those meaningless facts that make a relationship were no longer true, our relationship was starting to fail. Small things were breaking us because we didn't have big things to hold us together anymore. The attraction that I got from seeing Lacey's blonde hair had vanished.

The thing is, I didn't want it to. I didn't want 10 years of love between us to break now. Now that I had her, it was hard to admit that I had stopped caring about her the way that I used to. I felt guilty about starting to drift away from her - and it was bothering me big time.

"We don't belong together anymore, Andrew. We don't know each other anymore." Lacey whispers, not able to meet my eyes.

Somewhere, I felt something tear inside of me but it felt more like band-aid ripping off and not a stab in the gut like I had expected it to be. She looks at me, waiting for me to say something and then she shakes her head and walks out of my apartment for the second time.

Collin Maloney was never a blip on my radar. The Maloneys were a big family; they took up a lot of Clinton Boulevard. I didn't know anything about the Maloneys until someone told me that they had ratted out one of the Waynes. My dad, who was a self-proclaimed gang leader and some other crazy stuff, had raised me telling me that rats were never gonna be our friends. So, that night, he went out with a couple of my younger uncles (uncles that were 17-ish) and killed the entire Maloney family. Collin came out 10 years later, claiming that he was also a Maloney and started going on a killing spree. Suddenly, half of my uncles were dead and so was my dad - all because Collin, alone, had decided to avenge his family's death. I feel for him, really, I do. Maybe this is selfish of me but I didn't start hating Collin until he killed my dad - and not even for the obvious reasons, too. I hated him for putting me in charge of a motley crew that I never wanted to be in charge of.

She gasps and Adam twitches in surprise. "Tessa! I forgot about Tessa!" She shrieks. "Are you coming?" She asks, turning to me.

I shake my head. "I'm just gonna stay here; I don't want you driving back in the Heights later tonight."

"I'm starting to think that I should call you a softie instead of a bad boy. I've never heard of a bad boy that cares about the well being of others." She says teasingly.

When she starts turning to leave, I nudge Adam, who jumps up with a start. I nod at Elena's retreating figure and he gets up with a start, realizing what I needed him to do.

As soon as the two of them left, I walked out the door and headed towards Maloney's block, ignoring the glares on my back as I passed their rusted metal gate. I knew that it was basically suicide walking into the Maloney complex but I couldn't see past my blinding anger. I couldn't stand the fact that Maloney couldn't handle his boys - couldn't give them at least notice of who was apart of the Wayne family. Although there was only three Wayne gang members in the Heights at this moment, the rest of them could easily outnumber the Maloney men.

The difference between the Maloney boys and Wayne guys? We're loyal. I was raised on the foundations of loyalty, respect and trust and, okay, maybe that sounds kind of lame, but it is what it is. Besides being a gang leader whose very name instilled fear in the souls of others, he was also completely lame. Sure, who scared me to the point that I literally could not look in his eye, but he was great.

"Is that a Wayne I see?" I'm snapped out of my thoughts by a boy (man?) with a voice that was way too deep and didn't belong to his body. I'd finally met Collin Maloney - and the kid was a fucking runt. I stand up straighter and slide my hands into my pockets, my thumb grazing the cold metal of the gun in there. I notice that with every move that I make, one of Maloney's guys backs away.

"Yes." I say coldly.

"And what brings you to the Maloney block, if I may ask, Your Highness?" Collin sneers.

I half expect him to stick his tongue out and blow a raspberry at me but he just strolls closer to me. "I want to know what you want." I say simply, staring right into Collin's nervous brown eyes.

"I want to destroy the Wayne family." He replies, a ghost of a smirk appearing on his face.

I hold back a snicker and lean forward. "Yeah? How do you think you're gonna do that? Your goons are shaking where they're standing and your hookers are, well, hookers."

A shadow crosses onto Collin's face and suddenly, his right arm is swinging towards where my head was. I duck immediately and swipe my leg to knock him down. See, at this point, any Wayne guy would've jumped in to help me fight but in Collin's case, his Maloney guys were all looking for a place to hide.

"You're not gonna win anything with a gang like yours, Collin." I smirk and nod at the guys that were all running for cover and make eye contact with the guys that were just sitting there, drowning themselves in booze. "If I ever find out that a Maloney man has approached any of the people that are known associates with the Wayne family, I will personally castrate you in your sleep." Collin nods fervently, fear and a smidgen of anger clear in his eyes.

As I'm walking out of their decrepit compound, I hear footsteps behind me. I turn around and find myself standing chest-to-chest with Collin, who looks like he's about to shit himself.

"I –"

My right comes around and I hit him square in the jaw. In a flash, he's on the ground, on his back, his eyes sparkling with malice. I sigh inwardly; this probably wasn't such a good idea. I probably just agitated he one guy that I shouldn't have. Maybe he was coming to apologize.

Somewhere in the back of my mind, I imagined my dad smacking me upside the head and mocking me. "'Maybe he was coming to apologize.' Are you fucking dreaming? This guy, no matter how lame and wimpy he looks, is going to be your worst enemy." My 'dad' berates while slapping my head.

"You're gonna fucking regret that."

I hear as I walk away, my shoulders squared. I turn around, smirking. "Regret what? Aren't you comfortable on your back?" I half expect Maloney to get up and run at me again, but he's just laying on his back, his mouth twisted into an angry grimace. I shrug and turn around again, shoulders tensed, ready for anyone of his gang members to get up and run after me - but no one does.

I make it out of the compound and back in the safe Wayne territory. I throw a couple dollars at Bernie, a semi-insane hermit that usually slept outside of my apartment building and usually didn't speak much.

"Is your name Andrew?" Bernie rasps, smiling a tooty smile. I nod, and Bernie stands up, grunting with effort.

"I saw two ladies exiting your building. Really beautiful, the two of them. Honestly, the dark haired one..."

I nod warily, finally remembering through my angry haze that Lacey and I had broken up. "Thanks, Bernie." I manage gruffly, turning around to go back into my apartment.

"Did I say I was done?" I hear as Bernie gets up to shuffle towards me, muttering something about aliens and guns. "The dark haired one gave me 20 dollars and offered me a shower up in your apartment...but I said no. She's quite a keeper. The other one...she just walked right by me, didn't even give me a second glance. That one's quite a, excuse my french, bitch."

I stare at Bernie, "And how did you deduce all of this about her character?"

Bernie blinks. "The way she walks, boy! The way she looks at the homeless. Like were nothing but gum on her shoe - which we might be, but she doesn't have to look like that! And, by God, if you don't bang that other girl, I will!"

"Bernie..."

Bernie shakes his head, and turns to walk away.

I stare at Bernie as he walks away, and for the first time, I think of what it would be like if Lena was my girlfriend. The thought of her being my girlfriend is, of course, extremely appealing. She's a beautiful girl and she's smart, funny and kind to boot. The thought flickers across my mind but it disappears just as quickly. At the same time, I was still trying to convince myself that I was still in love with Lacey...even though I probably wasn't.

Wrong. We had. I climb the side railing of Lacey's house and climb up onto her balcony and towards the window that I was most familiar with in time to see Lacey falling onto the bed with some guy that has blonde hair. She's moaning loudly and squirming on her bed and in my head, I'm wondering why she never sounded like that with me.

Suddenly, I'm feeling emasculated and angry and very, very confused but the one thought that floats to the top is that Lacey had changed more than I thought she had. She turns her head and opens up her eyes that are suddenly filling up with shock but no regret. I was hoping for regret. Maybe she was too shocked to push the guy off of her but I watched as she kissed down her body and started pulling off her shirt before I finally snapped out of my stupor and climbed down the side of her house.

I slide into my truck and listen as it groans alive. I peel away from her sidewalk and start driving to the house of the girl that I knew would fix me. I reach for the key in her hiding spot and unlock the house door, still numb, still not sure what I was going to do. I mean, what do you really do when the girl that you had been intensely in love with had so easily discarded you for another guy in a matter of seconds? I trudge to Elena's couch and throw myself on it beside Adam and Tessa, who are staring at the TV in complete silence.

"What happened?"

Elena shuffles into my view with two cartons of ice cream and three spoons. I don't answer, instead standing up and taking the carton of ice cream and the spoons. I put it in Tessa's lap and then dig in, entirely aware of Elena's questioning stare at my back. Adam sits up and snatches the carton out of Tessa's lap to which Tessa snaps angrily and hits him on the head. Soon, the two of them are just smacking each other and Tessa hitting him with everything she had in her. I hear Elena heave a sigh as she sits on the recliner to the left of us.

Finally, the slapping sounds stops and Tessa leans on Adam's shoulder and starts to cry.

"Why are relationships so hard?" She sobs, her chest heaving. Adam sends a 'help!' look at me but I shrug, finishing off the carton of ice cream. Elena gets up and sits herself in between Tessa and I and I finally notice how tired she looks.

She gently pries Tessa off of Adam's arm and presses her face into her shoulder. "Everyone is a dick, Tessa." Elena says softly, stroking the other girl's hair.

"I want to drink." Tessa sobs, wiping away her tears. Elena starts to protest but I cut in, deciding that that was a brilliant idea.

It wasn't actually a very brilliant idea. After telling Tessa that I had booze in my car (you know, just in case I had a surprise family function) she decides that we should go drink at the beach, seeing as it was already 10PM and everyone was likely gone.

I grab the pack of beer and go lay on the sand and Tessa lays down beside me, sighing. "What's up with you and Lacey?" She says, grabbing a beer from my box. I shrug. "I went to say sorry," I start, downing half the bottle and continue, "and found her making out with some douche bag."

Tessa hisses and shakes her head. "That girl became a total bitch after Sophomore year." She says, also downing her beer.

"So what happened with you?"

She sighs, "Well, the piece-of-shit that I more or less fell in love called me a skanky bitch and said that I drink too much. I don't." She finishes as she finishes her bottle and opens another one. I smirk at her and one of my eyebrow raises. She shrugs. "Tonight, I drink all I want."

Elena walks into view and shakes her head at us, sucking her teeth. She walks off again and out of my line of sight, probably going back to her car.

"I think we should start a drinking game." Tessa says, already slurring slightly.

"Yeah? What are we playing?" I ask, giddy.

"Every - Everytime that Elena walks by us, we're gonna finish a bottle of beer."

"Dude…I don't think I have enough beers."

Tessa giggles as Elena walks back into our view, snapping open the beer bottle cap and quickly downing it.

"Come on, Lay, let's get durunk!" Tessa slurs, laughing maniacally.

I shake my head at Tessa but finish a bottle of beer nonetheless. Around the 6th time Elena comes back around, I'm more than buzzed and she's starting to look more beautiful than usual. I stand up and stagger after her, pulling her towards the surf. "I want to - I want to kiss you." I say as I lean closer to her. She's staring up at me with her dark blue eyes that are suddenly changing to Lacey's eyes. I kiss her and pull back, a smile stretching onto my lips. "Lacey." I say goofily before I turn around and walk back to Tessa, who is snickering at whatever weird thing she had just seen.

Tessa rolls over and is suddenly glaring at me before turning back onto her back. "You know…Lena really…really…really…likes you." She slurs, stabbing at the sky with each word. "I wish Trent had really…really…really…liked me." She mutters before promptly shutting her eyes and letting out a very unladylike snore. In my drunken stupor, I try to remember why the name 'Lena' was so very familiar to me and it seemed just within reach - the memory of her name - but everytime I almost grasped it, Lacey's face popped up in my memory and the memory was flitting off to some other dark area of my mind. I sigh contentedly and smack Tessa who snorts and rolls over, her back to me.

Sometime that night, I had drifted off to sleep and the next morning, I found myself with a crazy hangover sleeping in Elena's guest bed. I pad out of bed and towards the quiet clinking in the kitchen. I can smell bacon and hear the sound of glasses being pulled out of cabinets and whispers for coffee and milk. As I turn the corner, Elena freezes and blushes furiously before taking her fork and scraping the pancake off of her pan and onto a plate. "That's for you." She whispers, clearly aware of my hangover. I nod and walk towards the plate, grateful for sustenance.

"My head hurts!" Tessa whines, turning the corner and padding into the kitchen, sunglasses on her face. "That's what you get for proposing a drinking game." I mutter, stuffing a strip of bacon in my mouth and chase it with water. The kitchen is silent as we all eat and I get up to put my dish away, awkwardly knocking into Elena, who winces as we our skin touches. I drop my plate into the sink and note her weird behavior before sitting back at the table.

CHAPTER 8

Lena's POV:

"He kissed you?" Adam asks, shocked. The kitchen was pretty quiet because Andrew and Tessa were still passed out in their respective bed rooms, probably about to wake up with painful hangovers. I nod once and drop bacon into my pan, sighing.

"Yeah, but I don't think he knew that he was kissing me." I say reluctantly, blushing when I remembered the kiss.

"What?" Adam asks, confusion clear in his tone.

I shake my head, "It was a mistake. He was totally wasted last night - I don't blame him." Adam snorts and walks next to me and I see him shaking his head out of the corner of my eye.

"Besides," I say, flipping over the pieces of bacon. "I don't even like him."

Adam chuckles, "Are we seriously back to that again? Seriously?"

I shrug, "Back to what? It's what I've been thinking since I met him."

"But -"

"Just because I'm good for someone doesn't mean that they want me - and what if I don't want them?"

"You do." Adam says, completely serious.

I turn around and stare at him, open mouthed. "How are you gonna tell me who I do and do not like?" I snap, glaring.

Adam backs away jokingly, his hands in the air. "Didn't mean any offense - man, you're pretty prickly."

You would be too, if the guy that you have a stupid crush on finally kissed you but he thought you were somewhere else. But, like always, I opted to say something else, "This comes from taking care of two drunken idiots for half the night."

Adam grins, "I take care of one of those drunken idiots every night. You'd think by now, Andrew would've gotten better at holding his liquor."

I snicker, "He's a wimp, obviously."

Silence drops like a comfortable blanket in my kitchen and a couple minutes later, Andrew pads in, his eyes squeezed shut, his muscles rippling underneath his shirt. I turn away before Adam can see me drool and blush.

I turn around and my eyes land on his six pack and I can literally feel myself blushing harder. I wince and push the plate to him. "That's yours." I mutter, trying to look everywhere but at Andrew. Somewhere in the kitchen, Adam is snickering and I bite the inside of my cheek, doing everything I can to hold myself back from throwing my pan at his head. I can feel Andrew's gaze on my head but thankfully it drops when Adam comes over to pass him a fork and knife.

Tessa shuffles in muttering something that I don't bother to decipher and soon, the kitchen falls silent again but this time, there's an awkward tension that lingers in the room. Tessa gets up abruptly and I jump in my seat at the sudden noise. "What the hell is going on in here?" She whisper-yells, careful not to speak too loud. "You two," She connects a line between Andrew and I, "aren't even looking at each other. And Adam is sitting over there giggling like he knows something that I don't - which is impossible, right, Lena?" I grimace and muster up an awkward smile. Suddenly, Andrew's head snaps up and his eyes meet with mines, his eyes wide with horror his posture stiff. I shut my eyes - he knows.

"Can I - can I talk to you?" He says.

"No, you can't. You can talk to her in front of -" Tessa snaps, wincing as she does so.

"Sure." I cut her off and walk around the island. I can feel the tips of my ears heating up and wince, wishing that I could magically hide how red I am.

We're in the guest room and Andrew is looking everywhere but me, clearly flustered. "I..." I start, trailing off, not sure what to say to ease the awkward tension.

"I'm sorry. It was a mistake." Andrew says suddenly, shifting on his feet.

I feel my face fall almost immediately but quietly plaster a smile on my face and tease him, "Yeah? So you didn't enjoy it?"

Andrew grins, "Of course I did!" I beam, forgetting my place and Andrew quickly adds, "But mostly because I thought you were Lacey."

When the feeling of disappointment caused my chest to tighten and my stomach to twist, I realized just how deep I'd fallen for Andrew Wayne. And then I stood there as he left the room, a grin on his face, the question of 'When?' repeating over and over again in my mind. It had started as a crush and I had been so sure that it would always just stay a crush - after all, I didn't think I was ready to just start liking someone after my fresh heartbreak. When had I fallen in love with that stupid, smirking, broad shouldered, clear blue eyed, tall, smart, witty, funny, brooding, sweet, kind and - and - when? I couldn't wrap my mind around the new fact that I was now one of his many fangirls. Of course, the one thing that separated me from those idiots was that I was actually his friend...but I wasn't sure how much longer I could be.

Like I said before, I'm not as pretty as Lacey - no matter what everyone else thinks. Maybe I'm appealing to the boys that think with their dicks but to Andrew, I clearly wasn't attractive in any kind of way. A couple months ago, this would've shattered me. I'd changed a lot in half a year. I was still the idiot that pulled over for wounded animals and I was still the idiot that cried when movies like Finding Nemo and Pitch Perfect were put on and I was still the idiot that strived for a 99 average. And, apparently, I was now the idiot that had fallen in love with a boy that was in love with another girl.

Damn, this is inarguably the most twisted web ever.

The next day was Monday - a day that I was dreading more than usual because I was dreading seeing Lacey was Andrew...something that I figured was inevitable, considering the fact that that girl was a conniving, manipulative little thing. For a while, I had tried my best to like her just because she was Andrew's girlfriend - and now? Now that I knew that she had brought someone to her bed just seconds after she broke up with Andrew, I had a valid reason to not like her. Just imagining her possibly finding a way to get

Andrew to forgive her had me feeling digusted - everything about Lacey was disgusting to me now.

"Elena!" I turn around and plaster a smile on my face and inwardly, I'm melting at how adorable Andrew's trademark smirk was. Over the course of our friendship, I had stopped thinking of his actions as playboyish and began to recognize them as endearing. Andrew Wayne was the kind of person that didn't smile completely because he believed that those should be reserved for genuinely happy moments...like when he's around Lacey. A while back, when my crush had first began, I had realized that Andrew didn't usually smile in front of me, instead opting for a playful smirk or wicked grins.

"Andrew!" I reply, smiling wider as Andrew stops in front of me, curiously out of breath.

"Let's do something today." He says, grinning devilishly. "Do what? Like, after school?" I ask, staring up at him questioningly. "No...let's skip."

I blink. Sure, there were times in my life where skipping was a very, very appealing thought and one time, I'd almost snuck out of school but I'd never actually done it. I was too chicken. And, I couldn't think of anything that I could possibly be wanting to do instead of being in school - which is actually pretty sad, now that I thought about it.

"Do you really want to stick around to listen to your history teacher mutter stuff about France?" Andrew interrupts my train of thought, probably knowing that I was actually contemplating staying in school.

I bite the inside of my cheek and squeeze my eyes shut. "Let's go."

He grabs my hand and I quickly stomp on the butterflies that had started flying in my stomach. "Are we taking your car or my truck? Nah, let's take my truck." He says, grinning maniacally.

As soon as we were situated in the truck, he grins at me widely, almost a smile and puts the key and puts his truck into drive. As soon as we're out of the school parking lot, the radio is on and he's humming happily.

Strange, I think to myself, on Saturday, he was getting wasted at the beach and making out with me. Now, he's insanely happy.

"What happened?" I ask, curious.

"Nothing happened. I just realized that I shouldn't be sad over a girl that's changed so much because I have another girl - one that's my very best friend." He relinquishes childishly.

My chest squeezes again but I muster up a bright smile. "I'd like to meet this girl - she seems like the best thing that's ever happened to you." I expect him to reply with a 'no' but instead, he turns to me briefly, his eyes glittering mysteriously, as if he had a secret that I wasn't ever gonna know about.

He turns back to his wheel, and smirks. "Actually, she is."

When I don't reply, he looks over at me and his smirk grows even more devilish and ruffles my hair.

He probably said it jokingly, but even when he said something small like that, my chest burst with unexplainable happiness and a smile always found a way to creep onto my face. When he smirked at me, it was like the sun was coming out and birds were chirping. Disney had gotten something right - when you're in love, everything is cheesier and pinker and happier than it was before. When he gave me greetings hugs I'd find myself blushing and my brain turned into mush. Around Stephen, the guy I had convinced myself that I had loved, I always knew what I was doing, always knew where I was. The sun didn't come out when he smiled at me and when he kissed me, fireworks hadn't exploded in the back of my head the way that Andrew's kisses made me feel.

His stupidly low, husky voice caused butterflies to fly out from my ears and my toes to curl with pleasure. And he did this thing with his lips where they curl up ever so lazily into his trademark smirk. Awhile ago, it made him into this bad boy that I was so afraid to be near but now? Now, I couldn't be anywhere but by his side. Everytime I thought about him the way I currently was, the revelation that he was my Alaska always hit me like a ton of bricks.

Never, in a million years, had I ever thought I was going to be Pudge, the boy in Looking for Alaska that found happiness in just being in Alaska's presence. I didn't think that that kind of happiness existed - that being near Andrew's pinewood and vanilla scent could make me this irreversibly grinny tand glowy and excited for a long time after. When I read Looking for Alaska, I didn't think that I could ever find that kind of love. Andrew is my Alaska and I was Pudge. Deep down, I had been waiting for Andrew to break up with Lacey - the Jake in my story - so that I swoop in and claim him as my own but instead, he had dropped me to friendship status with a kiss that wouldn't come off of my lips no matter how many sugar scrubs I tried.

Andrew was slowly breaking my heart but he did it ever so delicately. So slowly, so painlessly that I didn't even mind it. That's something very new because since when did someone enjoy having their heart broken? Maybe they're just masochists - maybe I'm just a masochist.

Suddenly, Andrew's truck slows to a stop and I find us in the parking lot of an ice skating rink. I turn to him and gesture at my flip flopped feet.

"I don't have socks."

He grins, "I do."

"I can't skate." I protest, fear of falling on my ass in front of him bubbling up.

"You can hold onto me."

"We'll get caught!"

"We won't." He assures me. "Please? For me?" His lips pout slightly pleadingly and my shoulders slump forward. His face brightens and he jumps out of the driver's seat, pulling his keys out and slamming his car door. I lean to pull my door handle open but it's already opening and his face is smiling when I step out. He gives me his hand and I blink before I take it, confused. "Why do you look so confused, Elena? Smile!" He yells, still grinning widely.

A smile stretches onto my face on its own and I curse my body for betraying so wantonly.

He pulls me into the rink and to the desk where the tickets and skates were being sold. "Two tickets and," He looks at my feet. "a size 5 and size 12, thanks." He reaches into his pockets and pulls out three twenties and passes the guy the money as the guy passes us the skates.

As we walk away, the guy behind the desk yells, "Have fun on your date!" I start protesting but Andrew shushes me and pulls me towards the benches.

"If they think we're dating, they might let us ride on the Zamboni!"

I roll my eyes at his childishness and he quickly pulls his skates on, frowning when he noticed that I only had one boot laced up and ready.

He helps me and then pulls me to the ice, grinning at how wobbly I was looking.

"Okay...let's go!" He helps me onto the ice and pulls me along with him.

I start slipping immediately, and I blush as I fall on my ass.

He starts laughing and I get up, frowning. I crawl towards the wall grabbing onto it like I was going to die if I let go. "Aw, that's no fun, Elena! Just let go!"

I shake my head fervently and he sighs.

"Fine, suit yourself!" He says singsongily, skating away from me backwards.

"Show off!" I yell, my voice wobbling as I slid at little bit more.

For what feels like an hour, I'm 'skating' around the rink, basically glued to the wall, afraid to let go. Suddenly, I'm being pushed from behind and my hands are no longer on the wall. Maybe this helps when you're on a bike but in an ice rink? No bueno. I'm suddenly flying towards the other side of the rink and I'm not very sure how to stop, let alone change direction. I shut my eyes, arms out, ready to collide with the wall when two arms wrap around my waist.

Andrew is chuckling, a wicked glint in his eye.

"Andrew!" I moan, my knees shaking. "Are you serious? I could've - I could've gotten a concussion or something!"

He's shaking his head, a smirk still on his lips. "I wouldn't have let you get hurt." Suddenly, I'm all too aware of how close we are and it seems like Andrew's head is bending and his lips almost meet mine. My eyes flutter shut and then -

"Off the ice! Time for the Zamboni!"

My eyes snap open and I clear my throat as Andrew loosens his grip on my waist and awkwardly wipes something on my face.

"There was something on your face." He says quickly before pulling me out and onto the benches.

I sit on the bench stiffly, disappointment rising in me like a tidal wave. I should've known. I was so ready for a kiss and I probably looked like an idiot with my eyes shut. I was so willing to ruin our friendship because, let's face it, we'd never work. I wasn't his type and I probably never be.

I get up and dust off my butt. "I'm gonna head to the bathroom. I'll be right back."

Andrew looks over at me and nods but his diverts his attention immediately back to the Zamboni on the ice.

I'm not looking up, still wallowing in my self pity when I crash into a rock hard figure.

I look up and my eyes meet with the face of a probable Abercrombie god. Immediately, my cheeks are heating up and I'm stuttering apologies. The guy is biting his lip as I apologize awkwardly and I finally stop my enslaught of sorries.

"God, I'm so embarrassing." I mutter, averting my eyes.

"You're really cute." The Abercrombie god says brazenly, his voice weirdly deep but kind of soft at the same time.

I look back up at him, staring in surpise at how ruggedly handsome he is. Very cute...like Nick Roux but with brown eyes. "I'm Collin Maloney. What's your name?"

CHAPTER 9

His name rings bells in the back of my mind but for some reason, I can't connect the dots.

"Have we met before?" I ask quizzically.

"Nah, I think I'd remember a face as pretty as yours." He flirts smoothly, smiling.

I roll my eyes inside but smile widely outside. "Well, my name is Lena. Lena Parker."

"Are you here with anyone?" Collin asks, still smiling.

"Yeah, my best friend Andrew."

Collin pouts adorably but I'm not fazed, instead thinking that Andrew is much, much cuter. "Aw, that really sucks. The good ones are always taken."

I blink. "I said he's -"

"Your best friend, yeah, whatever, blahblahblah. It always starts out as a best friendship until someone falls in love. It never works out." Collin says knowingly.

I roll my eyes. "I doubt that'll happen to us."

Something catches his eye behind me and he blinks rapidly. Suddenly, Andrew is beside me, his face a mask of anger.

I blink. "Maloney." He growls, his eyes flashing. Fear rises inside of me belatedly as I remember why his name was so familiar to me.

"Oh my God..." I whisper, staring at Collin.

He didn't look like a sociopath...and he definitely didn't look like a killer or even the leader of a gang. Even though we were barely talking to each other for 15 minutes, I could tell that the guy was too soft to hurt anyone.

Andrew, however, glared at Collin with his lip curled. "Why are you talking to Elena?" He forces out, his voice low and angry. A smile stretches even wider onto Collin's lips. "Oh, my. Is this the 'Lena' that I'm supposed to stay away from? Oddly enough, I couldn't remember that little fact. Now I understand why you don't want me anywhere near her. She's quite the looker." Collin croons, a malicious glint in his eyes. When neither of us responds, he continues. "But, alas, you're a Wayne...and Waynes seem to always have what I want."

Andrew steps forward and I'm quick to grab his arm, shaking my head.

Collin's eyes widen a fraction at our interactions and then he steps back, still smiling. "I'm going to go...and Lena?" He says my name silkily, as if he liked the way it felt in his mouth. "It looks like one of you has already fallen in love...and maybe they don't know yet." Collin says while staring at Andrew. He walks away, his gait loping and graceful, almost like a predator.

"It looks like one of you has already fallen in love..."

Was I that transparent? Was it that obvious?

"...and maybe they don't know yet."

No...he can't be talking about me. He was looking at Andrew the entire time. Maybe Andrew...no. I wasn't going to get my hopes up just so that they could get crushed. I was hoping for too much. There was no way.

"Elena?"

If he liked me, I wasn't sure what I was going to do. Scream? Laugh? Cry? Dance? What would happen between us anyways? We'd probably break up and that left me with a broken heart and probably a broken friendship. Wishful thinking. I was wishfully thinking that Andrew would magically fall in love with me and he'd sweep me off my feet and...

"Elena?"

I snap out of it, and look up, our eyes meeting. He doesn't say anything so I blurt out the thing that was really pressing on my mind...

"Collin is really, really cute."

Andrew's eyes darken and an expression that I wasn't too sure about flickers onto his face before he semi growls. "He's not 'cute' he's dangerous, Elena."

I shrug. "I didn't say that he wasn't...I said that he's attractive ...appealing to the eye. If he wasn't out to get you, I'd probably get his number. Or something." I say, remembering Collin's Nick Roux-esque face.

"Elena..."

"What?"

"I didn't know that Maloney is your type of guy."

I grin, "I didn't even know I had a type!"

Andrew doesn't miss a beat, "He looks like a boy. I didn't know that you went after boys." He says as he leads me back into the rink and towards the benches, helping me take my skates off.

"Well, please point me in the direction of a man." I mutter, rolling my eyes.

"There's one sitting right here."

I look up to see Andrew pointing at himself, smirking. "I don't see a man anywhere." I say, looking all around Andrew. He fakes hurt but I roll my eyes. "Aw, did I pawp your bwig weego?" I pout. Andrew puffs up his chest comically and shakes his head. I burst out in laughter that leaves me bent over, my stomach hurting from laughing so hard. When I'm done wiping the tears from my eyes, I finally see Andrew...and the big smile on his face. Yes. A smile. A real smile.

My heart soars as Andrew starts laughing too.

God, I was so totally whipped.

Andrew drops me off in the school parking lot and watches me get into my car before he drives off, creepily winking at me. I turn my car on and then turn around to drop my bag into the passenger's seat, promptly emitting a scream when I notice that someone else is in my car.

"Holy fucking shit what the fucking hell are you doing in my fucking car!" I yell, ignoring the fact that I had dropped the f-bomb three times and probably was spitting all over the place.

Collin turns to me his expression calmed. Me? I had thrown myself against my car door, trying to get out. Unfortunately, Collin had my carkeys out of the ignition in a flash and locked up the doors every time I tried to get out.

After a couple of minutes of me just trying to unlock the door, Collin sighs. "Are we going to be doing this all night? Honestly, if I had known that you're dumb enough to get in the car without looking first, I probably would've abducted you at your house." I stop trying to unlock the door and turn to him, confused.

"Why are you going to abduct me?"

"Because you mean something to Andrew and that means a lot to me." He replies simply, nonchalantly putting his feet onto my dashboard and adjusting the seat so that he was now reclining.

"But..."

"Don't try the 'parents' card. No one is gonna call the cops because your parents are in Mumbai."

"Wait, how do you -"

"I sent them there. God, can your questions be anymore predictable?"

I pause, "What did you mean when you said that one of us was already in love?"

Collin blinks rapidly and stares at me, confused. "You can't see it? I know Wayne. I might hate him, but I know him like the back of my hand and he likes you. Loves you, maybe." Collin cocks his head and stares at me, searching my eyes.

I shift awkwardly, feeling violated.

His eyes suddenly brighten with excitement and then, "And, oh my God. You love him!" Collin looks like he's holding back a squeal and I feel myself heating up.

He snatches the phone from my lap and dials Andrew's number, placing it next to his ear, grinning maniacally. "Hello?" He pulls the phone away from his ear and presses the 'speaker' button.

"Where's Elena?" Andrew growls angrily.

"Come on, Lena. Don't be afraid. Say something." Collin urges, still grinning.

"Andrew…" I start. I trail off helplessly and look up at Collin who looks like he's on the verge of laughter.

"Your little pet is fine, Wayne. Now, tell me why you didn't tell me that you're in love with her?" Collin teases, still reclining lazily in my passenger seat.

"Maloney, if you don't get out of that car I'll -"

"You'll what? Set the gang of Waynes that are off vacationing somewhere after me? That's right, Wayne. I know you've been bluffing this entire time." Collin spits out, his face darkening. "I'm gonna kill her. I'm gonna skin her and then hang her upside down in your dirty little apartment. I'm going to kill her the way that -"

"Don't you dare!" Andrew yells into the phone, his voice strained.

"But first…I'm gonna let you have her. When you least expect it, I'm going to come and you're never gonna see her again. When you're finally happy and together, I'm going to come and kill her…just like when you killed my family." Collin says, his voice icy. He hangs up and turns to me, the dark clouds no longer on his face, a sunny smile on his face instead. "I won't kill you…anytime soon. I'll see you in a while. Goodbye, little Lay." He leans forward and kisses me on the cheek, his lips making the rest of my face feel dirty. He opens his door and steps out, tossing me my keys as he saunters away from my car, whistling happily.

Five minutes later, Andrew is pulling into the school parking lot and parking his car sloppily next to mine. I hear a slam of a door and then my door is being yanked over and I'm being pulled out of my car. In my haze, I thank whoever that I hadn't put my seat belt on yet.

"Elena?" Andrew is shaking me, his eyebrows furrowed, his jaw clenched. "Elena!" He yells again when I don't respond the first time.

I blink my way out of my haze and look at Andrew. "He said...he said he's going to kill me. But he said he's going to do it later." I say, still blinking. "He said...he'd do it later." Somewhere, in my shocked state of mind, I decided that this was one of the funniest things ever and started laughing.

Andrew is standing there stiffly, staring at me as I laughed, his chest heaving up and down. Finally, I stop. "Andrew?"

"Elena. He could've killed you." He says lowly, his jaw still clenched.

I roll my eyes, "Oh, shut up. He obviously didn't so relax."

"But..."

"Collin said -"

"Why are you on first name basis?"

"He seems pretty nice."

"He wants to kill you! Are you fucking insane?" Andrew shrieks in disbelief.

"That's besides the point -"

"Oh my God, Elena! That's the point! If you died I'd...I'd..."

Another car pulls into the school parking lot and Adam gets out of it, someone tall following him. I smile when I see them and start waving, my smile brightening as their figures come closer.

Adam grins, "Wow Lena! I didn't think you'd ever be this excited to see me!" I roll my eyes and smack him on the shoulder and wave at Bernie, the homeless guy that I had seen outside of Andrew's building.

"What the hell is the hermit doing here?"

I whip my head around to glare at Andrew, and start waving excitedly at Bernie.

"Bernie!"

"You're much more beautiful than I remembered!" Bernie says flirtatiously, wiggling his eyebrows.

"Why, thank you!" I wrinkle my nose. "Remember how I offered you that shower? I'm thinking you should come home with me and take it."

Bernie grins but then his face falls into a more serious expression. "Adam tells me that you've got the Maloney boy after you. When I was still a Wayne, all I remember is the Maloney family going crazy. Stepping into all kinds of territories until one of the members sexually assaulted one of the Wayne women. They're a crazy bunch, they are. When Adam told me that one had cornered you, I told him to drive me here to beat him up but it looks like Mr. Wayne is ready to do that himself." Bernie leans closer to me, smiling. I hear Andrew move beside me but I turn around, shooting him a warning glance. "That boy is...infatuated." He whispers, a grin clear in his voice.

"Don't be silly, Bernie! Now come on, let's go home."

"Home?!" Andrew yelps, starting after me.

"Yes, home. Bernie needs a shower."

Andrew blinks and shakes his head slowly. "You've gone crazy."

I shrug, "That's your fault."

Adam steps up and stands behind Andrew, grinning. "Don't worry about her, Andy. Bernie is quite capable." I notice that Adam nods at Bernie in respect and I stare at him curiously, making a note to myself to ask about that later.

Bernie steps out of the shower and smiles at me happily while he tugs on a pair of my dad's old sweatpants. He comes out shirtless and I find myself gaping at how fit he is. Of course, he didn't have a 6 pack like Andrew, but his pecs were very well defined and so were his arms. With all the dirt scrubbed off his body and his teeth gleaming white courtesy of a new toothbrush, he didn't look half bad.

"So, Bern. Tell me what Adam meant back in the parking lot!"

Bernie glances up from me as he slurps his cereal sloppily. Of course, it was 8PM but I was too lazy to cook. Bernie, however, was grateful for anything. He grins at me and I blink at how much he looked like Bradley Cooper in that moment.

"Well, that boy didn't wanna bring me - said I'd dirty his car (which I did) - so I got him in a headlock and punched him in the stomach until he said he would." He says, still grinning happily. I blink at him several times, not sure how Bernie had been able to get Adam into a headlock.

"Bernie…"

"Yes, Miss?"

"Didn't you know that my name is Lena?"

Bernie's face brightens, "Lovely name for a lovely girl. You're mighty beautiful, Lena. Surprised the younger Wayne boy hasn't snatched you up." He says thoughtfully, his spoon halfway to his mouth. "Well, not that surprised. That blonde girl is quite the minx." He shoves the spoon into his mouth and then grins at me again. "Honestly, that boy wants you more than he knows."

I open my mouth to ask him what he meant but my house door is suddenly crashing open.

"Elena!" Andrew yells, his jaw clenched, eyebrows furrowed.

I blink at confusion as Adam calmly walks in behind him, rolling his eyes as he stared at my newly broken doorknob. "What the hell?" I shriek, jumping out of my chair.

Bernie snickers behind me and mutters, "I told you so!"

I shoot him a glare and I glance at Adam, now angry. Adam raises his hands in surrender and shrugs.

He opens his mouth but Andrew beats him to it. "I was calling you to make sure that you got home alright and you didn't pick up!" He mutters, his eyes narrowed as he glares at Bernie.

Adam snickers, "He literally called your phone more then 10 trillion times, Lena. It was ridiculous. I told him it was probably off or something but he insisted on coming to check on you."

I spear Andrew with an icy glare. "What the hell am I gonna do about my door? If I don't get it fixed soon, anyone can get into my house. Is that what you wanted?"

Andrew doesn't reply and I realize that he's not sure what to say. The room is filled with tension until his entire face lights up and grins happily at me.

"We'll stay over tonight." He declares, still grinning.

I glare at him, "Bernie is staying over tonight. Just Bernie." But Andrew isn't taking 'no' for an answer. He's already walking to the bathroom, kicking off his shoes on the way, throwing a devilish smirk over his shoulder.

"I told you so." Bernie says, smiling widely as he walks past me and towards the guest room I had shown him to before.

I glance at Adam, who is still smirking. I sigh. "If you don't wipe that stupid smirk off your face right now -"

"Adam! Don't mess with Elena!" I hear Andrew yell from the bathroom.

Adam grins, "He doesn't know it, but he likes you."

"Oh, shut up with that. He doesn't like me. I'm like his sister or something else that's completely platonic." Adam shrugs, still grinning. "I don't know...I've never seen him break down a door for a girl before..."

I smile at him mischievously, "Has he broken down a door for you before?"

Adam nods immediately and my smile grows even wider. "So does that mean he likes you?" Adam stands there, his mouth opening and closing before he lamely retorts, "No! He's like a brother to me!"

I smile and lie, "He's like a brother to me, too."

But then Adam's eye is twinkling; "Don't lie to me, Lena. I can see it in your eyes. You're in lo-ove!"

I glare at him and turn away, also padding to my guest room. "Get my door fixed before my parents come home or else I'm never talking to the Wayne boys ever again."

"Don't be like that, Lena!" I hear and laugh as I pass by the bathroom door, Andrew walks out, smirking at me.

"So...I'm just your 'brother'?"

I blink as he gestures at his shirtless torso. I gape at him, my cheeks immediately flaming at the sight of him.

"I..."

He steps closer, biting his lip as he drops his hands onto my waist. My jaw is still dropping and suddenly I'm completely aware of every single hair on my body. He's dragging me backwards into the bathroom and the door shuts behind me. We're alone and then - and then...

He's lowering his head, his eyes hooded, his eyelashes fanning. I'm blinking rapidly and despite what my mind is telling my body, my hands find their way to his bare torso. His rock hard, completely flat torso and I'm also biting my lips. I'm in a daze, the only thought that manages to run through my mind is how weirdly perfect our bodies fit together. Suddenly, his hands are dropped from my waist and his head is snapping up, a lazy smile on his face.

"Am I still just your brother?" He opens the door behind me suavely and steps out, tossing me a smirk over his shoulder.

I shut the door behind him and lean over my sink, my chest rising and falling hard. What the hell just happened? I think to myself, my mouth dry. I had been so ready to kiss him in my bathroom with two other men in my house. I wasn't thinking...well, I was, but all I could think about was how incredibly handsome he looked with his eyes half closed and his shirt off. I splash cold water and my face and slap my face a couple times before sighing. I was trying to suppress my attraction for a boy that oozed sex.

What seems like a couple minutes later when the red in my cheeks had gone down I finally got the nerve to open my bath-room door and walk back into the living room where I could feel Andrew's gaze follow me as I plopped down between Bernie and Adam.

"Why are you so red?" Adam asks, grinning as he nods sugges-tively at Andrew. I spare a glace at Andrew and find that he has a placid look on her face but the traces of a smirk are left on his lips.

Of course, the combination of Adam's question and Andrew's ghost-smirk cause my cheeks to flame again and I groan. "I don't want to talk about it."

Adam elbows me playfully and I shoot him a (hopefully) withering glare. He shrinks back but still wiggles his eyebrow, still grinning stupidly. Bernie grunts beside me and then turns to look at me, a grin now on his lips.

"I reckon that Miss. Lena and Mr. Wayne have..." He trails off but also wiggles his eyebrows, causing my ears to heat up as well.

Andrew snickers over at his end of the couch and I groan, embarrassed. "Oh my gosh, Bernie! I thought that you were on my side!"

But Bernie shrugs and pulls an innocent face. "There are no sides, Miss! I was just stating the obvious."

I drag a hand down my face and sigh. "Nothing happened between us, you idiots."

"On the contrary," Andrew starts, throwing a wicked glance in my direction. "I seduced her."

Adam laughs beside me and elbows me. "He seduced you, did he?"

"That's not how it happened!" I whine weakly, shooting Adam a glare.

"I overheard her telling you that I'm like a brother to her." Andrew pouts. "Friend zoned, I can take. But family zoned? That's a low blow - especially from a beautiful girl like you. I'd say that I'm out of the friend zone now, right?"

Although I was still embarrassed, I managed to stutter, "N-no. Even Adam isn't as far into the fr - friend zone as you."

Adam protests beside me but I sit stiffly, still glaring at Andrew, humiliated.

"Don't pout, Elena. It doesn't look good on you." Andrew says, still grinning.

I roll my eyes. "I'm pouting because I don't want to think about kissing your stupid crusty lips, Andrew."

Andrew fakes an appalled look; "My lips are not crusty!"

Ugh, he's right. They're not. I think to myself, inwardly moaning.

Bernie mutters something and then shoots the both of us dirty looks. "You two are almost adults; settle this the right way. Just kiss her!"

I shoot Bernie a glare and shake my head. "He already kissed me!"

"I was drunk and I thought you were Lacey!" Andrew protests, mock pouting.

Bernie lets out a low whistle, shaking his head. "Damn, Mr. Wayne. You've dug yourself into a deep hole, yes, you did."

I ignore Bernie and plow on; "That kiss was enough to traumatize me completely." I watch as Andrew's face falls and he actually looks wounded. "But, to be honest, your abs are A+ - I'll give you that."

Bernie chuckles and slings an arm around me. "I think it's time for all of us to go to bed, little Miss."

"Go to bed?" Andrew repeats staring at the two of us, thoroughly confused. "You guys aren't going to bed together, right?"

I smile innocently up at Bernie who is grinning at me. I hear Adam snicker in the background and then Bernie and I shrug simultaneously. "I don't know, Andrew. Are we?" Bernie quickly pulls me toward the bedroom, chuckling under his breath. At this point, Adam was laughing so loud that neither of us could hear Andrew following us. I drag towards my room, with all the intention of shoving him down the hallway towards the guest bedroom but suddenly Bernie's arm is ripped from my shoulder and Andrew is standing beside us, his eyes narrowed.

"Really?" He asks, shocked. "You really were planning to let him into your room?"

I blink and divert my attention to Bernie, who's shoulders were shaking from trying to hold his laugh in. I shrug, "We weren't going to do anything...he didn't have anywhere else to sleep!"

"He could've slept in the guest room!" Andrew retorts, frowning.

"Yeah, but the bed space is gonna be all taken up with you and Adam in there." I reply simply, trying to bite back a smile.

"I..." He says, genuinely at a loss for words.

Bernie finally speaks up, barely holding back his chuckles; "Well, I think that maybe the Miss and Mr. Wayne should sleep in the same room. I can share it with my boy Adam."

Andrew looks satisfied, a smile appearing on his face. He turns around to shoot a grin at Bernie and I take that moment to shoot daggers at Bernie, irritated that he had switched sides last minute. Andrew turns around and I glare at him as he pushes his way into my room, whistling when he saw the size of my bed.

"I can work with this."

"Andrew, sit down." I ask, watching as Andrew starts pacing around my room, his hands in his hair.

"I can't get over the fact that you'd let Bernie into your room and you pick up strays in your car. You...ugh. You invite danger into your house!"

"Bernie isn't dangerous."

"Well, he could be!"

"Right...but he's not."

"Jesus, Elena. You've become one of my best friends," Andrew says, his eyebrows furrowed. "and I don't know what I would do if you got hurt."

"If I'm one of your best friends, why does it matter whether or not I see you as a brother?" I reply quickly, watching as several emotions I couldn't decipher flickered across his face.

He turns away from me, his back towards me and I see his shoulders heave as he sighs. "I can't explain that." He turns around, his face now pained and I feel something punch me in the gut.

Figures - the only guy that I really, really wanted after Stephen couldn't even look at me without putting himself into emotional distress. Of course, there's always Collin - butthat guy told me that he wanted to skin me alive and hang me upside down like a piece of meat. I flinch as I remember the way he said my name, silkily and seductive. Collin was definitely scrawnier than Andrew but, come to think of it, Andrew was built like a machine. Not body builder ripped, but his shoulders were broader than anyone else's that I knew. I think of Lacey and hold back a sigh, disgruntled that I wasn't shorter and didn't have blonde hair. Then again, I can't even compare myself to Lacey - she had something that I would probably never have. Even after Andrew seeing her making out with another guy, he was still infatuated with her - something that I decided stemmed from his probable undying love for her.

Man, I think to myself as I watch Andrew settle down at the edge of my bed, I would give anything for him to look at me the way that he looks at Lacey.

I wanted to read into his sudden bouts of jealousy and how angry he was when he found out that Collin had almost killed me, but I chalked it all up to him being protective. I guess with the body and his own personal complex, he was just really, really protective of me. I guess that I was being an idiot with my feelings - liking a guy that would never like me back because he's in love with a girl that has her head too far up her ass to see how much he loves her. Funny, how things worked out for me.

I chuckle to myself when I remember that I was trying to fight off my feelings for Andrew at a time like this.

The next morning, I'm startled awake by someone angrily pulling me out of my bed and whispers that I could barely understand. I'm being shaken back and forth and worried whispers and screeches of disbelief fill my hearing. I wince and force my eyes open, no longer bleary when I realized that my parents had returned home.

"Elena Emma Parker, please explain to me why there is a boy in your room and two other boys sleeping outside of your room and the front door of our house broken down!" My mother whispers furiously, her eyes wide, gaping at me.

As I opened up my mouth to try to calmly reason with her, I feel Andrew sidle up behind me, probably shirtless, yawning loudly. "Elena, what are you doing up so early?"

My mother gasps and I shut my eyes, holding back the intense urge to drag a hand down my face and moan. I jab an elbow into Andrew's rock hard and, you guessed it, shirtless stomach and half a second later, he's stuttering apologies and garbled explanations. I jab at him again, my cheeks flaming because this time, I was fully aware of his bare skin and he steps back and away from me.

"Mom. Last night, I came home to our front door broken down and, fearing the worst, I called Andrew, who called his two friends - Bernie and Adam - and they came over and volunteered to watch over me. Andrew is like my brother and he came into my room probably to make sure nothing happened to me. He probably fell asleep; they're very protective people." I explain, keeping a mental note of all of the lies that I was spilling in that moment.

"And why didn't you call any of your girlfriends over?" She asks, not buying it.

"Do you really think that any of my scrawny female friends can even win in a fight with a big mindless oaf looking for trouble, Mom? Really?"

Her face softens with understanding and she mutters a reluctant 'thank you' to Andrew before her lips purse and she turns to me, her face sheepish. "I think...maybe you dad might've taken a bat and harmed those other two guys, dear."

Andrew sighs behind me and shuffles out, waving at my mom as he left, probably looking for Bernie and Adam. Mom watches as he leaves (well we both did, to be honest) and she turns back to me, a wicked gleam in her eyes. "He's a hunk." She says, biting back an obvious smile. I shut my eyes again and shuffle towards the bathroom, ignoring her squeals of excitement behind me. As I turn into the bathroom, she yells, "Don't think I've let you off the hook, Lena! We're going to have a talk about your choice in male company!"

Chapter 10

As soon as I step out of the bathroom again, I make a beeline for the kitchen where I hear the rumble of Andrew's familiar voice and Adam's snicker. My dad is standing in front of the stove wearing his ridiculous apron, a grin on his face as Bernie started talking about the time that some lady chased him off her property. I shake my head as my mom titters around the boys, a wide smile on her face as her gaze lingers on Andrew's model-like face. The kitchen falls into silence and as I'm ready to round the corner and reveal myself, my mom says, "So, which one of you is dating my Lena?"

I hear a couple choking noises and something falling on the floor.

"Is it you, Andrew? Honestly, it makes no sense that anyone is that protective that he got two of his friends to come over to watch a girl for the night. I mean, you guys look lively - wouldn't you rather be out partying? Meeting girls?" My mom continues calmly, her tone tinged with false innocence. I mutter a couple of expletives, every bone in my body wanting me to round the corner to stop her investigation. Of course, the bones that mattered didn't want me to go at all.

"Actually, Andrew has just gotten out of a relationship." Adam says uneasily, breaking the awkward silence.

"Really?" My mom says excitedly. I shut my eyes again, easily imagining my own mother jumping in excitement in the middle of the kitchen. "Wait. How about you, Adam? Are you interested in Lena?" She asks, a grin clear in her voice.

Someone chokes as Adam answers 'yes' calmly. And then someone else chokes as Adam goes on to say, "She's a very beautiful girl and I'd like to ask her out."

I take that moment to round the corner and stare at the group of people innocently. "Who would you like to ask out, Adam? I sure hope it's Tessa..." I say, spearing him with my glare.

Adam doesn't mess a beat, instead opting to grin widely. "Actually, I was talking about -"

"Let's go home." Andrew interrupts abruptly, shooting Adam a look through narrowed eyes, obviously angry at something that I couldn't figure out. Adam gets up, shrugging, throwing me a mischievous grin, causing red flags to start waving in my head. Andrew shoves Adam, causing the grin to falter for a second before he's in my face, pulling me into a very warm hug that I returned out of instinct. I smiled at him, questioning him with my eyes, not sure what was going on. He shakes his head and ducks down, pressing his lips to my cheek.

I hear a strangled noise and Adam snickers before letting go of me and walking calmly out my broken front door.

"Bernie!" Andrew snaps, irritated. I turn to see Bernie sloppily inhaling his pancakes and bacon and then waving goodbye happily at me. "Thanks a lot, Miss!"

As soon as the three boys left, my mom rounds on me, smiling so widely that my cheeks were hurting just looking at her.

"Your father and I were gone for, what, another two months and then this? When we came home three months ago, you were still moping around the house with not a friend in sight, let alone male ones and now we're home again and suddenly you have three male friends?" She shrieks, excited. "And," she continues, grinning. "I hear wedding bells between you and that Andrew boy!"

I stare at her drolly, confused. "Adam is the one that..."

"Yes, yes. I know about Adam. Clearly, though, there's something going on between you and Andrew. The two of you ooze chemistry. I feel like I'm reading a teen romance novel!" She sighs, content. "Of course, this morning your father had a conniption seeing that many males in the house while we were gone. You owe me one for getting him to calm down and stop from beating Bernie with a bat."

"Andrew doesn't like me like that, mom." I say tiredly, waiting for the grin to slip off of her face. Instead, she stares at me, tilting her head to the side, searching my face eagerly.

"Oh my gosh..." She says, her jaw dropping. "My little girl is in love."

I open my mouth to protest but find that I can't. My mom might be a little insane sometimes, but I couldn't lie to her. I got my dark hair and my blue eyes from her along with my pale skin. The height, however, I had gotten from my father. My mother was 5'3 of energy and unconditional love for me. I found that while staring down at her, I couldn't lie to her face. When I didn't protest her jaw snaps shut and a smile stretches onto her face - again.

"Honey, Lena is in love!" My mom yells, her eyes never dropping away from my face. The sound of pans dropping filters into my air and I sigh as my dad comes thundering out, his face cloudy, his lips twisted into a pucker.

"Who's the boy?" He thunders, his jaw clenched angrily.

I roll my eyes, "Dad..."

"You're too young to be in love - you don't even know what love is! Just two months ago you were being potty trained!" He shrieked, his face reddening with each word.

My mom and I blink at him, confused. "Dad...that was like 15 years ago..."

He reddens even more and starts opening and closing his mouth, searching for words to shriek out. My mom sighs and sidles up to my dad, wrapping an arm around his 6'3 stature. I watch as she comforts him down to a reasonable state of mind and my insides melt. I wanted that kind of relationship with Andrew - the kind where my touch was able to stop him from lunging at a villain.

"Who is it?" He asks again, his voice softer this time.

"Do you really want to know -"

"Andrew!" My mom interrupts, beaming.

My dad blinks and then looks at me, his head tilting to the side. "I always thought you had a thing for those wuss boys. Stephen was a wuss."

I cringe at the thought of Stephen and my dad sighs. "Well, if it had to be anyone, I'm glad it's Andrew. At least you're in love with someone that loves you back. It could be worse...it could've been that Bernie guy. He looks way too old to be associating with Andrew and Adam."

"He doesn't love me back..." I say, trailing off awkwardly. My dad blinks and then rolls his eyes. I note that my mom's arm had tightened around his waist.

"Of course he does. Why wouldn't he?" My dad says, his eyebrows furrowing.

"There's another girl." I sigh, my shoulders slumping forward.

My mom squeals and my father and I shoot her wary looks as she steers the both of us to the living room couch.

"Gosh, you're gonna have one of the most beautiful stories to tell your kids when you grow up. Your love story is gonna be the cutest thing in the world - !" She sputters, smiling dreamily. "But first, you need to get over this stupid idea that he's not in love with you. Maybe he wants to love her but I've seen the way he looks at you and it's not just lust. He loves you. Why else would he get so unreasonably jealous when that other boy asked you out?"

My dad blinks next to her and purses his lip. "Now, sweetie, I don't think that you're wrong but...don't you think that maybe he just doesn't love her yet? Maybe he isn't over the girl." He says reasonably, smiling kindly at my mom, whose cheeks puffed up.

"Well, okay. That makes sense but...I still like my theory better." My mom relents reluctantly, shooting my dad daggers. He smiles softly at her and presses a peck to her lips and I coo, watching as my mom flushes. Of course, 22 years of marriage did nothing to their love for each other except strengthen it.

I'm startled awake by the vibrating of my phone. I roll over, determined to ignore it, sure that it'd stop eventually. It did. Two minutes later, the phone starts vibrating again and I ignore it again until it stops. Then, you guessed it, it started it up again. I roll over and pull the phone from it's charger and bring it to my ear, now extremely annoyed.

"Hello?" I whisper into the phone, blinking at the flashing green 3:49AM on my alarm clock.

"Lena, I need your help." Adam says. I hear him sucking his teeth as something crashes behind me and yells of disapproval fill my ears. I sit up straight and slide off of my bed and towards my bathroom, washing my face and swishing my mouth with mouthwash.

"What do you need?" I finally say, sighing.

"Andrew is...smashed. And I need you to come and help me bring him home; he keeps asking for you." Adam relents finally. Rustling sounds fill my eardrums and then a muffled, "Andrew, get down from there!" startles me back into movement. I tiptoe down my hallway and towards the kitchen, swiping up my car keys.

"Where are you?" I ask finally as my car turns on and I pull out of my driveway. Adam recites his address and in 20 minutes, I'm pulling into a parking lot next to a playground. I get out of my car, making sure to lock the doors and look around for Adam and Andrew. I hear them before I see them; Adam is yelling for Andrew to get off of the swings and Andrew is chortling and hiccuping. I walk towards them and in a flash, Andrew is off of the swing and running towards me, occasionally stumbling. I blink in surprise as he flies into my arms, nestling his head in my chest.

"Lena!" He says happily, hugging me even tighter.

I look up to see Adam walking towards me, his eyebrows furrowed. "Two seconds ago, he was ready to punch me in the throat and then castrate me." He says, pursing his lips. "I don't know what's going on with him. When we got home, he told me to go to the grocery store and when I came back, he was completely wasted. I couldn't stop him from leaving and then...this."

Andrew straightens up, crushing me into his chest. I protest but he tightens his grip on me even tighter and I hesitantly sink into his warm chest. "Y - you know what we should call him, Lena? A-dumb! Get it! Because he's dumb!" Andrew starts chuckling and then he's losing his balance and the two of us are on the hard asphalt. He still won't let go of me and I blink in wonder.

"I don't know why he got so drunk! He was fucking fine before." Adam says, sighing.

I look up at him and sigh. "He's not gonna wanna go home anytime soon so just go on a walk. I'll see if I can get him to sober up." Adam nods and turns and walks away, obviously relieved to let someone else take care of drunken Andrew.

"Andrew..." I start, uncertain. "Andrew, can you let go of me? Please?"

"You're warm!" He protests, whining. I snort and peer up at him. I feel his arms tighten around me one more time and then suddenly he lets go. "Let's go to the dock." He pulls me by the hand towards a dock overlooking a lake and then he suddenly plops down at the edge, sighing.

"Why did you get so drunk, Andrew?" I ask hesitantly, sitting down beside him.

"Lacey...you...Maloney..." He says, trailing off drunkenly. He lets out another hiccup and sits up, staring at me differently. "You know...you're actually very pretty." He mutters, tilting his head to the side.

"Actually?" I repeat, eyebrows raised. Andrew colors red and then he starts to stutter awkwardly, scratching the back of his neck with his hand.

"I'd understand if Adam wanted you to be his girlfriend. I wasn't able to but now I get it. You're very nice, Lena. Much, much different from Lacey. I like it. Or do I? Do I like Lacey anymore? I don't know. I don't know anything." He rambles, his eyes glazing over. He stands up, pulling me up by the shoulder. "Maybe I like you." He leans down, his eyes wickedly gleaming. And then with one quick movement, I'm shoving him into the lake - along with myself.

Suddenly, the both of us are submerged in lukewarm lake water. I quickly break the surface of the lake, wincing at how nasty I felt with wet clothing against me. Andrew breaks the surface a couple seconds later, coughing up water and shaking his head. We both swim to shore and then lay our exhausted bodies on the grassy shore.

"If you didn't want to kiss me you could've just told me instead of pushing me into the lake..." Andrew says, finally breaking the silence between us.

I snort. "I couldn't think of any other way to get you sober."

"So you had me drink dirty lake water?" He asks, his voice coloring with shock. I sit up and shrug at him, pulling the wet clothing away from my body.

"You're sober now, right?" I ask, pulling myself up. "And don't kiss me or ever try to kiss me like that again." I add quickly, hurt.

Why are you even hurt? I thought to myself, confused. Well, besides the fact that Andrew had basically just tried to use me as an experiment...I shake my head, now irritated.

I didn't like how my first kiss with Andrew hadn't been while he was sober. I didn't like the fact that he thought it was Lacey. I didn't like how the only reason why he kissed me in the first place was because he thought I was Lacey. I didn't like how he made me feel; I didn't like how my normal confidence about my appearance was suddenly wrecked because Andrew didn't look at me the same way that he looked at Lacey. I didn't like that he tried to kiss me again because he wanted to check something - I'm a human, not a test subject and I just...I didn't like how everything about him made me overanalyze and overthink. I was never one of those people.

"Elay...nuh." Andrew slurs, rolling over loudly and awkwardly in the passenger seat of my car. Somehow, in my overanalyzing haze, I had managed to get a guy with 5 inches and probably 40 pounds on me into my car. "Why..." He starts, his eyes clouding up. "Why...don't you want me to kiss you anymo...re?" He says, hiccuping in the middle of his sentence.

I throw a glance at him as I pull out of the playground parking lot and crane my neck to yell for Adam, who had walked 10 feet to the left and parked himself on a curb.

"Why aren't you answering my question?" Andrew whines, huffing as he slouched back into the car seat again. Adam slides into the backseat smoothly, sending a questioning look at me as Andrew lets out a groan and turns around to scowl at him before turning back towards me and sighing.

"What happened to him?" Adam asks, amused as Andrew moans again.

"He's wasted." I answer dryly, while flicking on my turn signal angrily. "Why do you keep on moaning?" I snap at Andrew, narrowing my eyes at him.

"Because he's here." Andrew says, pouting petulantly. I blink, confused.

"Adam is your best friend!" I protest, pulling over randomly.

Adam snorts in the backseat, rolling his eyes. "He's jea-lous, Lena."

"Don't call her that! Don't even talk to her. Don't say her name and don't -"

"He can call me whatever he wants." I cut him off, furrowing my eyebrows.

"Why? Why can he do whatever he wants around you but I can't? Is it because he's your boyfriend?" He exclaims, turning his head away from me childishly.

"Adam isn't my boyfriend." I say slowly throwing Adam a questioning look. He shrugs, smirking.

When Andrew doesn't answer, I shrug and pull back out into the highway, choosing to ignore him...and then I start hearing sobs. I turn around and stare at him before snapping my head back up front, bewildered. Why was he suddenly crying? Almost as soon as I asked myself that question, it dawned on me.

I had gone through most of my high school experience pretty much doing everything I could to ignore these kinds of people. I had listened to every rumor, googled every article there was to do so and managed to go through most of my life without encountering these people - even Tessa wasn't this kind of person...and now? Now, I was sitting on a car driving this person. Why hadn't I seen the signs?

"I forgot to mention that Andrew is an emotional drunk." Adam chips in unhelpfully from the backseat, surprisingly chipper despite the fact that I was sending him a glare through my rearview mirror.

I quickly glance over Andrew, who had curled himself into a ball in my passenger seat, his head in his lap, shoulders shaking...and sobbing uncontrollably. What had I done to get myself into this kind of situation? I was a good person - I was the kind of person that stopped her car to help people cross the road. The kind of person that didn't beep when someone was jogging at a crossw alk...I'm a good person. What had I done to deserve an emotional wreck in my life?

"Andrew..." I start helplessly, not sure what to say. I had never been good at comforting people - I always opted to walk away in such situations. But now, trapped in a car with a sobbing mess, I wasn't sure what to do. I couldn't just pull over and leave them stranded? I make a weird noise and sigh.

"Why won't you let me kiss you?" Andrew sobs, looking up at me with a tear stained face.

"I..." I trail off helplessly and try to motion at Adam to help me out. He shrugs and makes a weird face before leaning back and looking back at his phone. "Andrew...you can kiss me whenever you want." I admit reluctantly, ignoring Adam's stare on my back.

"So...does that mean I can," he pauses to hiccup, "kiss you now?"

CHAPTER 11

I sneak a glance at him and find that he has a childlike grin on his face. "No." I watch as the grin falls off of his face and I sigh.

"But why? I bet you'd let Adam do it." He says, scoffing and now sitting up, his face angry and his jaw set.

"Because I don't want you to and I wouldn't let Adam kiss me, either." I say simply, turning into my driveway.

"That's a lie. You would. And I think the real question here is, why does it matter, Andy?" Adam inserts (again, he's the most unhelpful person I know) curiously, sticking his head in between our seats to stare at Andrew.

Andrew turns back to me and starts crying again, his face twisted up. "The problem is that I don't know why I care! You're just my friend and I don't want you to be anything more than my friend but I want to...I want to kiss you! That's not how it works! I'm supposed to be in love with Lacey!" He whines, still sobbing.

I cock at eyebrow at Adam, who is now snickering. "The last time he was this emotional was the time after his dad died and he got all emotional and started begging me to love him forever. This is comedy gold; jeez, if any of the Maloney guys could see him now?" Adam makes a cutting motion along his neck and mimics himself sputtering blood out and choking to death. "Can't have anybody knowing that the big, bad Wayne is actually a wimp."

Andrew turns around to stare at Adam, his jaw dropped. "I'm not a wimp! I'm strong! You said so!" This time, I'm the one that snickers. Adam is blushing profusely, trying to look everywhere but me. "That was one time, Andrew. Stop bringing that up everytime you get drunk."

Andrew puffs up his cheeks and blows out the air quickly, shooting Adam an innocent look and then smirking. "I bet Lena wouldn't let you kiss her right now."

"Are we still on th -"

Adam leans forward and pecks me quickly, catching me by surprise and giving me a mini seizure. "What the hell -" I start, completely confused and caught offguard.

"You were supposed to stop him!" Andrew whines again, shaking his head, his eyes starting to water up. I gape at him and Adam starts snickering again before leaning forward to press another kiss on my lips. "Adam, stop that!" Andrew complains, the tears now flowing again.

"Why don't you do it then? It's fun!" Adam suggests brightly, smirking at Andrew.

Andrew pouts; "She said that she doesn't want me to!"

"Is that really going to stop you? Really?"

I blink as Andrew leans forward, his lips puckered up, making him look like fish. And then he's coming closer and internally, I'm swooning and falling into his stupidly clear blue eyes...and then he hiccups. Maybe if he were sober I would be be okay with him hiccuping just as he was about to kiss me but as it was now, I wasn't. His hiccup caused him to blow his warm breath across my face and overload my senses with the rancid smell of beer. As he comes even nearer, I feel a set of eyes on the side of my face and I finally remember that I have an audience. Just as his lips are about to touch onto mines, I push him away with both hands.

"That's gonna stop me!" Andrew whines, pouting and folding his arms onto his chest. "She doesn't want me to kiss her! Why did she let you kiss her?" He says, throwing a glare at Adam, who is now sitting back, grinning.

"Because I'm not drunk. Maybe if you were sober she'd be more inclined to let you make out with her face." Adam replies simply, causing Andrew to launch into another fit of sobs. I glare at Adam, who shrugs and casually opens his car door and steps out and towards my house, completely uninvited. I throw a glance at the clock on my dashboard and sigh. 5 in the morning. It was basically time to get ready for school anyways.

I tap Andrew on the shoulder and he turns around to stare at me, still crying. "I don't even know why I'm crying! I hate it when I get drunk because I'm always crying!" He says, crying even harder. "See!"

I grimace at his crying face; a face that would rival even Kim Kardashian's. "How about we go inside; I think that would be a good idea...going inside. I'll find clothes for you to wear and then I'll drive you to school, okay? Is that okay?"

Andrew nods and sniffles. "Can you make me something to eat? And do you think I'm gonna have a hangover even though I didn't go to sleep? And also do you think Lacey still loves me? And do you still think that I'm strong? I really hope so." He says, loopily pulling up the hem of his shirt and squinting his eyes at his 6 pack. I curse at the sight of his incredibly flat stomach and open up my side of the car.

I expect him to come out as soon as I did, but he's just sitting in the passenger seat, slumped over. I turn to ask Adam to help me but his attention is all on his phone. I sigh and walk over to the passenger side, knocking on the window. Andrew's body twitches and then he's sitting up and his head is leaning onto the headrest and I realize that he had fallen asleep in the five seconds it had taken for me to get out of the car. How the hell was I supposed to pull his body out of the car now? I yank open the passenger door and pull him out of the seat, causing him to fall out with a thump, now awake.

"What the f - Elena?" He asks, squinting up at me confusedly.

"Get up. We're going inside and you're gonna brush your teeth and eat so you can go to school." I reply dryly, turning on my heel.

He groans and struggles to his feet. I hear him staggering up the driveway behind me and then up my front porch steps and towards my house.

"I'm guessing he sobered up a little bit finally?" Adam says, finally looking up from his phone.

I shrugged, "I made him fall out of the car. I'm thinking he needs to eat something to soak up all that alcohol. And a shower. My parents should be gone by now...if they decided to go back to work a day after their vacation. They like you anyways so I mean...whatever. Just get inside." I say, pushing the door in. I turn around, sighing. "By the way, you guys still need to fix my damn door."

Luckily, that morning, my parents were basically passed out and didn't hear anything. My dad had gotten up once because Andrew had dropped a plate in the kitchen but he walked out and stared blankly at the scene and then turned around and walked back to bed.

"Where are we going?" Andrew moans, angrily shutting off my car radio. I shoot him daggers and flick it back on.

"School. Where else?"

"I can't go to school with this bad of a hang over!" Andrew complains lowly, irritated. I roll my eyes.

"Well, too bad." I shift my attention to Adam, who, again, opted for the privacy of the backseat and his phone. "And Adam...do you even go to a school? Any school?"

Adam looks up from his phone and shrugs, "I go to your school. I just don't...go to your school."

"So you haven't been to school?" I ask, surprised.

"I went for the first month and then I stopped coming." He says nonchalantly.

A knock on my windshield stops me from asking Adam why he stopped coming and I blink in surprise as Tessa leans down, grinning. She mouths something incomprehensible and then nods her head at the high school's double doors.

"Tessa goes to school here?" He asks casually, now turned back to his phone. "That's weird, she never mentioned that."

"Why would she?" Andrew finally joins our conversation, his eyes narrowed. Adam looks up and shrugs innocently. "I don't know. Maybe I'll come to school today..." Adam opens up his door and steps out and walks towards the school, whistling. Andrew and I exchange looks, confused.

"Do you think…"

"No…he wouldn't go for her…" Andrew replies uncertainly.

Andrew and I settle ourselves in the back of the classroom as usual. I start pulling my books out and, as usual, Andrew is just sitting there, his arms crossed on his chest. Whispers start building in the room as kids start filling and I spare a quick glance at Andrew to see how he's faring.

"…cheated on Lacey with that whore, Lena."

"Mark is already all over Lacey."

"She's so hot."

"Look at him today! What an asshole!"

Ms. Grie walks in but the room doesn't stop its whispers. "Are you okay?" I ask just as Adam strolls in, throwing charming smiles at every girl that swooned as he walked past them and towards us.

"What the…" Andrew says, suddenly sitting up and glaring at Adam.

"Lena!" Adam exclaims jovially dragging a desk next to mines and plopping down in it, grinning at me widely.

I shut my eyes and count to ten. Nothing could make this class any worse. Nothing, except being sandwiched between a hungover Andrew and an overly chipper Adam for 45 minutes. "What are you doing here?" I say, my eyes still closed. I can feel the glares of every single girl in the room on me and I take that moment to curse mentally.

"You're the one that suggested that I start coming back to school…" Adam trails off, a grin in his voice.

"I didn't know that you were in my AP English class!" I protest weakly, dropping my head onto my desk as Adam settles himself.

Andrew snickers beside to me and I lift my head up to give him a glare. His snickering dissolves into a coughing fit as Ms. Grie starts her lesson. "You'd think you'd be more excited to have Adam here. You have a crush on him, after all." Andrew mutters, looking straight ahead. I blink, confused. What was he thinking? I didn't have a crush on Adam...in fact, Adam and I had a perfectly platonic relationship.

I open my mouth to deny it but Adam replies first. I turn to look at him and note that he has a frown on his face. "I'm not the one that she likes. Jeez, Andrew. Are you blind?" I shoot Adam a 'please don't' look but he shrugs and turns towards Ms. Grie.

Why would it matter to Andrew, anyways? Even if I like him, there was no way that he could possibly be over Lacey yet. It'd only been a couple days and Andrew had latched onto her love for her for 10 years. It appears that my problem stems from being second best to Lacey - all the time. It's a real struggle to be second best to someone all the time. To be someone's back up plan. I'm the person that piece of English homework that everyone forgets to do; the chore that people leave behind when things get crazy. I always get left behind.

If it were anybody else, I would've considered that maybe he liked me. Maybe he was finally getting jealous. Maybe. But no, it's Andrew and he'd stated several times already that I was just a friend to him. Just a friend.

I groan and focus my attention on the lesson that Ms. Grie was trying in vain to teach to my class of bored teenagers. "This is dumb." I mutter, scrawling all the notes that she had written on the board into my notebook, sighing.

"That's because you're dumb." Adam teases, reclined in his seat.

The bell rings and I scramble to exit the room, determined to not be caught between Adam and Andrew. "Wait. Adam, who does she like?" I turn around as stupid fear grips me. Adam's eyes meet mines and his lip quirks up into a smirk as he turns back to Andrew and shrugs. "I don't know, Andrew...but it's not me."

Andrew turns to me, his eyes narrowed. Adam steps out from behind Andrew and casually slips out of the classroom door, leaving Andrew and I alone in the classroom. I clear my throat awkwardly and back up, intending to slowly retreat but my leg gets caught on the leg of a desk. I teeter and shut my eyes, ready to fall backwards and split my skull open but Andrew's familiarly warm arm is wrapped around my waist and he's pulling me back to my feet.

As soon as I'm upright, his eyes are back to being narrowed and he's frowning at me. "Are you going to tell me who you like?"

"Why does it even matter?" I reply instantly, my eyes now narrowed.

"This isn't elementary school, Elena. Just tell me who you like!" He complains. His face darkens when I don't reply to him and then he leans in, staring at me. "You don't want to tell me...is it because you like Collin?"

I gape at him bewildered. Andrew being Andrew decided my silence meant that I was agreeing with him.

"Elena -!" He starts, his voice strained. "This is a whole new meaning to falling in love with a bad boy! Collin has killed before! Please answer me. Do you like him or not?"

But I'm too shocked to say word. How did he even come to that conclusion? I'd only met Collin once - twice, if you count the time that he decided to threaten my life in my car. When had I even showed remote interest in the psycho? Sure, he was attractive but I didn't know him. The threat to my life had definitely dampened whatever interest I could have had with the guy and when I finally snap out of my thoughts, Andrew's arm is pulled away from my waist he's stomping away with stiff steps.

"Andrew..." I call out weakly. But he's already out of my sight and I sigh, resigned. I only had two more periods to go before I could go home and drown myself in chick flicks and Calculus homework.

I face plant into my desk, groaning when my forehead met the hard desk. Getting through those other classes had been such a nightmare; school seemed like a dream after the weekends that I had started to have. I found myself looking around at the other kids and wondering if they were also involved in gangs and shot other people. I wondered if any of them had secret lives; lives like Andrew's. A couple times I had stopped myself because they all looked too mundane to lead extraordinary lives but so did Andrew and Adam.

Someone drops their book in the desk next to mines and I flinch, snapped out of my thoughts. I don't bother to lift my head, instead opting to let out a groan.

"What's up with you?"

I groan and finally look up. "Why do you have this class with me?" I whine, dropping my head back onto the desk. Adam shrugs beside me and then drops his head onto his desk so that his face is facing mine.

"Blame the main office. Now, can you please tell me why Andrew thinks that you're in love with Collin Maloney?" He asks, his voice hard.

I groan again. "I don't like him! I don't know why or even how Andrew got that idea because," I lower my voice, "we both know that I like him and not Collin." Adam is silent for a couple minutes before sighing.

"Why didn't you correct him?" Adam asks, curious.

"Because he just kept going and I was in shock! I've never even expressed interest in Collin - for god's sake, Collin even wanted to kill me!" I reason, sighing again. "I think he's mad at me now." My voice drops to a whisper as the Study Hall attendant walks in.

"He's not mad at you." Adam starts, his face softening. "Andrew is really protective; especially when it comes to you. I don't believe that he'll ever attempt to break down Lacey's door if he thought she was in danger. He wouldn't go the Maloney compound to threaten an entire gang on his own because he thought that your safety was at risk. He wouldn't ask me to walk to your car everyday and he sure as hell wouldn't be around if you didn't matter to you. He might actually like you, Lena."

I snort. "We're only ever going to be friends. Andrew is more interested in Lacey than he'll ever be with me."

Adam's face takes on a look of surprise, then shock, then curiosity and then disbelief. "Wow..." He says, his voice filled with awe.

"What?" I ask, frowning.

"You're really clueless." Adam says, his eyes wide.

"To what? Andrew? I know him better than I know myself..." I say, trailing off uncertainly when Adam starts shaking his head.

"You really don't if you genuinely think that he doesn't...well, you don't if you think he still likes Lacey after what she did to him." Adam whispers back furiously, his eyebrows furrowed.

"They have history!" I argue, confused.

"History doesn't mean anything if there aren't anymore feelings in the present!" Adam retorts instantaneously, his face darkening. "That girl is trouble and he knows it. She's walked out of his life twice now and he's the idiot if he decides that he wants to get back with her."

"But he has feelings for her. He still likes her - love doesn't just disappear overnight!" I screech, sitting straight up in my seat. Too late, I realize my mistake. I can feel the everyone's gaze on me and my face heats up. Adam snickers beside me and I wince, embarrassed.

When the class turns back around, Adam turns back to me, his face serious. "If that's what you want to believe, then so be it...but I'm telling you that he doesn't have those feelings anymore. Also, maybe you should ask him?" He turns back to his desk and sighs.

"Please?" Andrew whines, pouting. I walk out of my closet, glaring at him.

"No way! Not after you snuck up to my room while I was half naked!" I exclaim, irritated. Andrew grins and lays back on my bed, stretching enough so that his shirt rode up and revealed his v-line. I feel myself drooling and quickly turn around to compose myself, completely aware of the blush that had flourished on my cheeks.

"Please, Lay? I swear, they aren't strange at all." Andrew pleads.

I turn around and stare at him, sighing at his puppy eyes. "I don't have anything to wear." I relent grumpily, padding over to the other side of the bed and plopping down, irritated.

"We can go shopping!" He exclaims excitedly, coming around to the other side of me and slinging an arm around my shoulders.

I raise an eyebrow at him, surprised. "You want to go shopping with me?"

His grin falters but it brightens back up a second later. "Yes."

I smile wickedly at him. "You're driving. And holding my bags." I pause, "And you're paying."

His grin falters again but then his entire face brightens up and he pecks me on the cheek. "Anything for my favorite girl."

I blush and he pulls me closer to him. I feel him grin into my hair and then the room falls silent. After a couple seconds, I clear my throat awkwardly. "Can you - can you let me go?" He shakes his head and chuckles. "I like this." I stiffen and try to pull away but he only pulls me against him tighter. He pulls the both of us onto my bed so that we're spooning and my face gets even hotter. My bare legs against his caused heat to spread all throughout my body.

"You like this too." He whispers in my ear teasingly, a smile clear in his voice. The tips of my ears heat up and I clear my throat and relax in his arms. "Why do you need a date to the wedding anyways? And whose wedding is it?"

"Because it'll be awkward if I go alone and it's my Uncle's. Wade. Uncle Wade. He's a great guy."

"Does that mean your other family members are coming back?"

He stiffens and pulls his arms back. "Yes. And they'd do everything to protect you."

I freeze, not sure how to reply to the tenderness in his voice. "Why?"

When he doesn't reply, I roll over, ready to interrogate him. The question is already on my lips but I realize that my door is wide open and he had already left.

"No."

"But -"

"No."

"Andrew!" I whine, pouting.

"Elena." He replies back, his lips pressed into a thin line. "I can see everything."

I look down at my dress and blush. I had stepped out in a simple lilac body con dress, expecting him to be wowed. "I have one more. Just one!" I promise, stepping back inside and sighing. None of the dresses that I had really liked had earned a 'yes' from him. He'd vetoed all of them. This one, I was sure wasn't going to get a no. I pull the little black dress off of the hanger and slip it on. I turn to the mirror and grin happily. No, this one wasn't going to get vetoed. It was simple. It had a square neckline and flared out at the ends like a skater dress. It hit just above my knees and scooped down in the back and had triangular cut out pieces just above the curve of my waist.

"Yes?" I ask nervously, shifting on my feet.

Andrew looks up, his stare blank. He clears his throat and sits up straighter. "Uh...uh...I -"

"I think that's a yes!" The saleslady chirps excitedly, grinning at me. "I've never seen someone stunned speechless like your boyfriend here! You're very lucky to have such a patient guy!"

"He's not my -"

"She's not my -"

The saleslady looks disappointed but her face brightens immediately. "You guys would be a great couple. You look like you belong together!"

I blush and turn back into the dressing room as Andrew stutters out an awkward reply.

Somewhere in my body, I really wished that Andrew and I were a real couple. It was weird, really. One second, I absolutely hated him for not loving me and the next, I was completely okay with. In fact, I can say that I even understand it. I realized that Andrew not wanting me as something more than a friend didn't settle right with me; but I also realized that I was being an idiot and assuming things because I didn't even know if that was true.

I step out of the dressing room, grinning at Andrew's bright red face. The saleslady is still chattering about how cute we are together and how she hadn't seen a couple as sweet as us in a long time. I walk towards Andrew, my grin grower wider and wider with every step. "Come on, babe. Let's go." The saleslady makes a squealing noise and smiles brightly at us. I don't expect it to happen but Andrew takes my hand, intertwining our fingers and causing a blush to spread across my face again.

As he paid for the dress, the cashier stared at us, also smiling. "Gee, you two are a couple made in heaven. I'd kill to have a boyfriend as handsome as you - actually, I'd kill to have a boyfriend at all." She says wistfully as she passes Andrew back his credit card. "Well, goodbye! Hope we'll see you soon!"

"So, babe, where to next?" Andrew says, smiling down at me.

"Shoes. Definitely shoes. I'm thinking nude pumps - wait, no. Sandals? No, black pumps." I say, staring back at Andrew, who had seemingly fallen asleep at the chair. I sigh and pick up a pair of black pumps, excited to find exactly what I was looking for. I walk over to the cash register and start to pull my wallet out when someone's familiar presence pushes into my senses.

"I said I'd pay." Andrew says huskily, sleep still coloring his voice.

The cashier coos and I blush as he leans forward to push his credit card across the counter. "You two are a beautiful couple. You're lucky to have him."

"I'm lucky to have her." Andrew replies, flashing her a charming smile. I almost pass out, completely dazzled by him. If only he was being serious. I think to myself, my mood sombering.

On the way out of the mall, Andrew wraps an arm around my shoulder and pulls me to him, causing me to melt comfortably into his arms as we walked. "I'd say that was a pretty successful shopping trip." He says, chipper.

I roll my eyes, "You were basically passed out or annoyed for half the time!"

"But you're happy, right?"

I nod, "Well, yeah. I didn't spend any money today." I look up at him to see that's he smiling down at me.

"That's all that matters then."

"He said that?" Tessa exclaims, her jaw dropping.

I nod, "Yeah, but I mean…I guess we're best friends now. So I'd get it if he wanted me to be happy - that's a best friend thing, right?"

Tessa stares at me and opens her mouth to say something but shakes her head, her expression pained. "Sometimes I wonder how you're a straight A student, Lena."

I blink confusedly, "Wait, what?"

"So, this wedding is for his uncle, right?" Tessa says, abruptly changing the subject. I shoot her a look but nod anyways, going along with the subject change.

"Yeah. Uncle Wade or something. Andrew's really close with him I think. He's one of the groomsmen, I think."

"Doesn't that mean that he's going to be dancing with a bridesmaid? Slow dancing?" She asks, her eyebrows raising.

The thought of Andrew's arms wrapped around someone else's body caused my stomach to drop. The thought of Andrew's body being touched by someone else made me want to vomit. I didn't like to think of how I'd feel if Andrew had started dating again. I simply denied that it was ever going to happen again; for me, if he ever dated anyone, they probably wouldn't be real because I would be in denial. I refused to believe that he'd date anyone. But, because I'm stubborn, I wouldn't admit to Tessa that I was going to be jealous. Instead, I sent her a hard look and shrugged. "Why does that even matter? He's just my friend. He's my best friend."

Tessa scoffs, "Doesn't seem like you want him to be your best friend."

"What? Of course I do!"

"Yeah, no. You want him as more - and don't even try to deny it. You're completely in love with that boy and he's probably in love with you, too." She scoffs, going back to filing her nails.

"I'm not in love with him!" I lie, blushing red. "And even if I were, there's no chance he'd even give me a second glance. The only reason why he's still around is because he thinks Collin wants to kill me."

Tessa's eyes narrow, "If you don't think that that boy gives you second glances then you're a fucking idiot. He talks about you when you're not around - even if you're gone for a couple minutes. He texts you first, he asks you how your day went. He gives you rides to school - geez, he even paid for that stuff!"

"He's just feeling guilty because Collin -"

"Wants to kill you, whatever."

"And he's just protective. It's not like he enjoys being around me; he just says it to make me feel better. Besides, I'm not his type." I say, sighing.

"And what is his type? Vindictive, slutty and crazy?" Tessa replies, looking up and glaring at me.

"Well, yeah."

"That's no one's type." Tessa snaps, rolling her eyes. She flips her blonde hair over her shoulder and fixes me with a glare. "You're insane to think that he doesn't feel something for you; you're missing all the signs, Lena."

What signs? There are no signs. I didn't think that Andrew could ever like me, let alone love me. Sometimes I didn't even love myself. "I don't see any signs. Wanna know why? Because there aren't any." I say, trying to force a tone of finality into my words.

Tessa looks up and puts her hands up in surrender, sighing. "Whatever you say. I just don't think he'd try to take you to a wedding to meet his family if he didn't care about you in a more-than-friends way."

"I'm hot." I say, shrugging. "I think he'd rather have a hot girl that knows by side instead of some weird, blonde slut."

She blinks at me and then laughs while shaking her head sadly. "You have all the answers, don't you, Lena?"

The room falls silent at the end of her question and I shrug. "I don't have the answers. I sure wish that I did, though."

Chapter 12

The wedding was being held in a garden somewhere in up-
state New York where mosquitoes and trees thrived. It was a
great place to be simply because I was excited to see Andrew in
clothing other than jeans and t-shirts. And, of course, I was excited
to meet the rest of the Wayne family that everyone was afraid of. I
found it funny that people so scary could have such a bad alcohol
tolerance.

In the beginning, the wedding was completely silent and entirely awkward. When Andrew and I walked in, a couple of his uncles
had strayed over, their dates looking completely bored and already
half the room was wasted.

"Andrew! You didn't tell us that you were out on the dating field
again!" The uncle booms, his eyes narrowing at the sight of me.
I lifted my chin in defiance and held on tighter to Andrew's arm,
shivers running up and down my spine.

Andrew chuckles and pulls my hand from his arm and inter-
twines our fingers instead, giving me a squeeze before continuing.

"She's my best friend." He replies vaguely, his thumb starting to rub a pattern into my hand.

"Well, she's a very beautiful young lady; does she know?" He asks, still not talking to me.

I blink, newly irritated. "Yeah, I know."

Andrew squeezes my hand again and pulls me closer to him. "She knows what we do, yes."

The uncle gives the both of us a searching gaze before a large grin spread onto his face. "Well, if she's okay with that and you really love her, then I guess she's a Wayne too." He steps forward and pulls me out of Andrew's hold and wraps his arms around me, laughing heartily into my hair. "We'll protect you with our lives - especially since you're a particularly beautiful lady." He says, winking at me.

Andrew pulls me back into his arms and starts guiding me towards a table, laughing. "Can't believe you just charmed Uncle Max. That was kind of a big deal, Lay." I don't say anything, still trembling from the encounter. "And he was right, Lay. You look beautiful today. Everyday, actually." I felt a blush forming on my face and I turn away and clear my throat awkwardly before mumbling 'thank you'.

He directs me to a table and I sit down, trying my best not to make eye contact with anybody. Meeting the other Wayne family members was a new kind of uncomfortable to me. I didn't want to look at any of them because I had a feeling that the Waynes were a family of people that were completely all-knowing. I had a feeling that if I looked at any of them, they would instantly know that I was completely in love with Andrew; and I couldn't have that.

"Andrew!" An airy, feminine voice chirped from across the table and every part of me wanted to look up and see who was calling him but I forced my head down and averted my gaze to the floor. "Who's your date?" The voice asks, taking on a sharp edge. "She looks beautiful but she's had her head down the entire time; have you scared her?"

Andrew clears his throat and drops a hand to my knee and squeezes it reassuringly. I take in a shaky breath and look up, praying that my face didn't give up too much. The girl who had asked about me blinks, surprised. She coughs and musters up a plastic smile. "Well," she starts, her eyebrow raising, "she's definitely a downgrade from Lacey."

It takes everything in me not to lunge across the table to behead her. I let out my breath and cock my head to the side, staring at her hair and then her dress, which is a vomit green color. "It's nice to meet you," I start in a saccharine sweet voice, "I'm Lena. What's your name?" The girl blinks, confused at my tone. She was probably expecting a mean jab or even tears, but I had played this game too many times to count and I always knew that killing them with kindness was the way to go. Andrew snickers beside me and pulls my chair closer to his so that he can wrap a warm arm around me.

"Her name is Annie." Andrew says, smiling at the girl who promptly looks like she's ready to die a happy death. "She's the girl that used to run around my house completely naked - I told you about her, didn't I, Lay?" He looks down at me and quickly winks, his lips hitched up cutely.

"That's Annie? Man, she grew up really prettily!" I say, smiling at her kindly.

Annie blushes even redder and shrinks down in her sink. Andrew takes that moment to lean over and kiss me in the cheek, earning 'aw's from everyone sitting at our table. "Well, if my opinion even matters, I like you." A booming voice says from behind us, causing the table to burst into excited whispers. I turn around and find myself staring at a man that looked like he was 6'3 and had a blushing, blonde bride on his arm. I blush and look over at Andrew, whose face looks like it's going to rip apart from smiling so hard. He tightens his grip on my waist and pulls me even closer so that my shoulder is basically pressing against his chest.

"Uncle Wade!" He chirps happily, causing me to do a double take. "This is Elena, she's my date."

Wade rolls his eyes, "She's obviously your date if all you've been doing this entire time and holding onto her and kissing her!" He booms, chuckling slightly. "It's funny because you're usually off looking for me as soon as we do one of these event type things -" The blonde at his side narrows her eyes and elbows him in the side, her eyebrow quirked. "This our wedding, honey. Not an 'event type thing'!" She whines, pouting. Wade quickly apologizes and turns back to us, apologetic. "This is Amelia - my wife." He says, his voice softening at the words 'my wife'.

Andrew laughs and pulls his arm away from my waist to find my hand. I smile at the bride who's eyes are twinkling with happiness. I let out a wistful breath as they walk away, finding a piece of me hoping that maybe one day, Andrew would look at me the way that Wade looked at Amelia. "What was that?" Andrew asks, turning to me concerned.

I sigh, "All I want is for someone to look at me the way that Wade looks at Amelia. It's dumb, but that's all I want." I pause to think and then quickly tack on, "And I also want a two story house, a big backyard with a pool and a stable income. I want a happy ending. I need a happy ending."

Andrew looks thoughtful and then grins back at me, "Wanna know what I want?"

I roll my eyes, "I bet you're gonna say 'food' and then drag me across the dancing floor to get some."

Andrew looks appalled at me and then he promptly stands up, still shocked. "You know me way too well, Lena. Way too well." I shrug, "You're literally in my personal space 100% of the time. It's hard not to know you this well." He looks pensive as he stands up and wraps a casual arm around my shoulders to direct me towards the buffet bar. Suddenly, he turns towards me, his eyes twinkling. "You know what? I want to -"

"Will the wedding party please step out onto the floor to join the bride and groom?" Andrew's arm falls from my waist and he steps away reluctantly, shrugging. "Wait for me." He says, smiling. I watch as he walks out onto the floor and taps a tall blonde girl on the shoulder. She turns and shoots him a dazzling smile and I sigh, my hope that Andrew might actually think I was pretty enough to date blown out of the water.

I knew that I would have competition but I never thought that my competition would be as beautiful as that girl. I couldn't fathom the idea of someone who had a face that literally glowed with beauty and I couldn't handle the fact that that someone isn't me. I turn away from the two of them and walk back to the table, resigned. I'd always have competition and I'd always be the loser. I was the underdog; the girl that was friend zoned - the girl that dreamed too hard. I watched as they floated around the dance floor, stuck in a trance so I was extremely startled when someone tapped me on the shoulder. I turn around and a grin slowly spreads onto my face at the sight of Adam.

He goofily bent over and held out his hand, "May I have this dance? I'd be lucky to dance with the most beautiful girl in the room."

I snort and grab his hand, a smile on my face nonetheless. He pulls me out onto the dance floor and wraps his arms around my waist and pulls me to his front, grinning slyly. "You look beautiful tonight, Lena." He whispers, his eyes connecting with mine and causing me to laugh at how ridiculous he was acting. He dips me playfully, causing me to burst into another fit of laughter and when I'm upright again, I'm even closer to him. "Andrew is so lucky that I would never steal his girl because if I would, you'd be swept off your feet by now." He teases. He stops us from waltzing and then looks down at me, a playful glint in his eye. And then he lifts me off my feet, causing me to let out a yelp of surprise and curl my hands even tighter around his neck. Adam chortles and then sets me on my feet, grinning widely. "Andrew is looking our way - oh man, he's furious."

"Why would he be -"

"Adam." Andrew bites out gruffly, glaring at the back of my head while doing so. "What are you doing with Lena?"

But Adam shrugs and smiles even wider; "I'm dancing, of course. Sweeping her off her feet. Wooing her. She's quite the stunner tonight, isn't she?" He says nonchalantly. I feel Andrew's glare intensifying and thank God that my back was to him right now. "Besides, you were having fun, right?" Adam asks, looking down at me mischievously.

"Of course I was! I always have fun with you." I reply quickly, laughing nervously at the end. The glare intensifies even more and

I wince slightly. I couldn't understand why Andrew was reacting so angrily; Adam is his best friend and we were just dancing.

Adam wiggles his eyebrows at me and loosens his grip on my waist and I turn around, smiling. My smile falters when I realize that Andrew is glaring at me, basically shooting daggers at my face. I wince again and step back, accidentally stumbling closer to Adam. "What happened, Andrew?" Just as he's about to answer, the leggy blonde from before shows up by his side, a cat-like grin on her face.

"Andrew," She purrs, her eyes twinkling, "where did you run off to? The song didn't even finish yet!"

My smile drops off of my face completely when I see how beautiful she is up close and I feel my stomach dropping, disappointed. Andrew offers her a grin and he starts to say something, his voice low and charming. Eventually, she turns to Adam and I and grins, showing off a row of pearly white teeth. "And who is this? Not a girlfriend, I hope."

Andrew turns to look at me, as if he was just now remembering that I was still there and his eyes dim a little bit before he turns back to the girl. "She's my best friend."

My mouth goes dry and take in a shaky breath, embarrassed that I had even dared to hope that Andrew would finally look at me differently tonight. Adam's grip around my waist tightens and he pulls me back towards him, as if he knew that I was now completely devastated. The girl turns to look at me, victorious, and I try my best to muster up a smile, before awkwardly nodding. "Yep. Just friends."

Andrew's head swings towards mine and I drop my head immediately, not wanting him to see my face. I knew that if he did, he'd know something was up and I'd be infinitely embarrassed. Instead, I turn back to Adam, who's face is stony and angry.

"So, can I have this dance?" The girl asks, her voice silky.

I wince again and start walking towards the table just as Andrew answers her 'yes.'

"That was a dick move." Adam growls out, shaking his head disappointedly.

"It wasn't. He didn't know what he was doing and -"

"Lena, stop making excuses for him. He knew exactly what he was doing. He probably didn't know why, but he definitely knew what he was doing - God, he's such a jerk." Adam rants, his voice hard. "Listen, you're so much better than that girl; honestly, he's making a mistake. He's just doing it to make you jealous and -"

"Stop, Adam. He's not doing it to make me jealous, he's doing it because he wants to. He doesn't like me. I'm just his best friend and that's all I'll ever be." I bite out bitterly, shaking my head. "I shouldn't hope for anything else."

Adam starts to talk again but I lift my head and he falters and then closes his mouth. "Let's just get you home. Is that okay?"

I nod and he stands up, offering me his hand. He turns around and waves at the other guests at the table and slings his arm protectively around my shoulder. Just as we reach the parking lot, I hear footsteps following after Adam and I and I feel Adam turning around and tensing.

"What do you want?" Adam bites out, angry.

Andrew's voice is desperate and tinged with confusion. "Where are you taking her?" He asks, his voice low. "She's my date."

Adam laughs sardonically, "Yeah? You haven't been treating her like one!"

"That's because she was with you!" Andrew replies lamely, his voice faltering at his last word. My head is still down and I feel tears start to build in my eyes and then eventually fall. The two of them are quiet and Adam pulls me to his side and I feel myself fighting to keep quiet.

"Just let me take her home, Andrew." Adam says tiredly, the fight suddenly going out of him.

Andrew doesn't answer, silent for what felt like hours. "Lena, I want to see your face." But I shake my head and try to turn Adam away but I'm too slow. Suddenly, I feel Andrew's presence right in front of me and he's pulling my face up. His face falls and the color drains from his face. Adam takes in a quiet breath and Andrew drops his hand from my face. Andrew's head swivels towards Adam, who looks shocked. "What the fuck did you do to her?" Andrew demands, now pissed off.

"I didn't do -"

"Bullshit! She wasn't crying before and she is now; what did you do to her?!" He yells, his face stormy.

When Adam shakes his head again, Andrew lunges at him, ready to punch him in the face. When he does, I feel my stomach dropping even further when Adam looks up, his face stoic. "It wasn't me." He starts slowly, his jaw clenched. "It was you, you fucking prick!" Andrew is instantly confused and he drops his hand, shaking his head. "How? What did I do?" Adam laughs sarcastically, "You brought her as your date to this wedding. Yours. And what did you do? You've spent the past three hours ignoring her completely, leaving her with me and your crazy fucking Aunts. Did you even think when you asked her here? Did you even think what it'd be like for her when you left to go chase after some other girl? That's right, you didn't. And now she's crying because all she was trying to do was be a good friend but you fed her to wolves to get your own family off of your back. This girl would do anything for you and tonight, you repaid her by being an asshole." Andrew looks over at me, crestfallen. "Lena -" Adam cuts him off, shaking his head. "Don't fucking talk to her."

Adam turns to me, putting his arm back around my shoulders and walks us away from Andrew. "Thank you." I say finally, when I was completely sure that I wouldn't sound like a congested whale. Adam shrugs. "That's what friends are for."

"Do you want frozen yogurt?" He asks wearily, trying his best not to look over at me.

For an hour, I was sobbing uncontrollably and I couldn't stop. I tried deep breaths and falling asleep, but the sobs kept coming. Do you ever cry about one thing and then end up gradually crying about everything else that's wrong in your life? That was me right now; to be honest, everything suddenly seemed wrong about my life. Grades, friends - even the damn weather was wrong at the moment. The car hadn't been silent since we left; every second was filled with loud sniffles and sobs and heaving breaths. With every second, I cried even harder.

Adam had stopped trying to talk to me half an hour after we got into the car; especially since I couldn't reply with anything but sobs no matter how hard I tried. My chest was heaving and tears were still streaming down my face and Adam was freaking out so bad that he didn't even have enough sense to drop me off at home.

To an outsider, we probably looked like a couple of lunatics. I had taken to rocking back and forth in the passenger seat and Adam's eyebrows were furrowed and his eyes were basically yelling, 'Help!'

at every car that passed by us. I try to take a deep breath again to dissolve my sobs and, surprisingly, it worked.

"I'm s - sorry." I finally say, stuttering with embarrassment.

Adam looks over at me, relieved. "Thank God you finally stopped crying - jeez, it's been over an hour!"

I roll my eyes, "I take back that sorry. You're an asshole." I say dryly, pouting. The car drops into a comfortable silence and I notice that Adam is finally driving towards my house. I turn to him, hesitant. "Adam, it wasn't all Andrew's fault. It was kind of mine, actually. I volunteered to -"

"Shut up."

"What -"

"You're being dumb; Andrew was completely in control of his actions tonight. He knew exactly what he was doing. Everything he does is calculating and he knows exactly what to do to push everyone's buttons. None of this is your fault; in fact, it's probably mine. I think I made him jealous." Adam says, flashing me a wicked grin.

"But -"

"Shut up. You're honestly an idiot if you think he wasn't jealous last night."

"I guess I'm an idiot, then. He wouldn't be jealous, Adam. He'd have to actually like me for that to be possible. You know what? I don't even know why I like that stupid prick. He's such a - an asshole!" I say, my voice hoarse from all the sobbing that I had just finished doing.

Adam glances over at me and rolls his eyes, snorting. "You're such a girl. You definitely still like him." But I pout and cross my arms over my chest; "No, I don't." I look over and realize that Adam had parked us in my driveway. "Do you want to come in?" I ask, already knowing that he was gonna say yes.

When we walk in, my kitchen light is on and I can hear my parents' voices loud and clear. My dad's familiar, comforting rumble combined with my mom's high pitched whine was a source of a happiness for me. I kick my shoes off and pad towards the kitchen, sighing.

My mom sees me first, her eyebrows pulling together and her lips dropping into a frown. "Honey? What are you doing home so early - is that Adam? Where's Andrew?" She spits out immediately, confusion coloring her tone.

"Hello to you too, Mrs. Parker." Adam says dryly, plopping down on a kitchen stool. My mom blinks at him and turns back towards my dad, whose eyebrow is raised almost comically.

"Honey, that was kind of rude." My dad admonishes softly, causing my mom to blush furiously. I roll my eyes at their cutesy relationship and pull a banana from the fruit platter in the middle of our kitchen island. My mom quickly apologizes to Adam before turning to me, her hands now on her hips.

"Now, please tell us why you're home with Adam instead of with Andrew at that wedding as his date?" She says, her voice starting to take on an irritated tone.

"He was being an, excuse me, dick." I reply drolly, biting into my banana as my mom's confused expression was replaced with indignation.

"Wait -"

"Now, dear -" My dad interjects, knowing that my mom was probably going to explode any second now.

"He was being a what?" She yells, irritation now taking over her entire tone of voice.

Adam sighs beside me, dropping an arm around my shoulders comfortingly. "He was being rude. He didn't dance with her all night - he danced with some other girl. He fed her to the wolves. He," Adam pauses to take a deep breath and turns to look at me, his blue-eyed gaze growing cold. "is a dick. And, he made her -"

Adam's rant is interrupted by pounding on my newly replaced front door. Impatient rapping on the front door echoed through the house abruptly, causing me to jump slightly in my seat, taken aback by the noise.

My dad exchanges a glance with my mom, whose face is now beaming radiantly. "Honey, it might not be him..." My dad says, his voice patient. My mom however, is bopping up and down excitedly, a wide grin on her face, her eyes dreamy. "It looks like little Lay is getting the fairytale romance that I always dreamed of."

Adam sighs, "Looks like Andrew finally showed up." The rapping gets harder and I hear an impatient groan. "And he's angry."

I sit up straighter before slouching tiredly, slightly annoyed. "What do I do - what am I supposed to say?"

Adam's arm tightens around my shoulder comfortingly. "I'll go with you, don't worry about it. We'll answer the door together and we'll figure everything else out. Together."

I smile gratefully and him and wrap an arm around his waist. "You're one of the best friends that I have."

His smile grows wider and he pats me on the shoulder comfortingly. "I'm starting to get sick because of this obnoxious sweetness, Lay."

As we walk towards the door, I hear my dad sigh and mutter; "I really wish she was in love with Adam instead of Andrew. I have a feeling that we're gonna have a major headache." My mom tsks beside him and I have a feeling that she was rolling her eyes. "They probably hear us, you know. They aren't that far away…"

Adam chuckles at my parents' banter and I sigh. "They're so weird. I'm sorry." I pull open the door to reveal an angry Andrew with a bruised jaw and tousled hair. His eyes narrow at the sight of Adam's arm around my shoulders, causing me to sink into Adam's hold, newly afraid of his wrath.

"Lena -" He starts, his voice hoarse and low. "I'm sorry. I didn't mean to - I didn't know what I was doing. I didn't know that I was hurting you. I -"

I almost take all of his apologies at the sight of the rumpled, desolate look in his eyes but instead, I take a step back and shake my head, gritting my teeth to fight back the urge to forgive him.

"You shouldn't have brought me with you tonight. I'm not mad at you - actually, I'm furious with you. Did you take me with you tonight to get that other girl jealous? It worked, obviously, but you hurt my feelings in the end. I feel used, dirty. And you - you had fun right up until Adam, who is the right definition of a good friend, punched you in the face to knock some sense into you. Thanks for the dress and everything but I don't know if I'll be forgiving you anytime soon so please get off of my porch and stay away from me for now."

When he doesn't move, I almost contemplate taking back every-thing I had just said - my confidence was faltering at the sight of his forlorn expression. I almost opened my mouth to apologize when

Adam pinched at my waist and pulled me to his side and cleared his throat loudly.

"Please get off her porch." He says calmly, his voice icy.

Andrew is still, watching as Adam leans forward to close the door before he finally springs into action. He pushes at my door and leans forward to grab the both of us and pull us onto the porch, breathing heavily after finishing his quick movements. "Lena, please." He begs, his voice cracking.

Chapter 13

I turn to Adam, my resolve already crumbling, already giving into him.

It hit me almost immediately that Andrew had me eating out of his hand - I couldn't even spend a second without him. I couldn't fathom being away from him and I couldn't even think about fighting with him. I realized that he was my rock and I had been leaning on him, depending on him so heavily that I had somehow managed to lose myself along the way and I had somehow convinced myself that everything was better with him. Funny, though, that with him, everything seemed to hurt 100% more. My most recent revelations caused me to decide that I needed to take a break from Andrew - I needed to stay away because everything would be so much easier without him nearby. Somewhere inside of me, something was screaming that I was making an idiotic decision and I needed to think again but at the same time, I knew that this was the time that I had to use to grow a backbone and stop being the damsel around Andrew. I couldn't stand that being around him caused all the bones in my body to turn to jelly and I'm suddenly just another whiny, needy girl.

I take in a quiet breath and clench my jaw. I step closer to Adam, taking in his warmth and trying to convert it to strength before I finally look up at Andrew with what I was hoping was a very steely gaze. "No. I'm not going to give in to you again. There's no point in you begging anymore because what you did tonight was fucked up, to be frank, and I don't know when or even if I'm going to forgive you anytime soon. I'm -" I stop, catching myself. I was ready to apologize to him, a habit that I had formed subconsciously over the years. I found that I was always apologizing for things that I didn't need to apologize for. "I'm not sorry for this. We just - we just need to take some time away from each other." My voice falters and starts to wobble by the end of my sentence and I almost take back everything (again) at the sight of his face but Adam wraps a comforting arm around my shoulders and shaking me encouragingly.

Andrew clenches his jaw and shuts his eyes for a couple seconds, looking pained. "And you, Adam. Will you take care of her?"

I look up at Adam, whose face is completely stoic. I elbow him and he blinks and quickly mutters out a yes before turning us towards the door. A piece of me is itching to turn around and fling my arms around Andrew one last time but I knew that that would send out mixed signals and I'd probably end up going back on what I was determined to do.

When we're back inside, Adam drops his arm from my shoulders and turns to me, a warm smile on his face. "I know that was hard. But you'll be fine. Who says you need that idiot anyways?"

"Stop being such a wimp!" Adam mutters, rolling his eyes.

I let out a deep breath, feeling my anger about to boil over. "How about you stop pushing me so hard! I can't do this!"

Adam scoffs, "Yes, you can. And I'm not even pushing you that hard - you're just a wimp." He shrugs and turns around. "Now, run from the top."

I shoot him a (hopefully) scathing glare and run from the top, all of my muscles crying out in pain. It'd been a couple weeks since my big blow out with Andrew and this was the first that I had willingly left my house. It wasn't that I was particularly hurt - to be honest, I was actually kind of angry with him. The problem was that I couldn't think of anything worth my while. Adam had come over too many times to count to try and coerce me out of my house but each time, I muttered a lame apology and excuse and then settled myself on the couch. Finally, I decided that I'd go out with him - and this is what I got.

Exercise. Can we please just take a moment to talk about how much I absolutely despise that word? I hate that word. I hate it. I hate that it isn't spelled with a 'z' and I also hate what it means. For me, exercise means that I have to take time out of my day to put myself through insurmountable physical pain because the promise of a body that was even just slightly fit was so unbelievably appealing to me. And, for the first time that I had gotten out of my house, I had willingly subjected myself to this torture - and with Adam, of all people. If it wasn't obvious from his arms and his intimidatingly hard torso, he was some sort of exercise buff.

For a week, I had contemplated the idea that Adam might have had feelings for me and for a moment, I actually thought that I did. Why else would he spend all his waking moments with me?

Quickly, however, I realized that he was just that kind of person - the kind of person that would always be there for you to be your rock; and he was also viciously loyal to his friends. On more than one occasion, he'd defended Andrew and I knew that it was a sore subject when people spoke about the Wayne family nastily.

Tessa, however, was not so easily swayed. She had called me one night and grilled me for hours about Andrew and I and when she was satisfied, she decided to start grilling me about Adam. I got annoyed quickly because I knew that she was trying to insinuate that he might have feelings for me. I didn't understand why she couldn't believe that he might just be a good friend and not someone that liked me. It was already far-fetched that Andrew could even like me; but Adam? That's like saying Earth isn't a planet - it's not possible. Finally, after more than an hour of her whining about me being dumb and blind, I snapped at her and asked her why she even cared so much. She didn't answer and promptly apologized and hung up, leaving me in a state of confusion.

When I finally make it to the bottom of the incredibly steep hill, I bend over, and heave. I can feel sweat everywhere on my body and I find myself feeling stickier than usual. I straighten up and freeze. My heart stops beating and I have to fight my compulsion to let out a blood curdling scream. Apart from realizing that everything in my life needed a major overhaul, I also realized that Collin Maloney is not a particularly harmless fixture in my life. I found myself being very scared of seeing him when I turned corners and seeing him in front of me right now caused fear to freeze me where I was.

"Hello, Lena." Collin's velvet voice caressed my hearing and, unlike before where I probably would've found it attractive, I found myself recoiling. His lips curl up into a cat-like grin and his eyes twinkle. "I noticed that you haven't been with that insolent little freak lately. Seems like you have a new toy now? Shame, though. I was really looking forward to skinning you alive."

"That - That's a real shame, yeah. I was looking forward to being skinned alive too. How did you know that that was my preferred way to die?" I ask, hoping that my voice was hiding that I was ready to curl up on the sidewalk and vomit all my feelings out.

Collin grins with amusement and winks at me, "Of course. I'd do anything to pleasure you," He steps closer and drops a hand to my arm, gripping it surprisingly lightly. "anything." He says, his eyes on mines.

I flinch at the sound of his voice and he pulls his arm back, and grins again. "I don't know what game you're playing with that little Wayne but I know that he still...has feelings for you. And you have feelings for him, too. Watch out, little Lena." Collin turns around and starts to walk away, whistling leisurely. Just as the fear is loosening its grip on me, he turns around, a creepy smile on his face. "And I highly recommend that you close your blinds when you change at night...and I really love those blue lace boy shorts that you wore last night."

My stomach drops again and as soon as Collin disappears around the corner, I bend over and start to retch, tears stinging at my eyes. The feeling of his hand on my arm burns into me and I can't help but feeling dirtier than I did before. At that moment, I found myself wishing that I had never met Andrew Wayne.

After telling Adam, I didn't go out for another week. When I went to school, he no longer allowed me to go on my own, forcing me to take his car with him. He skipped all his classes to follow me around the school and constantly had a protective, brotherly arm around me. At one point, he even tried to follow me into the bathroom, begging me to allow him to wait outside of my stall.

Tessa had given the both of us looks, her eyebrow cocked and her lips turned down in a frown. She follows me in, offering Adam a tense smile. As soon as the both of us were in the safety of the bathroom, she turned on me, her lips pressed into a thin line. "Do you like him?"

I blink and feel my mouth drop on it's own, completely bewildered. "Tess, no!"

But she shakes her head, her eyebrows drawn together. "I don't get it. How do you get two boys to fall in love with you - how did you get Adam, of all people, to even give you a second glance? Please. Tell me your secrets; I sure as hell haven't been able to get a second glance from that moron."

By this point, my head is spinning with a plethora of questions. I wasn't quite sure where Tessa got the notion that Adam was even slightly interested in me or how she could even possibly think that he looked at me as something that wasn't a sister. As her last words process in my mind, my jaw drops and I'm unable to control it. "Wait; you've been trying to get Adam's attention? Adam's?"

Tessa blushes beet red and her eyes drop to the ground as she tries to stutter out a sentence nervously. "W - Well, yeah. H - He's attractive and he was really nice to me when I was drunk and...I don't know. It's probably dumb. He deserves better."

"Tessa," I start, not sure what to say, suddenly uncomfortable. "listen, he -" Before I can finish the rest of my sentence, I notice that Adam was suddenly in the room, his eyes narrowed, his hands curled at fists at his side.

"Lena! It's been over 10 minutes!" He exclaimed, his lips twisting into a scowl. "I thought something happened to you!"

An eyebrow rises on its own, and a scowl of my own grows on my face. "There are no windows in here - the only other person in here is Tessa; you're telling me I can't trust Tessa?"

Adam doesn't soften or stand down. Instead he seems to get angrier and shakes his head. "You don't understand, Lay. You are my family now. I can't help but be over protective! You - you infuriate me! If I wasn't afraid you would sneak out -"

"There are no windows in here!" I interrupt him, suddenly feeling livid. Or maybe it wasn't so sudden. Maybe everything has finally hit me. I was being hunted by a mentally unstable gang leader, the boy I like doesn't like me back and I ran out of pads and had no money to buy more. Maybe, in that moment, I was trying to release all my pent up frustrations on the first person to take on an angry tone with me. Vaguely, I remembered feeling bad about yelling, but my blood still felt hot and I was still seeing red.

Adam takes a breath and clenches his jaw. "I didn't know that. I don't use the girls' bathroom!"

I'm about to open my mouth to say something else when I realize that I have no real reason to be angry at him. He was just trying to keep me safe; he was definitely being dumb about it but he had good intentions. I let my mouth soften into a smile and sigh. "I'm sorry, Adam. I just need my space. I know you're just trying to keep me safe. Hey, I know what. Maybe you should go hang out with Tessa tonight; you know, instead of watching me."

Adam studies me and then looks over at Tessa, who I had noticed had turned a bright red. "Why Tessa?"

I shrug. "Maybe if you hung out with her you'd understand why I trust her."

Adam sighs, "I'll pick you up tonight, Tessa. But Lena...you know there's only one other person I'd trust to watch you."

Chapter 14

I found myself sitting on the couch, wringing my hands nervously. All that had ran through my mind that night was that Andrew was probably coming over tonight. I couldn't think of what was gonna happen between us; I couldn't think at all, quite frankly. Even after a month of being cut off from him completely, his name still made my heart beat erratically. Even after a month, knowing that he was still watching to make sure I was okay still made my mouth dry and my toes curl. I had been hoping that my attraction to Andrew was just some dumb thing - that it was going to away with time, but now that I was given time, I realized that what I had with him was something that wasn't going to dissolve anytime soon.

I'm snapped out of my thoughts by my bell ringing. I stand up, smoothing my hair nervously and quickly adjusting my shirt. I walk towards the door and pull it open, armed with a nervous smile.

"Lena, hi." Andrew says, his voice as seductive as usual.

My mind draws a blank as I take in the sight of him. It feels like everything in the room had stopped - the air had gone still and out of my lungs.

"Lena?" He asks again, stepping towards me, concerned.

Scared of my own reaction to his closeness, I freak out and step back, shaking my head, words of no use. When I recognize the all too familiar look of desolation on his face, I shake myself out of my funk and then clear my throat and take in a deep breath. "Thanks for coming tonight, I know it must've been hard for Adam to call you."

Andrew blinks and furrows his eyebrows. "Wait, what? Adam didn't call me - why would he?"

Before I can reply, Bernie comes running in, out of breath, sweat glistening above his brow. "I saw the door open and I assumed the worst. Thank God Mr. Wayne is here because if he weren't, Adam would've killed me."

My lips fall into a frown as I look between the two. "I'm sorry, but what?"

Instead of answering me, Andrew turns back to Bernie and smiles. "Hey, why don't you go home? I got it from here." Bernie clenches his jaw and narrows his eyes before stepping into the house and locking the door behind him.

"I don't think I'll leave her on her own with you, Mr. Wayne. Maloney is getting to be too much to handle. I know your feelings for her - and you'll be too blinded by them to protect them from him."

Andrew's eyebrows furrow and his lips press into a thin line, his face expressing concern. "Wait, why did you assume the worst when you saw the door open - why are we mentioning Maloney more often…Bernie, please tell me that Maloney didn't get near her."

When Bernie doesn't answer, Andrew turns to me, desperate. "Please, Lena. Please."

I don't reply, suddenly afraid of what he was going to do after he found out.

"He did. That sonofabitch got near you - why didn't you tell me, why didn't Adam tell me?" When no one answers, the room gets eerily quiet; the kind of quiet you'd expect before someone starts yelling. But Andrew doesn't speak for what feels like 5, 10, even 15 minutes and suddenly, I'm very, very afraid.

"Please, Lena. Please don't tell me that the reason you didn't tell me was because you were mad at me. Please."

"Andrew, I -"

"I fucked up. I'm so sorry. I fucked up that night and I'll even admit it. I'll write it in the sky, I'll tattoo it on my forehead but oh my God, Lena. Please, please don't tell me that the reason that you risked your safety was because we got into a fight." He says, his voice low and desperate.

I shake my head and bite the inside of my cheek, finding myself fighting from talking to him. I try to look for Bernie, but he had somehow inched out of the room despite the palpable tension between Andrew and I.

When I finally decide to speak, my voice sounds loud in the completely silent room. "Why do you care?"

And that was when all hell broke loose. "Why do I care? Why? Of all the questions you fucking ask me - out of every fucking thing, anything at all, you ask that? Why do I care? I care because you're my best friend - because you mean so much to me; because you fucking - you're all I thought about for this past month. Adam told me nothing - not a thing about you. He didn't tell me whether or not you had breakfast, what you'd been doing. I wasn't allowed near you - I had to fucking sneak into your house to talk to you and you want to know why? You could've died, Lena. He could've killed you, you fucking - how close did he get?"

"He had me by the arm." I respond curtly, shocked by his response.

"He touched you?" He says quietly, starting to shake with anger.

I step closer to him, almost hesitant but reassured by the fact that he would never hurt me on purpose. I step closer until I'm right in front of him, close enough to take his hands and hold them; close enough to rub circles onto his hands; close enough to look up at the face that I had missed so much in the past month. I watch as he visibly relaxes and sinks towards me. His face is shuttered and his broad shoulders are caving in and towards me. A single curl is laid flat against his forehead, away from his perfect coif.

"Where was Adam?" He says, his voice deep and husky with emotion.

"We were running together and I ran a little fast. I ran away from him." I say, hoping that Andrew wouldn't get angry with Adam.

He pulls his hands away from me and pulls me close to him. I feel him pressing his face into my shoulders and leaving a kiss there before inhaling deeply. I feel myself shaking all over the place and I wrap my arms around him and relax into his embrace.

"I don't know what I would've done. I don't know what I would do, Lena. I wouldn't know what I would do if you had - if you had died." Andrew says, his voice cracking on the last word.

I pull him tighter and shake my head, feeling tears beginning to form in my eyes.

"I'm so sorry, Lena. I'm sorry for dragging you into this and putting you in danger. I wish we had met differently - where I wasn't apart of all of this. I wish -"

I pull myself away from his chest and look up at him, shaking my head vigorously. "I wouldn't have it any other way."

Our eyes lock and it almost looks like Andrew is lowering his head and just when it seems like he's only a moment away from kissing me, the front door bangs open and Tessa and Adam walk in, bickering loudly.

The bickering stops and I feel Adam's gaze on my back and Tessa takes in a sharp breath.

"Lena..." Adam says, his voice dangerously low.

I feel Andrew starting to pull away and I quickly let go and grab onto his arm with two hands. "Andrew, no. It wasn't him. It was me."

Andrew looks at me, full of disbelief and anger. "Lena -" "Lena!" Andrew and Adam speak at the same time and Adam steps closer to me, his face half relieved and half angry.

"Are you sure about this, Lay?" Adam asks, searching my face for any indication that I might be lying.

I nod and try to muster a smile, even with Andrew's heated gaze on me. "I'm sure. How was your date tonight?"

"It wasn't a date." Adam responds quickly, turning back around to shut the door.

Tessa rolls her eyes, "It was a date. And I know you enjoyed it, too."

Adam walks back to stand next to her and offers her a sardonic grin. "I enjoyed it up until you hit on the waiter."

Tessa groans, "All I said was 'hi', Adam!"

I shoot Adam a wicked look and laugh. "Did you get jealous, Adam?"

Andrew relaxes as the tension starts to dissipate as Adam starts to get red and flustered. He licks his lips nervously and shifts on his feet uncomfortably. "I didn't get jealous. I just think it's proper etiquette to not flirt with other people when you're on a date."

"Wait, but I thought that it wasn't a date?" Tessa teases, kicking off her shoes and plopping down on the couch.

"Adam, it sounds like you were jealous, man." Andrew adds in, chuckling at the end. "Never did I ever think I'd see the day that you'd be this red."

Andrew drags me to the couch and pulls me down beside him, throwing an arm around my shoulders and pulling me closer to him.

Adam quickly tries to change the subject, "Where's Bernie?"

A door opens and Bernie walks out, sighing. "I got here after Andrew and he's the boss. I tried to stay as close as possible but these two were getting all lovey-dovey."

I blush, embarrassed at how transparent my feelings were to everyone besides Andrew. "I - I wasn't being lovey-dovey."

Andrew snorts. "Shut up, Lena. I know that you have feelings for me."

CHAPTER 15

The room gets silent almost immediately and I try to break the silence by scoffing. "Why - Why would I ever?"

I look up at him when I realize that he hasn't replied and suddenly, everyone else in the room is getting up and muttering excuses to leave.

Andrew grins at me, "Well, because I'm handsome and funny? And I care about you?"

I try to scoff again, but it comes out as a cough. I glance at the clock and realized that somehow, almost an hour and a half had gone by and I was now too mentally and physically exhausted. "I'm tired. If you want, you can go home."

"You really think I'm gonna leave you alone after what I just found out?"

We spend almost half an hour arguing about where it's going to sleep. In the end, we settle for the guest room across the hall from mine.

The next morning, I find myself struggling to open up my own bedroom door. After a couple seconds of throwing myself against the door repeatedly, I was now completely awake and trying to figure out what the cause of the door jam was.

"Andrew!" I call through the door, hoping that maybe my voice would travel to across the hall where I knew he was sleeping. The door opens up less than a second later and I blink, stunned into silence at the sight of Andrew's disheveled appearance.

His hair was matted down on one side and I could see visible drool at the corner of his mouth. His shirt was wrinkled, as if he had used it as a pillow and he was blinking blearily at me. When I open my mouth to ask him how his night went, he pushes me backwards into my room and shuts the door behind him before pulling us to my bed and forcing me to snuggle under the covers with him.

To be honest, this was actually kind of my ideal Sunday after-noon. I find myself turning towards him and shutting my eyes. Just as I start to fall asleep, I feel his grip on me tighten.

I wake up before Andrew and pull my head away from his warm chest and look up him, studying the way that his long eyelashes fanned out and the way that his lips were so delightfully, deli-ciously pink. I stared at the way that his skin was smooth and the way that while sleeping, he was so delicate looking. Well, as delicate as a gang member can look. I pull away from him gingerly and mumbles something but doesn't protest too much. I slide out of the bed slowly and make my way to the kitchen where I find Adam and Tessa bickering quietly near the granite island. I stop just before I turn the corner and try to grasp pieces of their conversation.

"- doing with her?"

"- loves her."

"- you know?"

"- obvious. He doesn't know yet."

"He doesn't love me. We're just friends. We're only ever going to be friends." I say as coolly as possible, trying my best to hide that I really wanted him to just like me back.

Adam tsks and turns to the stove, turning on the fire and sighing. "I'm getting really tired of this nonsense, Lena. Almost anyone can see that he likes you, at the very least."

"He doesn't!" I protest to Adam's turned back. He starts noisily pulling pans out from the cupboard and I sigh, settling myself into one of the stools. "I think it's obvious that I like him. I'm pining for someone that could never like me the way that I like him and -"

"Like who?" Andrew's voice cuts through the noise in the kitchen and everyone freezes. Silence falls over the kitchen and I shift uncomfortably on the chair. I shoot Tessa a 'help me!' look but she shakes her head and turns towards the stove. "Lena? Who do you like?"

I clear my throat and shrug. "Like? Like who? When did you hear that? Ha, that's ridiculous." I say nervously, squirming in my chair when he comes around the table with a searching gaze.

"You just said -"

"If I liked someone I'd tell you." I say, trying my best to sound normal and not like I was lying to his face.

He doesn't say anything and sits back instead, resigned. He looked almost hurt that I didn't tell him but keeps it to himself.

Adam finally turns around, shaking his head. "Damn, Andrew. Don't you think she would tell you something as important as that? Don't you think she would've told you, her best friend?" The tension in the kitchen was palpable to everyone but Andrew. Adam and Tessa were sending me glares that said that I shouldn't have lied to Andrew. They kept looking at him and then at me and then raising their eyebrows, trying to motion that I should tell him.

Collin's POV:

She really didn't know. How could she not? Well, actually, how could he not know? How could he not know that he liked her? I stared at Wayne's little 'gang' sitting around the kitchen island with smiles on all of their faces. I couldn't stand that – couldn't stand that they were happy while I was sitting outside spying on them, bitter. I wanted so bad to pull out the gun in my pocket and shoot them – shoot all them – while they were defenseless. While all of their guards were down. But I couldn't. No, that would ruin the game that I had started. It would ruin the ending that I had in mind.

It was becoming near impossible to get near Lena without having a gun pointed at me or having someone trying to skewer me. I had almost started to consider changing targets – maybe to Adam. But no, going after him was definitely a suicide mission.

Going after Lena was going to be the plan. It made the most sense and at the moment, she meant the most to him. It would hurt him just as bad as it hurt me. I just wanted him to hurt as bad as I did. I wanted someone to feel the way that I do. I needed someone to hurt.

I watched as the blonde girl, Tessa, threw her head back and laughed and in that moment, I almost felt bad for trying ruining all of their lives.

Almost.

I wished that Andrew would finally realize his feelings for Lena so that I could swoop in and ruin everything. I wanted so badly – so badly to do that. To just ruin everything as soon as he realized. But even now, even as he was staring at him wistfully, he still didn't know. It was as if everything was sending him signs but he was too blind to do anything about it. I get up from the bushes and step away and out, sighing. I was done spying for the day. It starts getting nauseating when you sit somewhere for too long thinking of ways to ruin peoples' lives.

I walk across the street and get into my car and start driving towards the cemetery, sadness beginning to fall over me like a wool blanket.

Sometimes, the sadness suffocated me. Sometimes it felt like there were layers to my sadness – like everytime I finally broke free of one layer, there'd be 15 more waiting for me. Everyday, I found myself struggling to get out of bed. Everyday, just remembering that I was alone added another layer to my sadness. I didn't know how to deal with it. I didn't know how to deal with this. It'd been so long since Mom, Dad and Anna had died but I still didn't know how to deal with it. I pull into the parking lot and nod at the attendant who flashed a sad smile at me and gave me the 'ok' to walk up to my family's mausoleum.

I'd spent a lot of time in the cemetery. I remember when I saw them closing the mausoleum door for the first time – I remember the fear that had suffocated me. The fear that closed up my windpipes but managed to move my body across to bang my fists against the door. Now, however, all I could do was stare at the cold stone door. I couldn't make myself move to the door. The sadness was a barrier for me. All I could do was stand there.

Have you ever lost someone? Have you ever been so alone in the world? All thanks to someone else's family? Have you ever? I have and I don't know what to do about it except exact revenge. The Wayne family will feel the loss. They will understand.

The light turns on and I sit up, staring as Wayne walks in, obviously bugged by something. "Maloney." He growls, his eyebrows coming down and his lips pressing into a thin line. He reaches for his gun but I'm not fazed.

"I was watching your little...crew today, by the way. She's pretty beautiful. She's perfect, actually. I can only imagine the joy it'll give me when I bring my knife and slice open her -" I cut myself off and stand up, shrugging. "It's obvious to everyone that you like her. It's also pretty obvious that she likes you back. What are you waiting for, Wayne? Are you really that blind?"

Wayne doesn't reply, instead glaring at me, looking like he was going to shoot me right there. When I'm just about to turn and leave, he grinds out, "She's just a friend."

But I turn around, a malicious smile on my lips. "Oh, please don't tell me that the reason you're holding back is because you're afraid I'm going to kill her?" Something flashes in his eyes and the smile widens on my lips. "I hope you know that I was planning to kill her either way, Wayne. And you should watch out because if they hear gunshots in this building, you're going to die. Let me out of here and maybe Lena's lifespan will lengthen." I say casually.

CHAPTER 16

Wayne's hesitation is enough for me to throw myself in front of him, disarm him and then clock him on the back of his head with his own weapon. His body falls to the ground, unconscious and a smile creeps onto my lips at my victory. I turn around and drop the gun beside him before chuckling to myself and exiting out the front door.

On the way out, I watch as a homeless man eyes me uncertainly. Out of the corner of my eye, I watch him get up and start shuffling towards me. I notice that his hair looks very clean for someone that isn't supposed to have access to a shower and I stop walking. I turn to stare at him and recognition sets in almost immediately. His jaw clenches and he shakes his head. However, instead of pulling out his weapon like anybody else would do, he sighs.

"Collin." He says curtly, nodding at me.

The soft, raspy voice instantly brings back memories and I step back, stunned. "Bernie?"

"Collin, the Waynes had nothing to do with -"

"So you're one of them, now." I say, ice leaking into my voice.

"Your father outcasted me, Collin. I didn't leave you -"

"It doesn't matter what happened. The Wayne family killed my -"

"They didn't." Bernie says, his eyes cold. "Your family was running crazy, Collin. They were raping, beating and drugging up everything. Your own mother -"

"Don't talk about my mother."

But Bernie lowers his voice and shakes his head. "Your own mother, Collin, was killed by them. You don't know what happened. The Wayne family didn't do anything to them. One night, they came to the base and started to shoot at everything. Almost a fourth of the people living in that building died that night. Even more were injured. And the Wayne that you're fighting against now - the one whose life you're trying to ruin - he doesn't deserve it. You don't even know for certain that the Wayne family wiped out yours. You don't know anything -"

"I know."

"You don't. The Wayne family did nothing to your family. They didn't kill anyone. To this day, we still don't know who killed them. And you - and you're just trying to kill an innocent civilian to make up for something that didn't happen."

Fury rises in me faster than the tide can come in. Who was he to try and tell me who and what killed my family? Who is he to tell me that my family didn't die because of the Wayne family? I'd like to think that I know better than anyone who killed my family.

"I know who killed them - it was the Wayne family. And you're an idiot to try and convince me otherwise. My family housed you when you had no one and here you are, switching allegiance. Never," I say, disgust heavy in my words, "did I ever think that you would end up supporting these idiots.

Bernie shakes his head forlornly, and shuts his eyes. "That Wayne boy was just as young as you when your family died. The Waynes weren't even in the Heights when it happened - can you even remember seeing any of them? Did you even see any of them?"

And, for the first time in this entire thing that I had been trying to achieve, I flinched and started to regret the things that I was doing. He was right, actually. I couldn't actually think of the Wayne family in the Heights at the time. I'd never actually seen a Wayne in the Heights when it had happened. You might be thinking, "Wow, why would you just accuse the Wayne family?" And right now, I'm trying to wonder why I had accused them as well.

Andrew's POV:

When I wake up, the pounding in my head makes me groan loudly and I roll over onto my back, wincing. Almost immediately, I roll over and try to find my gun while fumbling for my phone. I press the number one on my speed dial and blink as stars start to invade my vision. Lena's soft, groggy voice fills my hearing and I sigh, satisified that she was okay.

"Call...Adam..."

I hear the rustling of her sheets and her panicked whisper-yells and I flinch, but let my eyes droop and close.

When I wake up again, Adam is standing over me, an empty bucket dripping ice water over my face. I blink and in a flash, Lena is by my side, her eyebrows furrowed, her pink lips pressed into a frown.

"How many fingers am I holding up?" She says, narrowing her eyes at me.

I blink rapidly and try to locate her hand but shake my head, fear gripping me. "I can't see your hand..." I say, trailing off uncertaintly.

A bright smile sweeps across her face and she sits back and nods at Adam, who drops to my side, his eyebrow cocked. "Looks like we're all moving into her house, Andy." I wince at the sound of my old nickname but try to sit up.

Lena pushes me back down, her eyebrows furrowed yet again, this time irritation setting into her face. "Don't try to sit up." The room falls into silence for a couple minutes and suddenly, a soft, feminine chuckle bounces around the room. "It's funny, actually. The amount of times that I've had to come save your life - or come save you from doing something stupid. You're quite the mess without me, aren't you?" She asks, a soft smile on her face as she leans over me again.

Adam laughs derisively and pushes Lena's head softly. "Yeah, it's almost like the two of you were made for each other."

"It's obvious to everyone that you like her. It's also pretty obvious that she likes you back. What are you waiting for, Wayne? Are you really that blind?"

The thought of Lena and I together had never really hit me as hard as it did until Maloney had brought it up. Was it really that obvious that she likes me? Was it? My eyes flickered over to her as she gently picked up my head and laid it on a pillow. She leaves for a couple seconds and comes back with an icepack, her lips pressed into a thin line of determination as she lays the ice pack on my head. She tucks her black hair behind her ear and I find myself staring at her face and realizing just how beautiful she was.

Of course, she had always been beautiful to me. She'd always been attractive to me - but somehow, at some point in our friendship, I had managed to push that attraction I had to her to the back of my head. But right now, as she was leaning over me, her hair falling over her shoulder and sending the sent of pine and vanilla into my nostrils, I found myself realizing that maybe - just maybe, I had started to feel something for her outside the realm of friendship.

I watched as her pink lips parted to reveal two rows of perfectly straight, perfectly white teeth and I took in a breath and hissed it out, causing her hand to jerk back to her body and a grimace to bloom on her face. "Sorry, did I hurt you?" She asks, her voice softer in respect to my pounding head. I shake my head and she sits back on her feet and looks up at Adam, who was watching me look at her. His eyebrow raises up and a smile twitches at the corner of his lips.

"Adam, let's bring him home - do you want to stay the night too?"

Adam smiles and shrugs. "Where else would I go? Come on, Andrew. We can't have a fine lady like Lena sitting around this dingy place in her pajamas."

I settle myself into Lena's bed and pat the space beside me, winking at her but feeling my stomach turn in anticipation of having her in my arms for another night. She comes over, yawning, not bothering to cover her mouth. She picks up her blanket and crawls in, settling herself right next to me, leaving two inches between us.

She rolls over to face me and she freezes, probably because she was unaware that we would end up so close together. My eyes drop to her lips and she lets out a shaky breath, blowing minty-freshness in my face.

"Lena." I breathe out slowly, my eyes lazily moving back up to meet her eyes. Her eyes widen and I hear her breath hitch. She tries to back away from me but I pull her closer to me. I rest my forehead on hers and smile lazily. "You're so beautiful." I whisper to her and she bites her lip. She looks like she's about to lean up to kiss me but pulls herself away and I disappointment causes my stomach to turn.

"Andrew..." She says softly, her eyes falling away from mine and dropping to where my hands were holding her wrists. "I need to tell you something,"

My heart starts beating a little faster and my mouth goes dry, a multitude of horrible things rushing through my mind. When her eyes lift back to look at me, her pink tongue dashes out to lick her lips quickly and I wince, feeling unbelievably aroused by the small gesture.

"I...I..." She starts unsurely, her eyes dropping from my face again. She falls silent for a couple of seconds but I don't press her. When she speaks again, my heart stops beating and my grip on her wrists loosen considerably. "I...when you look at me, it feels like my heart is going to beat right out of my chest. When you smile at me, or sit near me, or touch me, it feels like I can die happy. You...this - us, means the most to me. When you...when we were separated for that month, I felt so empty and I...God, this is so dumb." When I don't reply, she panics and looks up at me, and my stomach lurches. "I'm sorry. I shouldn't have told you - I just. I didn't want to lie to you anymore it's okay if you don't feel the same I just wanted you to know - God, I'm so dumb; I..." She pulls her wrists out of my newly loosened grip and slides away from me and out of bed and starts pacing nervously.

"I - I have to go." She says, her voice hoarse, tears building in her eyes.

When the door shuts behind her, it's almost as if time sped out. I pull myself out of bed and limp towards her, trying to ignore the stabbing pain in the back of my head. I find her standing out on her back porch, shoulders heaving, her hands in fists at her side.

I come behind and touch her shoulder to turn her around and pull her into a tight embrace. "I didn't know what to say." I said, burrowing my face into her neck.

She freezes, but I can feel her hot tears on my shoulder. "I'm sorry." She heaves out, shoulders still shaking.

"No, I'm sorry. I should've said something. I didn't mean to make you cry - please don't cry, Lena."

But it's as if my words make her cry harder and I let go of her, my heart breaking at the sight of her tear stained face. Funny how she was still more beautiful than the moon even while crying. "Lena, I didn't know what to say because I never thought you'd feel that way about me. I feel the same way. When I look at you, I feel like everything is right in my life. Please, stop crying - I - Oh God, please stop. If Adam sees your eyes tomorrow morning he's gonna punch me in the face."

She lets out a shaky chuckle and I dare to step closer to her, my eyes falling on her pink lips again. I let my head dip closer and closer to hers until she closes the space between us and presses her lips against mine.

In that moment, I swore to myself that I would never let any-thing hurt her. In that moment, I realized that somehow, in the 7 months that we had been friends, she had become my world - my everything. And I was okay with that.

CHAPTER 17

Lena's POV:

"Andrew, stop tugging at your collar like that. We'll be fine. You'll be fine -" I grab at his arm and pull him to a stop in front of me, a smile tugging at my lips at the sight of him looking so anxious. "What are you worrying about? If anything, it should be me that's worrying." He smiles down at me and stills himself.

"I'm just afraid that I'm going to mess up again. Just like last time."

I lean up and press a kiss against his lips but pull back before he gets too into it. "You won't mess up this time. I know you won't."

We get into the car and drive in comfortable silence to Uncle Max's (Andrew's Uncle) house. We pull into the driveway of a place that looks like it belongs to a billionaire and my jaw drops, amazed at the beauty of the place.

Before I know it, Andrew is at my side of the car, holding the door open for me. I step out into the cold winter air and shiver and in a flash, Andrew is getting ready to take his jacket off for me. I roll my eyes and click my tongue. "The house is only a 5 minute walk away. I'll be fine. Keep your jacket on."

When we step into the foyer, everyone stops moving and I recognize Max and Wade, both of whom I had met back at the wedding that Andrew had dragged me to. They pull away from their conversation and walk over, grins on both of their faces.

"Come on, Lena! Take off your jacket and come to the dining room. It's almost time for dinner!" The two men swarm around me and start trying to take my jacket off for me hurriedly. As soon as my jacket is off, both Andrew and I are ushered in the dining room, where the same crowd of people from the wedding were all seated around a table.

As Andrew and I stand there awkwardly, a couple of gorgeous girls break away from the group and come over, chattering excitedly.

"Andrew!" One of them says, a wide, white smile on her face - a smile that faltered when she realized that he had me pulled snug against his side.

"Ava," He says uneasily as she comes closer to us - not really us, actually. She was basically right on top of Andrew while his arm was around my waist. "Ava, you remember Lena, right? She was my date to the wedding."

Ava flips her blonde hair prettily over her shoulder and turns to me, flashing a blinding smile and causing me almost to flinch at how her entire face lit up with beauty. "Yeah, Lena as in your best friend, right?"

I wince but Andrew starts rubbing at my side comfortingly.

"Well, she was. Actually, she still is. But she's uh, she's my girl-friend now. We're together." He says. He leans down and presses a kiss against my temple and I turn to smile at him. When I turn back to Ava, I notice that her smile had faltered considerably and I almost start jumping with joy but restrain the urge.

"Oh, wow. I didn't know that you'd ever date a girl that wears dresses that tight. Looks good on you, though. Not slutty at all." She says, her voice now dripping with sugar. Andrew continues to rub at my sides and I sigh, my shoulders slumping just slightly. It was going to be a long night.

The knowledge of Andrew and I's relationship spread around the room like wildfire and in between the visits that his Uncles and cousins paid us, I usually caught a drop-dread beauty shooting me withering looks or daggers. Each look made me want to sink into his side until I literally wanted to hide myself inside his suit jacket.

"So." He says nervously.

"So..."

"I'm sorry. This was horrible. It was horrible tonight, I didn't expect Ava to react like that I -" He starts ranting as we laid on my bed. "I honestly didn't think that this would happen tonight. I'm sorry." We both roll over to face each other and I find a smile on my face at the sight of his worried one. "Don't be sorry. That was pretty entertaining, to be honest. I think I got enough dirty looks tonight to last me a lifetime."

Andrew groans and shuts his eyes while dragging a hand down his face.

"Honestly, you should've told me that you were really popular with the ladies before you came tonight. And you probably should've told me that they're all beautiful, too. Blonde beauties." I say, flashing back to every single girl that had angrily stared at me. "They all looked a lot like Lacey, actually."

"Yeah, they're all pretty beautiful." He agrees, a dreamy smile stretching across his face.

I feel my stomach turn uneasily and past insecurities envelope me. What did I have that Lacey didn't? I wasn't ugly, no, I knew that I was some sort of attractive. But I knew that I was nothing like the girls that Andrew usually surrounded himself with. Blonde, tall, tan and really passive aggressive. I knew that I was different from his usual girls. My hair was dark, sure I was tall but my skin was really pale and as far as I knew, I wasn't that passive aggressive. Some part of me, a tiny, tiny part of me brought up a strong point. What if he was only with me because he felt like he had to be? Like this was an obligation - something that he was only going to do because I trapped him into this. Somehow, when I had confessed, he had convinced himself that the best thing for him to do was just go along with it. Maybe he didn't want any of this; maybe he didn't want any of part of this relationship and that maybe, just maybe, I was annoying to him. I feel my lower lip quiver and my eyes start to fill with tears. I roll over onto my other side, away from his face and pull the covers over the both of us.

It made sense, really, that this would be possible. In the 7 months that we were friends, he didn't ever show any indications that he might've liked me even a teensy bit. And then suddenly, when I decide to tell him how I felt in a burst of recklessness, he told me that he reciprocated the feeling and suddenly we were in a relationship? Suddenly, I was able to wake up by being showered with his kisses? Suddenly, I got everything I wanted? No, this didn't make sense. There was no way that Andrew had fallen for someone like me. I wasn't even his type - I didn't even belong in his world. As far as I was concerned, we were more different than anything.

I lay there, the thoughts swirling around in my head and then stopping all of a sudden. I notice that Andrew's breathing had gone steady and that he was probably now asleep and I take that moment to force myself out of bed and towards the guest room where I knew that Adam was asleep in. Somewhere in the back of my mind, it registered that this probably wasn't a really good idea but I was also hysterical and panic was starting to claw at me, using my insecurities to weaken me.

I shake Adam awake and he sits up, his blanket falling away to bare his hard chest. "Lena? What's wrong?" He asks when he realizes that I had been crying.

"Adam, I don't - I don't know - I -" I say, stuttering and fumbling. My breathing starts to come out in short breaths and I bend over, suddenly heaving. The tears start to fall harder and I realize that everything was going so wrong but so right in my life. Adam wraps his warm arms around me and pulls me to his chest, rubbing my back and whispering sweet nothings into my ear.

"Why are you crying, Little Lay?" He says, wiping at his now wet chest.

"I'm sorry. I just - I -"

"Wow, this is the most articulate I've ever heard you." He says, an eyebrow raising.

I take a deep breath. "Tonight, I realized that I'm not Andrew's type. I - I'm not blonde, or tan and I don't know what I'm doing with him. For 7 months, he didn't think of me as someone he would ever date and then out of nowhere, we're together? That's just so shady and I just...I don't get it. What are we doing together? Is it obligatory? Is someone forcing him to be with me? That's what it feels like and I - I don't know how to deal with this feeling." I start to cry again and Adam pulls me into his arms again, nestling his face into my hair.

Suddenly, he pushes me away from him and presses his lips into a thin line. "You are beautiful. You are kind, you are smart and you are the best thing that has ever happened to him. He's lucky to have you. He's lucky to hold you and kiss you and call you his girlfriend. Don't you ever doubt that he wants to be with you, because believe me he does." Adam says sternly, almost angrily. "Don't you ever compare yourself to Lacey or Ava or Annie because you are so, so much better than them." He pulls me back to his chest and I close my eyes, basking in the warmth of his bare skin against my face. His warmth reminded me of family, of something completely platonic. The lights go out and I close my eyes and take deep breaths and find myself floating away to blissful sleep.

The next morning, I'm awakened to the door of Adam's room banging open. I wake up and blink blearily at Andrew's worried expression.

"Andrew?"

And then everything falls apart.

"Lena, what are you doing? Why are you sleeping in Adam's bed? On Adam's chest? Why doesn't he have a shirt on - what is going on here?" He asks, his voice low and dark.

"Wait -"

"Is something going on between you two? Is there something I should know?"

"Andrew, it's really not what it looks like." Adam says calmly sitting up and wrapping an arm around my waist protectively.

Andrew's eyes flickers down to where Adam had instinctively put his arm around my waist and his expression darkens. "I can't believe this. I -"

"We're just friends." I plead. "Andrew -"

"Friends don't sleep with friends who are half naked - friends don't sneak out of their boyfriend's arms and sleep with their boyfriend's best friend. Friends don't - friends don't do shit like this, Lena. You and Adam are more than friends - you're something else. I should've known. I should've seen this coming."

Adam and I stand up together and he draws me closer to his side, as if he knew that Andrew was about to lash out and explode. I pull myself out of Adam's arms and come closer to Andrew and he blinks at me, as if he was just now realizing that my eyes were swollen and I looked like complete shit.

"Lena, were you crying last night?"

I was hesitant to reply to him, not sure how to explain that the reason I had crawled into bed with his best friend was because I was insecure about myself.

"She was." Adam answers curtly, sidling up to me.

Andrew stops talking and turns to glare at Adam. "Can you put your fucking abs away, Adam? It's not fucking helping your case."

I look up to see that Adam is grinning. "Why would I put my shirt on? Lena loves me shirtless."

I reach a hand up and hit him on the head. "I think we both know that I prefer Andrew shirtless."

Adam pouts and bends down to pick up a shirt. "I'm just gonna leave the two of you in here to discuss. I'll see you later." Adam bends down and presses a kiss against my cheek. I turn to give him a scathing look but he winks at me before leaving the room.

Andrew closes the door behind me and turns to me, a scowl on his face. "And what was that?"

I sigh. "It was just a friendly kiss, Andrew. I swear -"

He comes closer to me and takes my hands in his. "Lena, what were you guys talking about last night? Why were you crying?"

My cheeks start flame and I duck my head. "It was stupid, really."

Andrew had never been the kind of guy that was good with expressing his emotions. It was true that he had been a dick several times - all of those times being when he got drunk and kissed me - and that maybe he was rude and had a hard time telling me how he feels. All I knew was that being in his arms made me happy; seeing him smile made me feel like my day was going to go so much better. I knew that his kisses made me feel like I was glowing from the inside out. I knew that talking to him, being around him and holding his hand made me feel like everything was going to be right. Maybe we had gone through a hard time; maybe we'd always be struggling like this but I knew that despite his faults and despite everything, I'd always love him.

The question is, would he always love me?

I feel him come closer to me and pull me into his arms. He rubs my back and we stand there in silence.

"I doubt that you would cry over something if it was stupid, Lena." He says, his voice tender.

I blink at his sudden change in tone. It went from the usual husky seduction to almost Adam-esque.

"I...I realized that we, you, well, mostly me...I don't know. I just don't. I realized that I was so out of place and that maybe I'm not good enough for you and that this whole relationship is obligatory.

I just wanted you to know that you don't need to be with me. You can be with someone better - someone like -"

Andrew groans and pushes me back so that he's holding me by arms. For what felt like years, he stared at me in disbelief before a smile spread onto his lips. "Are you serious?" He stares at me again and then pulls me to the bed, where he settles me onto his lap. He presses kisses on my neck and I can feel his smile as he does it. When he stops kissing me, he starts to rub circles onto my hand. "I want to be with you, Lena. It took me a long time to figure out that you're everything I need and everything that I'd ever want because I'm dumb. When I look at you, I see a house and 55 kids and 20 dogs. When I look at you, I want to kiss you long and hard and do it again and again forever. Don't you ever think that someone could possibly be any better than you because they really can't be. You're perfect for me, Lena. I wouldn't want anyone else. You're more than enough. You're perfect and there is no way that this is an obligation. Maybe for you, but I'm in this for us. Us against the world." He takes a deep breath and I turn around to smile at him.

"That was so unbelievably lame of you."

"You like lame me, though." He says, smiling wildly. We fall into a comfortable silence before he starts chuckling. "I can't believe you thought that this entire time I was with you because you felt like I was forced into this."

I roll my eyes. "I mean it's weird that I confessed and you immediately ran after me when for 7 months, you showed no signs!"

"I always thought that you and Adam had a thing. He's always taking care of you and holding you when I'm not there. You always run to him instead of me and it's weird. It's weird for me. It's almost like you guys are dating sometimes." He says honestly, his voice low and gruff.

"Adam? Me and Adam? Adam and I? Are we talking about the same Adam? Adam is like my brother. I always run to him because he knows me best because someone forced him to be my security detail. I swear, last night was purely sister-brother bonding. When I look at him, all I see is someone that's probably gonna be walking me down the aisle."

"It's not far-fetched, really. You guys are always together. He's your shoulder to lean on and I'm not."

A smile pulls at the corners of my lips and I look up at him and press a kiss against his lips. "This is weird. I'm not used to this tender side of you. I almost feel like I'm talking to Adam right now."

Andrew laughs and pulls me even closer to him so that I'm straddling his lap. The room falls silent and his eyes flicker up to mine. "I will never hurt you. I will never let anything hurt you." It falls silent again but the silence is quickly ruined by the sound of Andrew's stomach rumbling.

I laugh and get off of his chest and offer him my hand. "Come on, time for breakfast, I guess."

Down in the kitchen, I watch as Tessa smiles at her phone while Adam flips pancakes by the stove. I blink at her presence and watch as Adam slides a plate over at her with a smile that falters when he realizes that all of her attention is on her phone. I make a mental note to pull her aside and ask her later but instead decide to settle in around the island and wait impatiently for Adam to cook our breakfasts for us.

"Everything solved, then?" He says, turning around and flashing a smile at me.

"Yeah, everything solved." I turn to smile at Andrew who's already looking at me. I almost lean in for a kiss but Adam clears his throat loudly. I turn back to look at him but he's staring at Tessa fixedly, as if staring at her was gonna make her wrench her attention away from her phone.

"Who are you texting?" I ask, trying to seem semi-casual. Adam's neck snaps over to me and he shakes his head not even noticeably but Tessa replies nevertheless.

"Trent."

My fork drops to my plate with a clatter and I feel Andrew's hand searching for mine in an attempt to calm me down. "Trent? As in Trent the guy that dumped you?"

Tessa looks up at me, a grimace on her face. "Yeah, maybe."

"Maybe? He's the biggest dick - I - There are no words for how big of a dick he is! He hurt you. You literally were laying on the cold hard ground. You were so drunk after that breakup that even the 2012 bonfire is showed up by that night. You - Tessa, what about you-know-who?"

She winces, "I don't need you to lecture me, Lena. I already know that I'm not doing the right thing. And I don't feel anything for him anymore. I'm done. I really don't want to hear it."

I sit back in my chair and shut my eyes before opening one and staring at her. "I'm just trying to watch out for you, you know."

She tries to smile but it's feeble. "I know." Tessa stands up and pushes back her chair and starts walking away from the island. "I think I'm going to go for now."

When we all hear the front door shut, Adam looks at me, his eyebrows drawn together. "Just the other night she told me that they were gonna be over forever. And who's this other guy?"

I shake my head and resist the urge to roll my eyes. When was Adam ever going to get less oblivious?

Chapter 18

"You have to go home, Andrew." I say, pouting.

"But I really, really don't want to." He says, a slight whine to his voice.

Behind him, Adam scoffs. "Shut up, dude. Let's just go home. She'll be fine for one night."

Andrew sighs and leans forward to press a kiss against my lips. "I'll see you bright and early, Little Lay!"

I groan, "God, Adam. Do you see what you've started?"

Adam chuckles and I crane to look over Andrew's shoulder just in time to see him shrug. "Come on, Andy."

Andrew pecks me quickly on the lips and then turns around and leaves.

As soon as they pull out of the driveway, I see someone stumbling out from behind the bushes. The person comes staggering towards me, bent over and clutching at his leg. The scene was all too familiar. Without a second thought, I find myself sprinting out of my house and crouched in front of the person that I thought was a stranger.

"Lena."

My blood runs cold and my hands drop from around where they were holding on to. I scramble up back onto my feet and step back, my hands now shaking. "Collin -"

"Lena, help." His velvet voice is now low and shaky and even though every single nerve in my body is screaming - literally screaming - the word no, I step forward and look at him right in the eye and say, "Okay."

He slings an arm around my shoulders and I try to support him by the waist and pull him into my house. "Go sit in the kitchen."

I run upstairs and pull out my first aid kit and then run back downstairs. He opens his mouth but I shake my head. "If I don't hear your voice then I'll forget who I'm working on and -"

"Thank you."

I shake my head and reluctantly step closer and look at the wound on his leg. "Did someone - did you get stabbed?" I ask as I douse his wound in hydrogen peroxide and then quickly dab at it with a clean towel. He hisses and his entire leg jerks upwards, almost kicking me in the stomach.

"I did." He replies curtly.

"This is really, really bad. The bleeding won't stop." I look up at him and find myself staring into his eyes. Emotions were swirling around in them. Pain, sadness, anger, fear - mostly sadness, to be honest. "I can...No, can you hold this against the wound? I'm gonna get something to tape down the gauze."

When I come back, Collin is staring intently at me. "Why are you helping me? I threatened to skin you alive - I threatened to kill you. I could be about to attack you right now. Are you that stupid or are you actually as kind as they say you are?"

I shrug, "You looked like you were close to bleeding out on my front lawn. How am I supposed to explain a dead body to my neighbors in the morning?"

Collin lets out a short laugh which is cut even shorter when I pull the towel from his leg and press the gauze over the wound. "That's funny."

I look up at him with a level gaze. "I wasn't joking." When I finish wrapping up his leg, I get up and walk to the kitchen. "Do you want anything to eat?" I hear the chair push back and freeze but then I hear him staggering over, his breath short. What the fuck was I thinking when I invited him in? How was this a good idea in any kind of way? Actually, easy, it really wasn't.

"You're offering me something to eat?" He asks, disbelief clear in his voice.

I turn around and look up at him. "Yeah, is that okay? I have spaghetti on the stove."

Collin blinks and scratches his head awkwardly. "Uh, yeah sure. That's uh, that's fine."

When I set the bowl in front of him, the room falls into a suffocating silence. I stare at him from underneath my lashes, trying to inconspicuously stalk him from across the room. I stare at him, "So, are you Irish or something?"

He looks up and blinks at me, as if he were surprised that I could speak. "Yeah. My last name is Maloney. You?"

"I'm...well, I guess I'm Russian somewhere and maybe a little German. I don't know, my

coloring is funny, as you can see. My last name is Parker, though. So I think that's kind of really American so I mean I'm probably just a mix, like the rest of America. Not purely anything, really. I'm rambling because I'm actually really afraid of you - you know, the times you, uh, stopped me in my car and, you know, almost -"

"I'm not gonna kill you." Collin responds tiredly.

Everything quiets again and I stare at him awkwardly as he finishes the last of his spaghetti. "Are you not gonna kill me...like now? Or,"

"No," He says, newly irritated. "I'm not gonna kill you at all. I'm not sure if I was planning on killing you at all in the beginning - well, I was, but I guess I wasn't sure if I was going to go through with it."

A part of me feels light, relieved. I couldn't wait to call Andrew and Adam and tell them that they didn't need to hover around me anymore - I was gonna be safe again. Everything could go back to normal. But another part of me, the rational part, is confused. What changed that made him not want to kill me? It wasn't like I wasn't grateful or anything - no, in fact, I really was. But it was weird. Out of nowhere, over an impromptu dinner and some first aid, Collin had decided that he wasn't out to get me anymore?

"If this isn't a too-awkward question to ask, why?" I ask quietly, trying to look at him levelly.

"I'm not built for killing. I'm not mentally strong enough, in all honesty. Until last year, just the sight of blood made me squirm. I don't know where I came up with the idea that I wanted to kill you." He pauses. "Actually, I do know. I was convinced that Andrew's family had killed mines, that I owed him the same amount of pain and sorrow that I have in my life. But in light of recent events, I realized that I was wrong. I have no reason to kill you." He hesitates again, "Also, you're really nice, actually and I think I would seriously go to Hell if I killed you."

I stare at him, puzzled. A million thoughts are zipping through my mind. What happened? Why did he think that Andrew's family had killed his? "Do you want more spaghetti?"

Collin grins sheepishly. "Actually, yes. I haven't really had a home-cooked meal for a long time."

After he finishes his third (yes, third) bowl of spaghetti, I finally decided that it was probably way past time for him to go home. He gets up and stretches but ends up wincing. "I forgot that I was mortally wounded. Thanks again, by the way."

I walk him to the door but when he steps out, he immediately steps back in, his expression grim. "I'm not leaving. Not tonight."

He shuts the door, deadbolts it, shuts all of my blinds and locks all of my windows. He limps to the back of the house quickly and does the same thing before staring me down. His face is a mix of worry and indecisiveness. Finally, he pulls me to the couch and sits on the table so that he's facing me. "There's someone out there and they don't have good intentions."

"Who -"

"I don't know. It's just a feeling that I have. This instinct for dinner is something that people generally tend to grow when they live in the Heights for extended periods of time." He says grimly.

I stare at him, and of their own accord, I can feel my eyes widen. "What do we do?"

He stops talking and buries his head in his hands. "Why do you have so many people after you? What has Wayne done?" He stops talking again and just when I'm about to ask him another question, he looks up at me. "We need to call them. Andrew and Adam. I'm not gonna be able to protect you because my leg but they will. If I let any harm come to you I'm sure that they'll mess me up."

He stands up and reaches for his phone, wincing when he had to move his leg. "Hello? Wayne, Adam. I'm at your girlfriend's house." He hung up abruptly and stuffed his phone back into his pocket.

"Why didn't you tell them -"

"They'll come faster. And I like fucking around with Wayne." He says, grinning widely.

20 minutes later, Adam and Andrew are inside of the house and Andrew looks like a cloud is following his every movement. His jaw is clenched and his hands are balled into fists. All in all, I'd never seen him so angry in my life.

"I was expecting you to be strung up and hung like meat when we got here but it looks like the two of you are literally just having a conversation." Adam says, a ghost of a smile on his face.

Andrew turns around and fixes Adam with a scowl before turning back to Collin and I. "What the fuck do you want with her?"

"Nothing." Collin replies curtly, shrugging and making his way to a couch far, far away from me. "I showed up on her front lawn bleeding profusely and she invited me in, patched me up and fed me. I could've died if she hadn't helped me and now I want nothing from her. A life for a life. I'm giving you hers because she saved mine."

And instead of relaxing (something that I hoped but didn't expect him to do), Andrew turns to me, scowling (if possible) even harder. "What did I say?" He says, his voice low and cold. I look up at him at the sound of his voice, and find that although his voice made him sound furious, he was actually just worried. Really worried. "Andrew, he was bleeding -" I say softly. "I don't care if half of his body was blown off - you can't just let strange people - especially people that have threatened on numerous accounts to kill you into your fucking house. You're defenseless. You can die, Lena." He says, worry betraying his previously cold demeanor and revealing to the rest of the room that he was worried.

I look over at Collin, who is staring at Andrew and I confusedly and then Adam starts to snicker. "Oh, Maloney are you in for a treat tonight."

Andrew and I ignore Adam and I stand up, feeling uncomfortable and just slightly embarrassed. "This is a part of me, Andrew. I can't help that I want to help everything and that's never going to change about me. You can't do shit about it -"

"I can fucking try." He spits out harshly, coming closer to me, still scowling. "Do you know how worried I was?"

"I do," Adam pipes up from behind him, his arms still crossed over his chest. "he looked like someone had cut off his head, the way he was running to the car. Actually, the way that he drove here was reminiscent of a chicken without its head."

Andrew and I both shoot Adam a withering glare but he's not affected by it, instead walking over to the couch and sitting down.

"Accept me for who I am, Andrew. I'm sorry. Don't be mad at me - it worked out in the end, didn't it? I'm still alive, aren't I?"

Andrew takes a deep breath. "The point is that you could've died. There are endless possibilities. You, the most important thing to me -"

"Hey!"

"The most important thing to me next to Adam, could've died. I just got you, Lena. And now you're trying to get away from me? Do you have a deathwish or something?" Andrew says, lowering his voice and staring at me with frustration clear.

Just as I'm about to answer, Collin clears his throat and stands up, wincing. "Wayne, I called you here because, as you can see, I'm mortally injured. I pray that you weren't worried enough to notice but when I walked outside earlier, I felt something weird in the air. Almost as if danger had a smell and we were surrounded by it. I'm sure it's gone now, but I had to be sure that she was safe. I think someone is watching her, getting ready to go in for the kill." He raises his hands in the air innocently. "It's not me, though."

Andrew turns around and scowls at him. "What, so you're guarding her now?"

Collin shrugs. "The both of you have lives, I have nothing better to do. One of you can't always be with her."

"No." Adam says, finally serious. "Sorry, but I don't trust you. You've been plotting to kill her for the better part of this year and it's weird that you're just ready to protect her now. I don't believe you...and we'll be fine."

Again, Collin shrugs. "Hey, I understand that. If it makes you feel any better, I'll always be around, watching her back. I've gotten pretty good at that these past months."

Andrew makes something that sounds a lot like a growl and starts to come towards Collin but I step forward and take his hand. He looks down at me, his jaw clenched, anger clear in his expression. I shake my head at him and he shuts his eyes and uses his other hand to drag a hand down his face. Then, he gently pulls my hand out of his and walks towards Collin, his shoulders rising and falling slowly, like he was trying to take deep, deep breaths.

"I'm not going to hurt you." I hear him say when Collin takes a weary step backwards. Andrew walks until he's right in Collin's face and I can tell, even from several feet away, that's he doing everything he can to not bash his face in. "But I will," he says, through clenched teeth, "if I find out that she has even one hair gone on her head because of you. You will die the slowest of deaths. Slower than slow. You'll be so dead that they might actually have to find a new word to describe the state that you're in."

Collin's head pokes out and he looks at me with an eyebrow raised. "Are you two seriously just friends?"

"We're not -"

"We are." I assure. Andrew's head swings around, and his eyebrows furrow.

"Do you really still not believe me?" He says, incredulity clear in his voice.

I shrug, "It's pretty sketchy that there's suddenly love for me from you after 7 months of no signs."

Andrew looks like he's on the verge of committing suicide or shooting something but he takes a deep breath and lets out a heavy sigh. "What's it going to take?"

I shrug. "Another 7 months of begging on your knees."

The room falls into yet another awkward silence and then I hear Collin clearing his throat. "You're right, Adam. This is pretty entertaining."

CHAPTER 19

C ollin's POV:

I sit in the back of Wayne's car, a grin on my face as I listened to their conversation. It had been silent for the first five minutes but both Adam and I could tell that he was itching to ask a question.

"Just ask." Adam says, disgruntled.

After a pause, "What do I do?"

"I don't know. Lena's a tough cookie to crack. I mean, I get her, I really do. Where the fuck did you even come from with these feelings - don't get me wrong, I know that you liked her, it was obvious to everyone. Even our friendly neighborhood psycho -"

I roll my eyes and protest. "Hey, that offended me."

"Yeah, well, so was you trying to kill Lena all those times."

I shrug. "Touche."

"Anyways. As I was saying," Adam interjects, "even our neighborhood psycho agrees with me. It was clear. But to her, it wasn't. Give her some time. Maybe stop being such a dickhead and pushing her into a relationship...and just be there for her. Believe me, she needs someone to be there for her. Her parents are never home, Tessa is always out getting wasted."

"Where are her parents, anyways? The time that I spent stalking her showed that they were never home." I say, ignoring Andrew's withering glare to me from his rearview mirror.

"We don't know. When they're home, they take really good care of her, but personally, I just think they like to travel." Adam says hesitantly, as if information about their absence was going to give me more means to kill her. He pauses and then says, "Yeah, Lena mentioned that they've always wanted to travel the world and they've been waiting until she could take care of herself so that they could start doing it."

The fact that she was all alone, all the time made fear grip at me even more. I could definitely understand why the Waynes were so obsessed with this girl. At first, I thought that she was just going to be one of Wayne's rebounds for that blonde that he was so enamored in. Quickly, however, as I watched the two of them together, I realized that there was so, so much more underneath their so called friendship. They were together every second of the day; understandable, actually, because I was trying to kill Lena all the time. But they never really acted like friends. Maybe the first month or so, the distance was obvious, the discomfort apparent. But the two quickly became more than just friends, and I had noticed it first. Lena hadn't realized it, probably didn't want to, but soon, it was becoming more and more apparent that the attraction she had for him wasn't purely physical.

It definitely was, at first. Physical, that is. Always touching each other, hugging, forehead kisses, hand holding, arm holding - if it was an extremity, they'd probably held onto it already. I remember the time when they started sharing a bed; she hadn't even protested. I had chalked their relationship up to purely lust; there were no feelings behind it. And Wayne seriously seemed to believe that, too. He knew that he was attracted to her body and he was being completely honest when he told me that he didn't really like her that way.

Well, until that was up until the wedding that they went to for one of his uncles. After he ran to her house and saw her in Adam's arms, crying and shutting him out of her life, things changed. For months afterwards, he was completely different. It was like he was missing her - all of her; not just her body. It didn't really come as a surprise to me when he confessed that he liked her too. But, Lena is right to be suspicious. But, I definitely agreed with Adam. The signs were all there. Even though she was too gullible, too willing and too caring for her own good. I'd seen her taking in Bernie, someone she didn't even know. She'd let me into her house, for God's sake.

And I think that's what saved her. Realizing that killing her would be more than horrible. She was too sweet. Too gullible and way, way too innocent. And, moreover, her offering to help me and feeding me a homecooked meal really sealed the deal. I just couldn't. To be honest, I wasn't sure I ever was going to. The thought of killing is disgusting to me; punching someone in the face is already sickening. The sight of blood used to make me want to faint or hide - maybe that comes from watching my parents get mercilessly slaughtered.

Watching them die should've made me a psycho. It should've turned me into a heretic, I should've become a sociopath. Instead, I'd been turned into a hermit without a home, someone that was too weak to lead but damn good at pretending. I'd spent a lot of time pretending to want to kill Lena and destroying the Wayne family. I'd spent a lot of time and I'd dedicated so much time to leading my gang, wishing that maybe if I was a leader long enough, my gang would start feeling like a family the way that Wayne's family was.

"If we let you out here will you stay here?" Adam asks, glancing at me from the rearview mirror.

I shrug. "Depends. If my spidey-sense start tingling, I might turn around and watch Lena sleep."

"You just referenced Spiderman and Twilight in one sentence. This isn't helping with the trust issues between us, Maloney." Wayne says dryly, rolling his eyes. Awkward silence envelops the car and as I reach for the door handle, Wayne grunts loudly and clears his throat. "Wait." He says begrudgingly. "Thanks."

I don't have to ask what he's talking about. I flash him a smile and wink. "Anything for you, of course." As soon as I step out of the car, I head towards my compound, whistling almost happily.

"Maloney." A cold voice remarks.

I straighten up and turn around, a smile (the wonky, crazy one that you're usually supposed to expect from psychos) on my face. "Hello."

But, whoever this person was didn't seem to believe in small talk. "Why aren't you bleeding out somewhere?"

My smile doesn't falter. "I'm not sure, should I be?"

The guy looks frightened, even if it was only for a second. That's what the crazy does to them. I mean, wouldn't you think twice while talking to someone who even resembles psychotic? But this guy doesn't. "I mean, considering the fact that I shot you, I think you should be."

My head cocked to the side, the smile growing wilder and wider. "You're the one that shot me? Interesting."

"Again. Why aren't you bleeding out? Who helped you?"

I shrug. "Why couldn't I have helped myself?"

"We know how you live, Maloney. No food, no water, no electricity. You bathe at the beach, you have no friends. Even your own gang hates you. We hate you. You should've died and I was just speeding up the process."

The smile drops off of my face and turns into a mock pout. "Well, that's not nice at all." I cluck my tongue. "What am I going to do with you?" I start to walk around him, eyeing him creepily.

And that's when he freezes and I can feel the fear starting to emanate off of him. I go to stand in front of him, the smile back on my face. "Tell you what," I start, smiling even wider. "maybe, if you tell me who orchestrated this whole thing, I'll let you go with an arm."

"They just sent me to shoot you. I - I don't know who."

"Are you lying?" I ask, stepping forward.

The guy looks like he was about to turn around but tips his chin up defiantly. "No."

I cock my head to the side. "Are you sure? I don't like liars, you know. And you certainly seem like one."

"I -"

The minute he's about to answer my interrogation, I hear the sound of a car pulling up behind me and I turn around. The guy behind me shifts, as if he was ready to run and I turn around and pull him back by his hoodie. "Don't even think about it." I say between clenched teeth.

I turn back around just in time to see Wayne leaning out of the driver's window, staring at the guy that I had struggling against my grip.

"What are you doing, Maloney?"

"He walked up to me and told me that he shot me." I say, shrugging. I turn to the guy. "That's what happened, right?"

"Well, I -"

"Right?" I say, the smile creeping back on my face. "What was that that you asked me? 'Why aren't you bleeding out somewhere?'"

"You're scaring the shit out of him." Wayne says.

"That's the point, Wayne." I reply, exasperated. "They don't answer you if you don't scare them shitless."

The kid yanks his body back and looks at me, eyes wide. "Don't bother coming back to the compound. Now that you're hanging out with the Waynes, you're not allowed anywhere near us. Get off of the property." He says, pulling out a gun.

I almost step forward and punch him in the face but then think better of it and step back, hands up. "I'm leaving, no need to get hostile." I say, the smile still on my face.

"Stop smiling like that."

"Like what?" I say, smiling even wider.

"Like you're - like you're crazy."

"Oh, but I am." I stare at him for a good five minutes before he drops the gun and turns around, running and not once looking back. I bend down and pick it up and turn around while putting the safety on. "I think my own gang put a bounty on my head."

Wayne and Adam exchange a look and it almost appears like they're silently arguing about something. Just when I'm about to interrupt them, Adam gives Wayne a sharp look and looks over at me. "Do you have a place to live for the time being?"

"Yes." I reply without thinking. Adam cocks an eyebrow and leans forward, past the driver's window, skeptical.

"What were you thinking of doing? Sneaking back into your compound and passing out in your own room? If they figure out you came back, they're gonna surround you and burn your room to the ground."

I almost defend my own gang and try to explain that they're not as savage as he thinks they are but my mouth shuts when I remember that they actually are that savage. "I don't have anywhere to sleep tonight."

Just when Adam is about to answer, Wayne turns and gives him a withering look, his mouth twisted in disgust. "Lena is going to be very angry at you if you let him sleep out in the cold, Andy. You know that."

"It's not even that cold - and who says she even has to know?" He retorts immediately, his voice low and cold.

I open my mouth to reply, ready to assure them that I'll find a way but then shut it, instead wondering to myself about whether or not I had a chance to get away from them if I just tried to creep off. Just when I decide to take a chance, Adam glances up at me, eyes narrowed. "And where do you think you're going? Get in the car."

"No -"

"No!" Wayne and I protest at the same time - his with admittedly more vehemence. Adam doesn't look amused. He stares at me, his brown eyes narrowing and his lips twisting into an angry line.

"Really, Andrew? How do you think that's going to settle with Lena? How do you think she's going to feel when she finds out that you're going to cast someone out into the cold? Don't think that I won't tell her, either. I will. Don't test me." Adam says, turning to glare at Wayne, who looks like he'd rather cut out his intestines than give me shelter. Again, I try to slink off but Wayne looks up, his lip curled with distaste.

"He keeps trying to sneak off - he doesn't even want our help. Why are we offering it?" He says, turning back to Adam, who rolls his eyes.

"I promise that I won't slit your throats while you sleep tonight." I say, trying to turn the conversation back to the lighthearted end of the spectrum.

"Thanks," Wayne says dryly. "that's really reassuring. Just get in the car. We're sleeping in the penthouse tonight."

"You're...rich?" I ask as we pull up to a tall glass building that was just at the border of the Heights and Glass Hills. I'm not sure what to make of the duo. Adam tries to put an arm around Wayne's shoulders but Wayne shrugs him off and I hear him growling even though I was a couple feet behind them. The two are obviously close - best friends and brothers and I wonder why I had chosen to chase after Lena instead of Adam. My answer comes when two minutes later, Wayne is on his back and moaning in pain.

Right.

CHAPTER 20

Lena's POV:

I don't know why I called Collin. Actually, I do. At the time, he was the best option. I crept out of bed and lunged for the scrap of paper that he had hastily scribbled his number on the day that he had caught me outside of my house. I knew that despite his past with me, he'd guard me with his life. I'd seen the way that he had stared at me and I knew that subconsciously, he had decided that he'd protect me.

And I knew that right now, I couldn't call Andrew. He wouldn't be able to think straight. When it comes to me, the first thing he does is rage until everything is better – and the thing is, nothing is ever truly better when Andrew decides to rage. I know that I also can't call Adam. Despite the fact that he's the most reasonable person when it comes to my safety, I know that he'll call Andrew because he tends to panic for a few seconds and he always tells Andrew first.

So I called Collin – partly because I knew that he would help and partly because I knew that he wouldn't tell Andrew or Adam. I just hoped he'd get here on time.

"Oh, Lena!" A gruff voice tries to sing my name and a shiver goes down my spine. I'm backed against the wall, a lamp in my hands, ready to swing at my would-be kidnappers. I wasn't sure what was going on. I was sound asleep when I heard crashing sounds. If not for the fact that I live on the second floor, I'd probably be running towards my car and driving to the Heights right now. My grip tightens on the lamp as the footsteps come closer to my door. "Lena, we know you're here!" The guy says again, his voice low and sing-songy. The knob to my door starts to turn and then, before I can blink, two big guys are in my room, malicious grins on their faces.

"W – What are you doing here?" I ask, my voice coming out shakier than I wanted.

The two of them look at each other, probably surprised that I had seen them coming and that I wasn't cowering against the wall. "This is the first time that we've ever been asked that question. You know, Markus, I thought we were pretty well-known in this gang business. Most gang groupies know who we are."

The blood drains out of my face and I take a cautious step backwards and try to get closer to the window.

"I advise that you get away from that window, girly. What we're going to do to you is far less than falling to your death." Markus says, smiling maniacally. "Markus!" The other guy says, his eyes narrowed. Markus' smile drops off of his face and turns to the other guy, frowning. "What, Brett?" But all Brett does is narrow his eyes and look at me, studying me. "Right, okay, I was just wondering if you even know what you did."

"I -"

Just when I'm about to answer them, I hear Markus fall backwards loudly. Brett turn around almost instinctively and raises his arm to hit the other person but I run forwards, quickly throwing my lamp at Brett's head. Brett falls forward with a thump and Collin quickly walks around the bodies and towards me, his eyebrows furrowed.

"You being alone is dangerous." He says, glancing over his shoulder at the two unconscious men on the ground. When he turns back to me, he's studying me with newfound curiosity. "Why did you call me? Why not Wayne or Adam?"

I shrug. "Why did you want to kill me and not Andrew or Adam?"

Collin studies me and then shrugs, a whisper of a smile on his face. "Touche."

I hear a grunt and suddenly I'm being yanked to the ground, my hands shooting out to help break my fall. I start kicking at Brett, who was trying to drag me towards him. When I'm finally next to me, he looks at me straight in the eye before wrapping his hands around my neck and pressing down hard on my windpipe.

I hear Collin start walking towards me and then he's at eye level with me, his face pressed against the ground as Markus sits himself on top of him, groaning in pain. Markus pushes Collin's face harder into the ground, "This is what you get for hitting me on the back of the head like that you son of a -"

I start to claw at Brett's hands, my vision starting to blur and spot. Collin's face starts to become unfocused and I start to struggle harder, flailing and ultimately kicking everything in the room. I hear a grunt as my left foot connects with something and Brett's grip on my throat relaxes enough for me to pull his hand off from my neck and roll over. It only takes 10 seconds for him to recover but it's enough for me to gather my breath and start kicking at him again. When my foot connects with his body again, I hear him groaning loudly in pain and I assume that I've kicked his crotch ar ea.

"Why you little -" Markus says, his eyes wide.

But I stand up as Brett's groaning in pain and grab the heaviest object in the room (my APUSH textbook from my nightstand) and throw at him. Collin gets up and quickly punches Markus in the fact, effectively knocking him up. Brett gets up, towering over Collin by 5 inches. Collin's knee rises quickly and Brett doubles over again, groaning. "God, what is it with you two -"

Before Brett can finish his sentence, Collin has him pinned against the wall, his forearm against his throat. "Who sent you?" Collin asks, his voice low and dangerous. Brett doesn't answer, instead shaking his head, a grin on his face. "Does it matter? Who really cares who wants her dead? We'd all celebrate just the same." He chokes out, getting blue in the face. "Who's 'we'?" Collin growls. I walk over to them but Collin turns towards me, his eyes narrowed. They drop down to my neck and I see him flinch. "Get out of here. I'll take care of this."

When I'm out of the house, I run to my car and quickly switch on my phone, my hands shaking. What did he mean by 'take care of this'? Was he going to kill them? Maim them? Was he going to skin them alive? Or was this his plan? Was he double-crossing us? Was he trying to get Andrew and Adam to trust him so that he could sneak in and kill me while I'm sleeping one day?

I have to dial and redial Andrew's number four times before I get it right. By the 3rd ring, he's on the phone, his voice husky. "Lena?" He says, sleep clear in his voice.

Although I'm now a couple blocks away from my house, I still whisper. "Andrew, I'm in trouble."

"Where are you?" He asks, sounding wide awake. I hear rustling in the background and the sound of his fingers snapping and someone else groaning awake. I tell him where I am and he hangs up abruptly.

In 10 minutes, he's standing outside of my car, which is pulled over next to a tree, his jaw clenched, his hands curled into fists. I open the door and jump out and into his arms, burying my face into his chest. My throat is sore and it feels like I'm going to die with every breath I take. It takes him a couple minutes to finally wrap his arms around me, but when he does, I find tears leaking out of my eyes.

Finally, the silence is broken when Andrew's curiosity bests him. "Lena, what happened?" He pulls his arms away from my back and pushes me away from him, his eyes landing on my neck. I see the fury wash over his face almost immediately probably at the sight of the bruises that had formed on my neck. When I don't answer him, he seems to get angrier. "Lena. Whathappened?"

"I -" I say, my voice cracking.

"Goddamnit!" He says suddenly, his hands falling away from my arms and balling into tight fists at his side. "It was fucking Maloney, wasn't it? I knew I shouldn't have trusted him. I -" He cuts himself off and turns around, his back to me. He punches the tree and I don't even see him flinch in pain. "Fuck!" He yells, turning to look at me. I shift out of the light, hoping to hide the bruises so that he can stand to look at me. "Fuck, this is my fault." He says to himself, his eyes dropping to the ground.

I step towards him hesitantly, scared that his mood was going to change if he caught sight of my neck for a third time. "Andrew..." He looks up at me, his eyes dark. "I woke up to the sounds of two men in my house. I got up, called Collin -"

"Collin?" He practically screeches, his voice hard, anger leaking out of every syllable.

I wince. "I -"

He doesn't let me speak. "What is it about Collin that you like so much? You don't think I'd protect you? Why didn't you call Adam? You don't think we wouldn't have given up our lives for you?" He says, his voice low, his gaze on a piece of grass to the left of me.

"It's not like that -"

"Then explain!" He yells, his eyes lifting up to mine.

I pause, watching the emotions swirling around in his darkened eyes. Rage, jealousy, sadness and the most obvious of all; hurt. "Andrew, I...I wasn't thinking. Well, I was, but I thought Collin was the best choice. I figured he'd be close by and -"

"You'd trust him? God, Lena, how stupid can you be? He threatened your life more than once. He stalked you; he cornered you in front of your house. And here you are, blindly trusting him. Do you not see how dangerous this is? Do you not see what's at stake here?" Andrew says, his voice rising slowly to a yell, causing me to flinch.

I feel tears start to blur my vision as I struggle to find out the shortest way to apologize. My throat is burning and so are my lungs. I had decided to hold my breath because I was least likely to cry that way.

He turns towards me, lifting my neck so he can inspect the marks. "Someone strangled you?" He says, his voice barely above a whisper. Andrew turns away from me again, cursing. "This is my fault. I shouldn't have gotten involved with you. This was a mistake. All of this was a mistake."

My stomach drops and my hands start to shake even more than they already were. I feel the sob building up at the back of my throat but I force myself to hold it in. No, I wouldn't let myself cry here. I wouldn't let him see the affect that he was having on me. The weight of everything that had happened tonight was crashing on me and it felt like someone had filled a box with two tons of rocks and thrown it on me. I didn't know what to do with myself. I knew that Andrew was blaming himself for my being strangled and maybe it was his fault that this happened; maybe someone else had a vendetta against him and had decided to take Collin's route and go after me. Maybe. Or maybe, it was someone else. Someone else that hated me because of Andrew. I knew that Andrew, himself, had lost control in front of me and he was hating himself for that, but despite everything that I knew for sure, I also knew that it hurt, more than anything, to hear the boy that I liked; the boy that I might have loved say that everything that had happened between us was a mistake.

Even though I had been trying to hold the sob in, when I realize that I have to take a breath, the sob forces its way out of me, making a loud, ragged noise that causes Andrew to whirl around.

"Lena." He says, his eyes softening, his voice lowering into something that resembled something uncharacteristically tender. He steps towards me and pulls me to his chest again, resting his cheek against the top of my head. "Lena, don't cry. Please. I'm sorry." He rubs circles into my back while whispering sweet nothings into my hair. "Please, I'm sorry." He says continuously as I sobbed into his chest.

"I'm sorry too." I manage between ragged sobs, causing him to remove his cheek from my head. "You have nothing to be sorry about. You were just being logical and I was just being a dick. I lost my temper." He admits, almost sheepish. "I'm sorry for everything, Lena. I'm sorry for hurting you so much, for ruining your life. I'm sorry. I wish I could change everything so that you were safe. So that I'd never have this image of those marks on your neck in my mind."

I fall silent and he continues, his voice low. "I hate seeing you in pain, Lena. I lose it everytime. I'd go to Hell and back for you; I'd fight with my bare hands for you. Anything to make sure you're safe."

CHAPTER 21

I don't know how to reply to him; not sure how to reply to his tenderness, his verbal affection. Maybe it was because of the fact that Andrew was raised in a gang but he was unbelievably physically affectionate. I'd never heard his proclamations. Right there, listening to him trying to calm me down, trying to calm himself down in the process was incredibly calming.

"I'm sorry for all of this." He says after five minutes of silence. "I'm sorry for ruining your life. You were going to have a future and now you're..." He trails off, but the silence is failed with possible scenarios of how I was gonna end up because of his involvement in my life.

Dying, getting seriously injured, falling into a coma, getting shot...falling in love, becoming apart of the Wayne family, being his...dying.

I remember him saying that everything was a mistake and another sob finds its way out of my chest. I didn't want him to think that this was a mistake. I didn't want him to think that I didn't want this to have happened. I wanted more than anything, in that moment to be able to stop crying and make a coherent sentence but I found that I was struggling to even take a breath that wasn't ragged. I burrow my face into his chest and wrap my arms even tighter around him.

At this point, I'm not even sure what I'm crying about. I'm not even sure why I haven't stopped - I'm not sure why I'm still sobbing but at the same time, I do. Everything changed. I had gone from a normal student to the kind that spends her days with her boyfriend, his best friend and their gang. I went from a girl without a care in the world to the kind of girl that had to look over her shoulder every two seconds. The kind that had a self-mandated curfew because god forbid I was out too late at night and got stabbed in the back.

After I broke up with Stephen, I wanted this to end. I wanted something else. I needed a change of a pace. I wanted it; I wished for it. But I didn't think that my life would do a complete 180 like this. Any other person would've dropped everything. Any person with any bit of sanity and reason would've left Andrew by now. Would've begged their parents to move to Moscow or Russia. Somewhere far and not on this continent. What was wrong with me that made me want to stay with Andrew; what was wrong with me that made me want to stay with him forever?

I had been shot at, threatened. I had been kidnapped, I had probably grown fifty gray hairs from this. I had been strangled and people were coming from nowhere to try to kill me - and all because of a boy with the clearest blue eyes in the state.

What was it about Andrew that made him into an addiction?

Was it the way that his lip curled up on one side whenever he saw me? Was it the hugs, the kisses (even the drunken ones), the lazy way that he would sling an arm around my shoulder, the way that he walked; loping and with a predatory grace? The way that he looked when I was with someone other him? Or was it the way that he treated me so tenderly, like I could break. Part of me still believed that he was only with me because he felt bad for me. Because he felt bad that he had dragged me into his life and almost got me killed but part of me could only remember the way that his eyes lit with fire whenever he saw me, the way that they seemed like blue suns when I walked into a room and caught his eye.

The realization hits me like a ton of bricks.

Was I...Was I in love with him? I didn't want to be. That much was obvious. The idea of loving someone that didn't love me back - someone that might not even like me back was painful. I didn't want to ruin anything we had but standing there, in his arms, his hand rubbing comforting circles into my back made me want to ruin everything and blurt everything that I was thinking.

Instead, I settle for deep breaths and eventually pulling away from Andrew and wiping the tears from my face. My throat is sore; partly because of the sobbing but mostly because of the strangling that I just went through. "I -" I clear my throat and square my shoulders. "I'm sorry for worrying you." I hesitate. "And none of this was a mistake. I don't regret any of this - of us. Our friendship...even the kisses."

Andrew looks down at me, cynical. "Even when you got stabbed? Even when you were strangled literally just now? Even when being involved with me meant that Collin Maloney was stalking you for almost half a year? Even when I made you cry?" For some reason, the last part - the part where Andrew mentioned making me cry, was the part that his voice cracked on.

I froze. I wasn't sure what to say to him. What could I possibly say to a bull headed idiot like him? How could I convince him that I do, in fact, cherish every moment we had together no matter what happened? How could I convince him that I don't care without revealing that I love him?

Fuck. I love him.

Fuck.

When I lift my eyes to his face, he looks like he's built himself behind a wall in the minutes that I was silent. When I step towards him, he steps back. I try to hide my flinch but it's useless anyways. Andrew would always be able to detect any one of my emotions. I stay where I am, but look at him straight in the eyes.

"You don't have to hide away from me. You don't have to - to doubt this. Us - whatever the hell we are. I like you. It doesn't matter that it's absolutely ridiculous given the circumstances. But I do. You mean a lot to me. And I wouldn't regret any of this. I've made friends and met people I don't want to forget. You've changed me. And I'm okay with that." I pause. "You know me better than anyone. You know that I don't regret this," I take in a deep breath, close my eyes and steel myself. "but I think that you do." I'm quivering by the end of my speech. I open my eyes and level them with his. And what I find there was heartwrenching.

I take a step back and shake my head, trying to shake this off. I pull my phone and text the address of the CVS I knew was just around the corner to Collin. When I start to walk away, Andrew comes towards me but I flinch away from him. "You need time to think. I'm not hurt," I'm a liar. "don't worry about me."

"What happened to you?" I say, my voice penetrating the silence in the car.

I see Collin glance over at me quickly before focusing back on the road. "What do you mean?"

"What...happened to you? All I hear about is how you...watched your parents get killed. But I never heard it from you." When the car falls silent, I look over at Collin. His jaw is clenched andhis knuckles are white, gripping the steering wheel. Hesitantly, I put a hand on his arm and he turns to glance at me, his glance softening. He turns back to look at the road and unclenches his jaw.

Maybe it wasn't such a good idea to ask him while he was driving my car. Just when I'm about to apologize to him for prying, he says something. "I found the bodies. I doubt that I would be alive if I had been in the room at the time. Whoever killed them were...thorough. The lines were precise, the blood was wiped off of the body. Everything was clean in the room except for the mirrors and the windows. Everything had the Wayne emblem on it. I never watched them get killed. I was only a kid - I didn't know what to do. I just thought they were...tired." He says bitterly, his jaw clenching, as if hating himself for something he couldn't possibly control.

"You don't have to continue," I start, my voice soft.

"I need to." He says, swallowing hard. "I sat down in between them as they took their last breaths. And for hours, all I could do was shake them and scream. Somewhere, inside my pea-sized brain, I knew that they were dead. I wouldn't wish that realization on anyone. I wouldn't wish the pain of feeling the warmth going out of your parents' bodies on anyone. For 9 years, I was in the orphanage. They treated me like shit. See, back in the day, they had problems providing for even government facilitated homes. No one ever showed me an ounce of kindness. And I remember feeling anger building inside my body for every minute that I was forced to be there; anger at the person that had killed my parents, anger at the people that made my life end up like this. Eventually, the anger faded to sadness and when I hit 17, I was depressed. They say that I'm a maniac. They say that I'm psychopathic, a sociopath...that I'm not cut out for any of this."

I don't say anything, waiting for him to continue.

"It felt good, Lena. It felt good to chase you down and watch you. I loved it. It was a distraction. It was routine. It didn't hurt me. It gave me the attention that I needed; even if it was bad." He says, his voice low.

"So, why did you stop? Not that I regret your decision or anything. Thanks for that, by the way." I say, flashing a smile in his direction.

"I realized that it wasn't right. I never asked to be treated like that. I never did anything. And I realized that you hadn't done anything. You didn't deserve the fear that I was putting into your life. I was ruining it. And then you fed me and helped me even after all the shit that I did to you. Can you believe that? You're the first person to be nice to me after 10 years."

"I...I'm sorry that you went through all of that." I say weakly, not sure what to say after the heaviness of his story.

Collin looks at me again, his lips pressed into a thin smile. "I'm sorry too." He doesn't say anything for a little bit and the car stops, pulling into a parking lot just outside of a large penthouse. "I know I was hellbent on ruining your life before but I'm determined to protect you with my life now." I know that the unspoken reason was because he wanted to make up for everything.

"What's going on with you and Wayne, by the way?" He asks, his tone lighter.

I glance over at him quickly and slump a little in my chair. "Nothing."

He looks over at me. "And that's a problem?"

I don't want to say anything but suddenly everything is spilling out of me. "Yes. It's a problem. I like him. I like him a lot. I like him so much that I think I love him and I don't know what to do with myself. It's like everytime we can step forward, he pushes me away or forces me backwards. It's like - It's like he doesn't want me with him but he does. And I don't know what to do. Not force him. I know that. I know that I can't force him - that would ruin everything. He's so...he's so hard. I want to run but I'm tied to him. I tied myself to him. And I think I hate myself for that. He's playing games with me or he's not. I don't know what he's doing with me. He said that he likes me in the same way that I like him but he doesn't even know how I feel - he doesn't even know that when he looks at me, my stomach explodes and I want to curl up into a ball of sunshine. He said that he regrets this - us. And that hurt way more than that goon strangling me. He hurts me more than anything that's happening to me right now." I laugh bitterly. "Funny how he thinks he's protecting me when in reality, he's messing up everything I've ever built for myself. I was never like this before."

Collin whistles. "You sound like that girl from that stupid vampire movie."

I wince. "I know. And I hate it."

"...But you love it."

"I do. Thanks for listening, though. And saving me. Thanks."

He glances at me again before shrugging. "It's not a big deal. Listen, Lena. Maybe you should tell him. Wayne. How do you expect him to know if you're keeping this to yourself?"

I stay silent for a second and then turn to look at Collin, whose eyes are still on the road. "That was surprisingly wise advice for a self-confessed psycho..."

Collin's lip quirks up at the corner and he turns to me, rolling his eyes. "These psycho jokes are never gonna stop."

I shrug. "Well, not on my end. In case you don't remember, this one time you held me hostage in your car and threatened to skin me alive..."

"And if you remember that, then how are you still sitting in this car with me? Trusting me to drive you home? How do you know that I'm not going to drive us into the woods and kill you and then drive away? How can you be so trusting?" He asks, his voice low, trying to imitate the velvety danger that his tone used to be.

The car silences for a couple minutes while I scramble to think of an answer. Why did I trust him so much? What was it about Collin that I trusted so much? He was right - he had threatened to kill me; had spent the last 6 months plotting my death. Andrew was right. Maybe I was a little too trusting. A part of me, however, couldn't not trust him. I had been frightened of him just a couple months ago. A couple months ago, I couldn't even look at him - couldn't even think of him without shuddering. But now? After looking at him closely, listening to him talk about his past, all I could think was that he was just like the rest of us. Collin had somehow found a way under my skin and into my heart. I had a soft spot for him. Maybe the trust stemmed from the realization? that he was just as vulnerable as the rest of us; that he had just as many problems as the rest of us. That he wasn't just a psychopath that was hunting me down for no reason - no, he was just as human as me.

When the car slows to a stop at a red light, I turn to him and he turns to me. I lift my eyes to his and stare at him dead in the eyes. "I don't know if I'm crazy. I don't know if it's because I'm too trusting, or gullible...or if you're just a really good actor. But I know that when I look at you, I see a human. I see someone with the same wounds that I have, a person that can feel the same things that I do - a person that's hurting. I don't mean to turn this into something dramatic - but when I look at you, I find a soul that I can trust - a soul that I do trust."

Collin's eyes flash with something that leaves too quickly for me to decipher but I notice that he looks relaxed. I feel his disposition lighten and he turns back to the wheel just as the light turns green. "So. Where am I taking you?"

I knock twice on the door and Adam opens almost immediately, as if he was waiting for me to knock on the door. Collin pushes me in and I see Adam scowl at him. I elbow him and he backs down. "Lena, where's Andrew?"

Collin clears his throat awkwardly and starts edging out and towards the kitchen area.

"We needed some space. He got a little mad that I called Collin before I called him." I say, trying to avoid looking at Adam in the eye. I'm waiting to be berated but instead, Adam pulls me into a bear hug.

"I can see those marks on your neck - God, Andrew must've freaked out. No wonder he was so frantic. He almost forgot to put on his pants..." Adam says, trailing off at the end of his sentence as he pulls away from me to study the marks on my neck. "Was he angry? Actually, don't answer that. He probably was." Adam pulls me over to the couch and sits down next to me, making tsk noises.

"He got so...he got so weird tonight. It was like he wasn't even himself anymore." I say quietly, flashing back to the thoughts of him almost punching a tree, him holding me in his arms and whispering sweet nothings into my hair. I think about how unsure he was, how out of character it was for him to not know what he wanted to do next.

Adam chuckles and I look at him just in time to see him rolling his eyes. "What, did he punch a couple of trees and pace a lot? Newsflash, Lay. He's like that whenever anything happens to you."

I squirm. "He's not, though. He's normally so...so arrogant. Tonight, it was almost like he wasn't sure of himself. It was like he was jealous, almost. Almost jealous that I called Collin before I called him - which is ridiculous; why would he be jealous of Collin?"

"Wouldn't you be jealous if instead of looking for you when he needed help, he went to someone else? What if he went to Lacey instead? Or someone else? How would you feel if someone you had feelings for gave you the idea that they can't depend on you? Maybe that's how Andrew is feeling right now. He may seem like he's sure of himself, but no one is that secure; least of all Andrew."

"But -"

"But nothing. I'm not even sure if he understands just how whipped he is, but he's so whipped. You calling Collin was almost like you telling him that you couldn't depend on him when you needed help. You calling Collin instead of him probably ticked him off because he already blames himself for everything that's happened to you. He blames himself for getting you involved

and to him, calling Collin was like you agreeing with him." Adam
pauses, almost to catch his breath. "Over everything, he values
your safety. He's so whipped, Lena. He's so in love with you and
he doesn't even know."

"He's not whipped, Adam. Tonight he told me that he regrets
everything." I lower my voice. "I'm nothing like the girls that he
usually dates. I'm not good enough for him. I don't fit in with his
lifestyle. I'm not badass, or beautiful like Lacey is. I'm just...me.
What do I have going for me that other girls don't have? A part
of me just thinks that he doesn't like me at all. That he's lying, you
know? Obligatory feelings. He doesn't want to hurt my feelings, so
he just agreed that he liked me too."

Adam sighs and takes my face in his hands. "Lena. How do you
expect to see that Andrew likes you if you can't even see why
he would? How do you expect to love someone if you don't love
yourself enough?"

"Adam, if that's how love works, then I don't know. I must love
myself, because I'm pretty sure that I'm in love with Andrew."

"If you're in love with him, why can't you see why he loves
you? You're beautiful, you're smart, witty, caring...you care so much
that it doubles as a flaw. You're trusting and innocent...you're
independent. You're everything that Andrew wants in a girl. That's
why he loves you."

Collin pads into the room and sits down on the couch across
from us. "I agree with Adam. Anyone, stalker or not, can see that
you're perfect for each other. This needs to happen. You and
Andrew. You guys are a power couple, obviously. It's like your
personalities were made to work with each other - holy shit - you're
like one of those romantic comedy couples. The ones that are

friends at first and then the girl brings out a side of the guy that no one ever sees and they fall in love and get married and have babies and live happily ever after -"

"When did you have the time to fit chick flicks into your schedule? Was it in between your 9AM session of being a psycho and your 12PM lunch?" Adam says, teasingly.

Collin snorts. "Actually, I fitted it into my night schedule. I was a stalker for 2 hours and then went and watched some chick flicks. I prioritized being a psycho, obviously."

Chapter 22

He pauses and turns to me, his eyes narrowed. "You know, think contemplate this a lot. You think about whether or not you love him...a lot. It's getting annoying. Like, in the beginning, it kinda made sense. You just met him, whatever. But now, now that you know him, you should be more, "holy shit I should tell him" instead of "holy shit"...you know?"

The room settles into silence after Collin's rant, an awkward silence with me questioning what the hell just happened and Adam who now had an expression that resembled shock and amusement. His eyebrows were raised so high that they literally blended into his hairline. "I think I liked you better when you were a psychotic stalker...This love guru shit is really creeping me out. Also, I'm pretty sure that being the love guru around here is my job." Adam teases, struggling to keep the amusement out of his tone.

Collin tries to shoot Adam a withering look but it's ruined by the twitch by the corner of his mouth, signalling that he was trying to fight a smile. The room falls into another silence and I settle back into my chair, my mind wandering.

"Wait, Collin...what happened to Brett and Markus?"

He shifts uncomfortably on the couch before averting his eyes. "Do you want to hear about everything?"

"I," I start, unsure. "yeah. Yeah I want to hear about everything."

"Well, after you left, I might have dislocated Brett's shoulder and broke his nose. Markus might have fallen out of your window - but don't worry. I made sure to open it before I threw him out. And after everything, I made sure to drag both of the bodies out. I wasn't sure where to dump them so I just left them across the street." Collin says, rushing everything out in one breath.

"Uh -"

"But, but...Brett woke up while I was throwing Markus out of the window so I might have broken his leg. Or his legs. I'm not sure."

I wasn't sure which part to be more worried about; the fact that Collin didn't seem apologetic at all or the part where he probably did all of this without even hesitating. In the back of my mind I hoped that my neighbors would've woken up because of the noise and called an ambulance for Brett and Markus.

"Let me get this straight - you don't have problems maiming a person but you have problems with a little bit of blood?" Adam asked, his expression incredulous.

"Okay, no. Maiming implies that I render them useless. I don't render all of them useless, just parts of them. Maybe an arm here, a leg there...a wrist, four ribs. When I'm feeling creative I like to break their jaws." Collin says, his expression calm. "I have a problem with killing partially because that's a hell of a lot of work and I'd have to put in way too much time covering everything up afterwards - and I hate paperwork."

The room falls silent and I suck in a breath, hoping with everything that I had that Collin was just joking.

"I'm not joking." He says, a dark look crossing onto his face. "I don't take kindly to people trying to kill -" I break him off with a protest. "We don't know that they were coming to try to kill me..." Collin shoots me a dark look and continues, "- my friends. I don't think I would've thrown Markus out of your window if the two of them hadn't tried to sneak into your house and kill you last night."

I sigh and settle back onto the couch. "Okay, moving on. I think the more important question here

is if anyone found out what they wanted with me. Why did the go to the trouble of breaking into my house and trying to kidnap me?"

In the middle of my sentence, Adam had gotten up off of the couch and started pacing, a hand on his hip and his eyebrows drawn together. Collin sat back, putting his arms behind his head. I glance at the clock while Adam paces and my jaw slackens when I realize that it was nearing 5AM.

"Brett and Markus are neutral guys. I don't understand...if it wasn't Maloney trying to get you killed and it definitely wasn't us, I don't understand who could've possibly sent them to you." Adam says, stopping in the middle of the room, his eyes narrowed. He turns towards Collin, who is still relaxed and reclining comfortably on the couch.

"Brett and Markus are hired hits. I wasn't the only one in the area with a grudge against Wayne..."

"Are there other gangs in this area? Are there other people or..."

"There are but..."

"Okay, so why don't we figure out who has a problem with Andrew out of those gangs and we'll go on from there. What else could've happened? What else...happened?"

Adam's face screws up in concentration. "The only other person with a possible vendetta against Andrew is Bernie but we figured that out - there's no problem between them anymore."

Collin snorts, "Clearly you guys don't know Bernie at all."

Adam sits up, now riled up. "Bernie has been a Wayne since -"

"Since after the Maloney gang got wiped out." Collin says, an eyebrow raised. "If Bernie thinks that the Wayne gang killed his family don't you think -"

"But there's no way that he thinks that - fuck, Bernie is like family to us!" Adam says, indignant.

Collin sits forward, "This makes sense, actually. Bernie being the culprit, I mean. He did try to throw me off the scent. He did approach me and tell me that you guys didn't do it. I knew there was something suspicious about him - the way he moved that night, like he had fallen out of something, like he was hiding something. It makes sense, how he disappeared after what happened to the Maloney gang."

"But - But I let him into my house. He's always been so kind to me - he..." I said, my voice barely above a whisper. Slowly, in that moment, I had begun to connect things. It made sense; how eager Bernie was to come help. He didn't even know me like that.

"Call Andrew." Adam said, his lips pressing into a line.

"So, basically, you guys think that Bernie is trying to kill Lena." Andrew says calmly, leaning against the wall farthest from me.

When no one answers, he turns his head to glance at Adam. "Do all of you think that it's Bernie or is it really just Maloney?"

Collin sits up lazily, sighing. "It was me, obviously. I'm the only one that can be objective here."

"You're also the only psychopath around here." Adam mutters, dragging a hand down his face.

"Well, not anymore." Collin says brightly. "It's the only thing that makes sense. He was so willing to be near Lena and help her. He's been watching her since the very beginning, just like I have. There are so many holes in this plot and it starts with him. Bernie doesn't know what loyalty is - in fact, I doubt that he even understands what being apart of a family is. He abandoned us without a second thought. He's out for revenge - that much is clear when I saw him."

"For what?" Andrew asks, his voice tight.

"You know why." Adam says quietly.

I watch as realization washes over Andrew's face. He straightens up and pushes himself away from the wall, suddenly pacing around the room. "That can't be why."

"What? What happened?" I ask, panic rising in my chest as Andrew's face contorts with anger and then fear. "Adam!" I say, turning to him as his head drops into his hands.

But no one answers me. I see Collin settling back into the couch, his arms crossed on his chest.

"I fixed it!" Andrew says, his lips twisted into a grimace.

"Hardly. Killing someone's daughter and sending them a fruit basket as consolation is hardly fixing it." Collin says, his eyebrow raised.

"I...I didn't kill her!"

"And that makes it better?" Collin says angrily.

Andrew's usually guarded facial expressions finally drop away and I can see the agony on his face for a second before it was replace with unbridled rage. "It doesn't make it better. I fucked up. I -""Okay, so you fucked up. Now what? What do we do?" Collin interrupts him, clearly agitated.

"Fuck, how am I supposed to know? I'm not a magic 8 ball - fuck!" Andrew says, his voice clear with anger.

"Maybe if you weren't such a fuck up, this wouldn't have even occurred!" Collin mutters, loud enough to have Andrew whirling towards him, almost frothing at the mouth.

Adam pushes himself off at the couch, his fists clenched. "You don't know what you're talking about, Maloney. Stop throwing accusations if you don't know what you're talking about."

Collin pushes himself out of his spot, his lips pressed into a thin line. "I know that someone killed Bernie's daughter - accident or not - and never apologized. And instead, sent a fucking fruit basket and some money to keep him quiet about it. You don't understand how hard it is to lose family. You idiots cannot possibly comprehend losing someone. He was a mess and now? It's your fault that Lena's life is on the fucking line." Collin gets up in Andrew's face, almost snarling. "This is your fucking mess." He says, shoving Andrew.

But instead of losing his temper like I had expected him to, Andrew stepped back and dropped to the couch, his head in his hands. "I didn't know it was Bernie. We didn't kill her! We were just trying to help her. We were just trying to help her."

I'd never seen Andrew so resigned before, so done. I'd never seen him so...tired. I squatted in front of him, my hands on his knees. "Andrew, what happened?"

"6 years ago, this girl...she got hit by a truck or a car or something, we don't know. It was the middle of the day, when the Heights weren't so fucked up. But no one was around. It was a hit and run - they just left her there. And we - we didn't know what the fuck to do...we didn't have phones...so we left her there and ran back to call 911...and when we got back, she was already dead."

The room falls into a silence that I probably wouldn't be able to destroy - even with a wrecking ball. Collin sits himself down onto the couch, his expression one of obvious disbelief. Adam was pacing around the room, his shoulders slumped forward and his eyes on the ground, as if he couldn't look at me. I stand up, ruining the stiffness in the room with my sudden movement. "What the hell is wrong with the three of you?"

The guys all looked at me, incredulous. I turned to Andrew and Adam, whose jaws had dropped. "How could you possibly think that any of that was your fault? You were two 11 year old boys - what could you have done? You couldn't have possibly saved her life in the middle of the fucking road." I whirled on Collin, who jumped, startled at the look on my face. "And you! How could you? How could you blame this on Andrew when he didn't do anything wrong - fuck, you are such a -"

"I thought they were the ones that ran her over - the way that Bernie talked about them made it seem like they were." Collin said, never lifting his eyes away from the ground.

"You guys are all fucking idiots." I say, plopping down onto the couch, my head in my hands. After a beat of silence, I look up at them. "So, does anyone know who did kill her? More importantly, does Bernie think that Andrew and Adam killed her?"

"I think he thinks they killed her and I doubt anyone knows." Collin mutters, annoyed.

"So what the fuck do we do?" Andrew snaps, irritated.

"Let's just kill him...fuck, it would really solve all of our problems." Collin snaps back, a disgusted curl forming on his lips.

"You can't just kill everyone that pisses you off!" Adam says, exasperated. "That's not how this works!"

"Well, maybe that's why you three have so many fucking problems!" Collin mutters.

"At least we have a roof over our heads!" Andrew snaps, his fists clenched.

Andrew and Adam glare at Collin murderously and Collin stands up, his fists now clenching. "The both of you need to fuck off." He spits out, scowling.

I stand up, making a noise in the back of my throat as Collin and Andrew lunged at each other. "How is any of this supposed to help? You guys are being fucking idiots!" I shouted, just as Collin and Andrew raised their fists. "I need the both of you idiots to understand that you're here for the same reason. I'm in trouble, and you both want to help. If you're going to fight the entire time then you might as well be signing my death certificate." I say, leveling the both of them with glares. Collin drops his fists and Andrew follows him, pulling his hand away from Collin's neck. "What we need to do is find Bernie and talk to him. There's nothing else that makes any kind of sense. We need to explain -"

"There's no use trying to explain anything - if he's been holding onto this grudge for as long as Maloney says he has, then there's nothing we can say to reason with him. What we need is -"

"What? Kill him? There's nothing else we can fucking do!" Collin shouts, annoyed.

When the room falls into another tension-filled silence, I attempt to break it (again) and fail (again). My head dropped into my head and I bite back an agitated groan. When I looked up again, the guys were all glaring at each other, trying to skewer each other with their eyes. I grimace, suddenly too tired to try to scold them again. I glance at the clock and my jaw drops when I realize that we had sat in silence for over half an hour.

"Why don't we just call the fucking cops?" I spit out, regretting it almost immediately.

The boys' heads all whipped towards me, glaring. They all started speaking up at the same time, protests and furrowed eyebrows scolding me.

I cleared my throat. "Are you morons done?" When no one answers, I remark dryly, "That was probably the first and last time the three of you are ever going to agree on something."

CHAPTER 23

"That was probably also the first time that you've ever made fun of us." Adam says, his eyebrow raised.

I ignore him, instead plopping down on the couch, my head in my hands. "What we really need is for you idiots to trust each other. We won't be making any kind of progress if you guys just -"

"What, so we should do trust games? Like holding out our arms and trusting the other person to catch us if we fall?" Collin cuts in rudely, his eyes narrowed and his lip curled, annoyed.

I shrug, "If that's what it's going to take, then yeah. Trust exercises."

The three guys start protesting, each of their voices rising over the others', stupid excuses being thrown out right and left.

"Alright, Collin. Now fall back." I say, trying to coerce the tall brunette to fall back. I had been trying to persuade him to fall into Andrew's arms for almost an hour now while Adam was sitting on the couch, rolling his eyes.

"Yeah, Collin fall back." Andrew sneered.

I narrowed my eyes and shot Andrew a glare, and he smiled sheepishly at me. "Collin, fall back now." I say, abandoning my sweet act and instead pinning him with a glare. All of a sudden, Collin lets himself fall back and I shut my eyes, knowing full well that there was no way that Andrew could catch him in time and that trying to get the boys to trust each other was probably a failure.

"Why are your eyes closed?" I hear Collin's questioning voice, sounding a little winded and my eyes snap open.

"Holy shit. Holy shit." I whisper when I realize that Andrew had caught Collin - no, he had done better than simply catch Collin. It looked like when he realized that he wouldn't be able to catch him using his arms, he simply slid under Collin, using his body as a cushion for Collin's fall. "Holy shit!" I scream, a smile spreading on my face. I clap excitedly.

"How does this even count as a success?" Collin says, an eyebrow raised.

I narrow my eyes at him. "Don't you dare try to undermine this, Collin. He caught you. Maybe not the conventional kind of catch, but he cushioned your fall. Now get off of him - it's Adam's turn."

Adam glares at me through narrowed eyes but nonetheless goes to stand in front of Collin, arms crossed, frowning. "He's going to drop me - just for fun. I can tell."

"No, he won't. Right, Collin?" I assure him, turning to Collin, daring him to even try to drop Adam.

Collin shrugs. "We're never gonna know what's going to happen if Adam doesn't stop being so lame and just -" Collin's arms shoot out to catch underneath Adam's armpits and a grin spreads over my face.

"Cute. Can we move on now?" Andrew says, clearly bored.

I turned to him, trying to ignore the butterflies that erupted when my eyes landed on his face. Instead, my eyes narrow and my lips press into a thin line. "This shit isn't meant to be cute. I'm just trying to help you three idiots realize that you need to learn to trust each other if worse comes to worse. I know that it's hard trusting someone that's wreaked so much havoc -"

"Maloney." Adam coughs out. I shoot him a glare.

"and that goes both ways. Adam, you've fucked with Collin's life just as much as he has with yours. You guys have truly levelled out the playing field with you idiotic -" I take a breath. "As I was saying...you guys need each other...No, I need you guys to get over whatever it is you're holding onto and just trust each other. For me. Because my life is the one that's hanging in the balance." I remind them, my voice softening as Andrew's face hardens. I almost want to stop my speech just so I can walk over and comfort him but instead, I opt to tear my eyes away from his and instead scan the other two guys. Their faces had also gotten angry. My voice falls even softer and a sigh escapes me. "I know the three of you guys have the same goals - you guys want to help me but you know that I would never forgive myself if any of you got hurt. Please, just humor me and go along with this."

Adam and Collin look at each other and after almost a minute of just staring, Adam shrugs and moves over to clap Collin on the back. "Let's go, bro. It's probably gonna take another two hours just to convince Andrew to turn his back towards you."

Collin's scowl falls off of his face and a grin replaces it instead. I try not to smile automatically but I can feel my lips twitching in the corners as the two advance towards Andrew, who was now clenching his jaw and scowling at the two.

"No. No...no." He protests, but Collin and Adam step closer, wicked grins on both of their faces.

"Andrew, it has to happen. You have to do the trust fall with Collin." I say, trying to keep the smile out of my voice.

He turns to me, pleading. "Please, please, anything but this, please!"

One of my eyebrows raise and I grin. "Anything?"

"This is probably worse than the trust fall would've been." Adam comments, grinning. I smack the back of my head and glance at my watch.

"Alright guys, we have two hours before we have to start heading to school -"

"School?" Adam yells immaturely, causing me to lean over and smack him on the head again.

"Yes, school. Do you remember what that is? Probably not, since none of you have been there for such a long time."

"It's only been a week!" Andrew mutters crossly. My dirtiest look is sent his way and he quickly shuts his mouth and grins at me sheepishly.

"We're going to school and that's final. There's been too much drama lately and we need to balance that out somehow..." I pause and then continue, "Okay, so Andrew, you're going to put a blindfold on and Collin is gonna guide you towards the flag that I planted on the other side of the room. And before you start protesting, you said anything. This counts as anything...nope, close your mouth."

"But -"

"This is not up for discussion!" I say, trying my best to sound like an angry schoolteacher.

"Turn left!" Collin yells belatedly, just as Andrew's hip crashed into a table.

Groans escape from both Adam and I and my hand comes up and slaps me in the face. It's been a full hour since we had started this excersize and weren't getting anywhere. Collin wasn't good at being a leader, and Andrew wasn't good at taking orders - even if it's for his own good. Adam and I exchange a look and I step forward, clapping and clearing my throat obnoxiously. "If you guys don't work this out now, I'm leaving. Yes, that means that I'm going to leave. Before you ask, I'll go to Tessa's house - or even worse, I'll just go home."

Andrew glowers at me and turns blindly, trying to locate Collin.

"On your left, dumbass." Collin says, rolling his eyes.

"Hey!" I scold, causing Collin to mutter a half-hearted apology.

Andrew drags himself back to where he thinks is where he had started, crashing into tables, the couch and Collin several times. "Okay," he says, while rubbing his elbow. "okay, let's try again."

Collin roughly pulls Andrew's blindfold down, causing Andrew's lips to drop into a scowl and his fists to clench. I hold my tongue and instead shoot Collin a glare, causing him to shrug unapologetically.

"Turn left - the coffee table is on your right. Okay, now stop right there...you're now right in front of that sharp thing." Collin says, craning his neck.

"What sharp thing?" Andrew asks, irritation clear in his voice, betraying his 'relaxed' posture.

"Relax, Wayne. Now, take one step back. Just one...and turn right. Now keep walking straight, take five steps straightforward..." Collin pauses. "Wait, one more step. Now put your right foot in and take your left hand out - wait, that's not how you do the hokey-pokey. Fuck."

I roll my eyes but smile, turning to Adam, triumphant. But Adam isn't paying attention to me, instead he's staring right at Collin and Andrew, almost as if he were ready to bolt across the room and defend Andrew if a fight broke out between the two of them. I tense up, realizing that just because the two guys might trust each other, a fight would still be inevitable - after all, Collin and Andrew are two completely different people.

Despite the fact that both guys came from the same background, the same kind of loyal-gang-normal-for-them-dangerous for us kind of family, they were both completely different people but the same in weird, weird ways.

Funny, though, how despite the entirely different personalities, the guys shared a lot of things in common. They had the same favorite colors, they both like having their hair short. the both of them are, or can be, very impulsive. They had much of the same dislikes and likes and the same set of problems. The difference between the guys is how each guy would handle those problems.

"Lena!" Adam whisper-yells, nudging me with his elbow.

I snap out of my thinking moment and glance at him before focusing in on Collin and Andrew in the back of the room, surprised that in the two minutes that I had slipped off in my thoughts, the two were still standing there with fsts firmly at their sides.

It looked like making his hands into fists was merely an after-thought for Collin - something that he did only after he realized he was probably about to have to engage in a brawl. Anyone that didn't know Andrew any better would've known that he was tensed up at the moment - that he probably thought of something that he didn't want to think about and was triggered and probably not gonna talk about it later.

That's something that I had learned about andrew. He was reluctant to talk about his feelings, and even more reluctant to talk about himself. The most that I know about him is that he's just really protective, loyal and just a strong person. He cared about people way more than he let on - was smarter than he let on, kinder than most guys and generally just not as big of an asshole as everyone might think he is.

Andrew's POV:

It's not like I had anything against Maloney personally - no, in retrospect, I guess you could say that being so near to the guy that had quickly earned my girlfriend's trust and was there for her when I couldn't be was getting on my very last nerve. Alright, I know, this probably isn't a good time for me to step back and punch the lights out of Maloney for being the better man (and I'm using the word better very loosely), and I know now definitely isn't the time to assuage my bruised ego.

In reality, I didn't want much from my current situation except for Lena's safety. To be completely honest, all I really wanted was for all of my friends (I guess even Maloney) to be safe. I'd grown attached to them, and although I'd probably never say it out loud, I'd probably risk my life for all three of them.

In the back of my mind, I knew that Lena's trust excercize idea was probably a good thing. I knew that trust is a big thing when it comes to fighting. I wouldn't still be alive if I didn't trust Adam the way that I do.

But nothing can really explain how I'm feeling at the moment. My fists are balled at my sides, my lip is curled up and all I can feel is frustration and complete and utter agitation at my current dilemma. There was nothing that we could possibly do except for call the police and that would seriously only result in more trouble. I remember feeling the guilt from remembering that night from so long ago; I remember it coming back up in waves, remembering the girl's death was something that I had tried so hard to never do.

In the back of my mind, I knew that there was nothing tht neither Adam or I could've done. We were just kids, just barely starting puberty - our voices were just starting to crack and we were only just starting to grow facial hair. I could never really talk about the incident, much like I'm not exactly great at expressing my feelings. I felt like it was strange that some people could do it so well - just sit down and talk about how they're feeling, how certain things make them feel.

Sure, I could talk to myself about it. Like right now, thinking about Lena makes my palms get sweaty and my stomach flutter. It makes my lips want to curl up into a permanent smile. I want to pull her to my chest and hold her and tell her that I love her and protect her until the both of us are together in another place - but at the same time, I'm confused and angry. Not only with myself, but with her.

Could she not see the way that I was looking at her? Sure, I hadn't really brought it to the front of my thoughts until recently, but it had always been there. I'd always treated her like I loved her, always like she was the world to me. It made me angry that I couldn't be a better guy - someone that was better at showing how he felt. It made me feel like shit, quite frankly.

Fuck, everything about our current situation made me feel like shit. There was nothing I could do to help her - I couldn't put her on lock and I couldn't call for help. The other Waynes were most likely out vacationing. At that thought, my lip twitches and tries to turn into a smile at how similar Lena and I are. The four of us, actually were more similar than I had originally thought.

A soft touch on my arm sends a spark of electricity down my arm and I raise my fist, almost based entirely on reflex. Collin steps forward, his jaw clenched but an amused look in his eye and I quickly unfurl my fists, quickly realizing that Lena was standing right next to me.

"Andrew?" She says, her voice soft, her touch even softer as her hand slides to a stop at my wrist.

I turn to look at her, not saying anything, too overwhelmed by how close she was to me. I was beyond astonished by how much I missed her even though we had only been apart for a couple hours. I quickly pull my wrist out of her grip, suddenly too overwhelmed by how strong her hold was on me.

Hurt flashes in her eyes and she quickly tries to recover but her voice is a little wobbly. "I - We have school tomorrow - today. It's almost 7. I just wanted to...I'm going to go home." She says, her voice regaining its strength.

Before I can protest, she shakes her head and a small smile plays on her lips. "I've literally been surounded by testosterone for almost 5 hours now and I'm starting to reek. I have no clothes here and I doubt that I'll be in anymore trouble if I go home. It's not big deal. School starts in almost an hour and a half anyways."

I open my mouth to reply to her but she's already turning to Maloney, who pulls her into a bear hug. I clench my jaw and bite my tongue, trying to hold off from shoving him out of a window and instead decide to let them have their moment. Lena turns back to me and waves, smiling brightly. "Alright, I'll see you later. No worries. It's all good." I feel like there's a double meaning in her words, as if she's telling me not to worry about our relationship, that it's going to be all good no matter what but again, my subconscious tells me that that's only wishful thinking.

Chapter 24

"Are you going to say anything?" Lena says, agitated. "Because apparently, Willa isn't going to let us out until you say something. And I still can't get over the fact that you got locked in your own safe room."

I look at the ground, sheepish. Willa had locked us in my safe room. Of course, the minute she had met Lena, she fell in love but she could tell that there was tension between us. She got Adam to take us and shove us into the safe room, where we had just been sitting for 15 minutes in silence.

How did we get here? Let me rewind.

As soon as she's out the door, Maloney turns to me, irritated. "Listen, you jackass. I don't know what the fuck you're doing, but you're going about it the wrong way. Lena isn't the type of girl that you play hard to get with. She's clearly already wounded. I don't know what the fuck you want to do but this is not the right way to do it. If you still like that other idiot then whatever but the least you can do - actual common courtesy is to fucking tell her."

A growl starts to build its way and I almost let it erupt out of me but the door opens again. I immediately snuff the growl out, expecting it to be Lena. I knew full well that if she caught me growling at Collin, she'd be pretty pissed off and would probably subject us to another trust exercise.

"Andy!" A voice yells from the doorway.

My head swings open to the person standing at the door, my jaw dropping as I realized who was standing there. "Willa?"

Willa stands there, trying to pull the key out of the door and also trying to not look awkward as she was juggling whatever it was she had in her other hand. Her hair was up in a haphazard ponytail, messy as usual. Her eyes widen at the sight of me, probably because I looked like I was getting ready to punch Maloney in the face.

"Andy - holy - fuck, is this a bad time? I'm sorry - I realized that I forgot my hoodie here and I figured I would just stop in and get it -"

"Will, you haven't been here for almost a year. Did you just notice that your hoodie was still here?" I ask, trying to bury the smirk. I knew that Willa was really absentminded - most of the time she was focused on her computer and hacking into 'high-security' sites.

She smiles sheepishly, "Sorry. And maybe I needed to borrow your safe room for a little bit. I'm not in trouble or anything - it's just...Oliver is being really loud."

"Are you still with that -"

"Yes. And what did we say about calling Ollie names?" She asks, frowning at me.

"We agreed not to...but if the shoe fits..."

Willa rolls her eyes at me. "Oh, shut up. Ollie took a bullet for you."

"If you could even consider what he did 'taking a bullet'..."

"I do. Is the safe room in the same place?"

I roll my eyes, "Will, since when can you move safe rooms?"

She opens her mouth and starts off towards the bedrooms. Right before she's at the entrance of the safe room, she turns around. "And Andy, why is Collin Maloney standing in your living room?"

I give her the look and she steps back, hands up in surrender. "It was just a question!"

When Willa is in the safe room, I turn back to Maloney, whose jaw is dropped. "Who was that? Is she related to you? And how does she know who I am? She's gorgeous, by the way."

Adam stands up and smacks Maloney on the back of his head while rolling his eyes. "That's Willa Wayne. She's Andrew's cousin."

Maloney turns to Adam, eyebrows raised. "When you said Willa, I didn't think..."

"What, that that was the Willa? Just because she's gorgeous doesn't mean that she can't be a total genius either." I snap, agitated.

"The stereotypes normally fit..." Maloney says, trailing off. I'm not sure how to respond to that, instead opting to sit down. "So where's the safe room?" Maloney says, grinning.

"It wouldn't really be a safe room anymore if we told you where it is, would it?"

"Au contraire - it might actually be safer if I knew where it was." Maloney says, smiling devilishly. "What are we supposed to do about Lena, Wayne?"

Before I could answer, I see movement in the corner of my eye and I shoot Maloney a look, trying to warn him not to say anything about our current conversation. I didn't want Willa to know. See, the thing about Willa is that everytime she came around, it was usually to fix internet security in the penthouse. But she also loved to get in trouble. She liked fixing things and she liked to fix trouble, most of all. God knows what would happen to me if she got stuck in the crossfire in my drama with Lena. Actually, I didn't want her to meet Lena at all. Besides basking in drama, she loved to freak all of my girlfriends out - and I wasn't going to have her scaring Lena off some more.

"Andy, can I borrow your internet?" She asks sheepishly, trying to smile sweetly at me.

I blink at her. "Wait, Will...what are you really doing here? It's literally 6 in the morning. Or something. Did you and Oliver get into a fight?"

"No, Andy. It's nothing like that...it's just...lastnightI-foundthiswebsiteandIcouldn'tgetthroughthefirewalls," she takes a deep breath and continues, "andIwassoagitatedsoIstayedupand-nowOllie is mad at me..."

"So you're hiding out here?" I ask, incredulous. "Will, that's not good for your health - jeez, you need sleep!"

Willa pouts, "But Andrew!"

"Willa." I say, my eyes narrowing, my voice warning.

"Fine. I'll go to sleep. But only after you fill me in on what's happening here."

"What do you mean?" I ask cautiously.

Maloney steps forward and I know that he's eager to speak but I glare daggers at him and he steps down, surrendering.

"Well, Dad says that you've run into some trouble here. He told me not to come, so I didn't, but then I found that website...and now I'm here...and if you need help..." Willa trails off but I know what's she's insinuating.

I glare at her and she steps back, hands up again. "Also, who is this Lena chick? Last time I saw you, you were hung up on some blonde girl? Lucy?"

"Willa..."

"Okay, okay! We'll talk in the afternoon. Morning. Whenever you come home. And bring Lena with you."

"Nice to see the three of you in class today." Ms. Grie says, narrowing her eyes on Lena, Adam and I.

"We were sick." Adam says coldly.

"All three of you?" She asks, seeing right through our thinly veiled lie.

"N - no. Just Adam and Andrew...my grandmother died."

"Can I see the obituary?" Ms. Grie asks, her eyes narrowed.

"What?"

"I want to see the obituary."

"Don't you think that's a little callous?" I ask, narrowing my eyes at her.

Ms. Grie pales a little and she stutters. "I - sorry."

The period flies by. Occasionally, I catch Ms. Grie glaring at Lena and I glare right back at her. Lena makes it so that Adam sits between us and spends the entire period avoiding my stares. I just wanted her to look at me, so I could plead with her to forgive me for pushing her away. I hadn't wanted to admit it, but Maloney was right. I was being a dick.

"Are we talking to Bernie or what?" Adam speaks up out of nowhere.

"Yeah, probably. We just need time. Willa is in the penthouse right now - it's probably not such a bright idea if we go talk to him with her there?"

"Who's Willa?" Lena asks, finally looking at me.

"My cousin. She's the only one you didn't get to meet when Uncle Max had that thing."

"Why can't we talk to Bernie if Willa is here?"

"Will likes to get involved. Oliver would shoot me if she got involved." I tried to explain.

"I want to meet her." Lena says, grinning.

"No." I respond almost immediately, remembering what had happened when Will had met Lacey.

Lena looks hurt, but she covers it up quickly with a narrow of her eyes and pressing her lips into a tight line. "I'm going to your penthouse, and I'm going to meet her."

"Lay," Adam starts gently, turning on his reasoning voice.

Lena glares at him. "Adam, don't you dare try to reason with me. If she's family I want to meet her."

So, yeah. That was basically why I was stuck in a room with Lena.

"What is there to talk about? I like you, you don't believe me."

"Really? How about how you shake me off everytime I come near you? How about that brush-off yesterday? What do you want from me? I'm never just happy with you, Andrew." Lena says, frustration clear in her voice.

I'm immediately hurt.

"I'm always happy and in love or if not, I'm frustrated but still in love. You make it so hard for me! You're so gorgeous and easygoing and your hair! Your hair pisses me off! Everytime I try to be angrry with you, you do something and suddenly all is forgiven. And you can't - you don't understand." She says, her face bright red.

I gape at her. "What am I supposed to do, Lena? How am I supposed to prove to you that I like you?"

"I don't know, Andrew! A part of me wants to believe, really, I do. I really want to believe that you like me, but at the same time, it's so...unbelievable."

I stand up, frustrated. I cross the room easily and stand in front of her, frowning. I cup her face in my hands and lean in, brushing my lips against hers. I fumble for words, her wide blue eyes throwing me off completely. "Lena. I don't know how to put it into words. I like the way that your eyes narrow at me everytime I say something dumb. I love the way that your hair falls over your shoulders, the way that you hold my hand. Tight, like you think I'm gonna run. I love the way that you smile, the way that you always try to find the best in everyone. I love how you waited for me. But I hate how you let random people into your house, how you don't understand the concept of danger. I hate how you don't trust me to protect you. I hate how you don't let me worry about you. I hate how you're so reckless. I don't know what I was waiting for. I'm dumb for waiting for so long but I need you to trust me now. I do love you. This isn't a practical joke. I've never been so sure of something in my life."

Lena doesn't say anything, her lips parted into a perfect 'o'. I start to step back and let go of her but she grabs at my wrists and then pulls me in for a kiss. It's nothing like our other kisses. It's passionate, like this was the last time she was ever going to kiss me, as if this was the last time she was ever going to see me. Her lips are sweet, just like her and with each second of the kiss, I find myself falling deeper in love with her.

When we break apart, her eyes are wide and her lips are swollen.

"So, I guess you believe me now?"

CHAPTER 25

"How did you even snag a treasure like her anyways, Andy?" Willa chirps up at dinner, mischief in her eyes.

"Seriously, how?" Maloney pipes up at the other end of the table, his eyebrows furrowed.

"Well, for one, I'm not a sociopath." I mutter.

My comment doesn't escape Lena's hearing (or anyone else's, actually) and she quickly smacks me on the back of my head. I smile sheepishly at her but she isn't having it, her eyes narrowing at me, warning me to not be a dick.

Maloney smirks at the other end of the table and he shrugs. "Some ladies are into sociopaths. They like them a little brooding. What do you like, Willa?" He says, smiling at her.

Willa opens her mouth to respond but I beat her to the punch. "Willa has a boyfriend. His name is Oliver."

"Andrew, Ollie is not my boyfriend!" She says, blushing beet red.

I roll my eyes. "Really? It sure seems like it."

"I - We - It's not like that! He's just a good friend."

"What, like Lena and I were 'just good friends'?"

Willa blushes an even darker red. "He...Ollie doesn't like me like that!"

"Yeah, that's what I told myself, too." Lena chirps before stuffing a spoon of mashed potatoes in her mouth. When she finishes swallowing, she smiles at Willa. "Don't worry, Willa. You'll get the guy in the end probably."

"He's a wimp." I mutter, a scowl finding its way onto my face.

"Not unlike you, Wayne." Maloney says, grinning.

I narrow my eyes but find that there isn't any actual disdain behind the action. It's weird, but in the last two weeks that we had been forced together, Maloney and I had developed a bond and even a little bit of trust. Now I can successfully hold a conversation with him without wanting to run him over with my car.

"So, Andrew. When were you planning on telling me that someone is trying to kill your girlfriend?" Willa asks casually before lifting her fork to her mouth.

"W-What?" I ask, feeling the blood drain from my face. Alongside having a fear of driving over bridges, my second biggest fear was Willa. Not just Willa, however. I'd witnessed her finding out that someone was hiding something from her and it wasn't a pretty sight.

"Someone is trying to kill Lena and you were trying to hide it from me." Willa says, her voice eerily calm.

"I -"

"Andy, we all know what happens when someone tries to hide something from me. You know that I can help at least figure it out - because we all know that you have no idea who is actually trying to kill Lena." Willa says, her voice rising with worry.

"Will, what the hell are you saying? Bernie -"

"Bernie is like family. He wouldn't do this. You've always been like this, Andy. You always jump to conclusions when there's so much more evidence that you could've found. Bernie couldn't have done any of this - he was either with Lena or watching Lena when this stuff was happening."

Confusion rises in me, "But Anna..."

"He's over that, Andy. It's been so long and Bernie isn't the kind of person to hold a grudge." Willa says, her voice soft.

Lena's gaze burns into my back and when I don't turn to her immediately, her hand grasps mine, her thumb rubbing against mine like she was trying to comfort me. I turn to glance at her and watch as her expression turns encouraging.

"Look, I know you're worried, Andy. But jumping to conclusions and blaming innocent people isn't the way to go. Let me help you." Willa says, her eyes imploring.

Maloney clears his throat. "Actually, I was the one that blamed Bernie."

Willa turns to him, glaring poison tipped arrows at him. "Great, now I have to deal with two over protective idiots?"

"Hey, what am I? Chopped liver?" Adam asks, his mouth full.

I ignore them and sigh. "Willa, you know I'd love to let you help, but Oliver would skin me -"

"But isn't he a wimp?" Willa says, her eyes narrowed.

Truthfully, Willa's best friend was a lot of things, but not a wimp. The last time I saw him, he had punched me in the face for making Willa tear up just a little bit - and that was the last time that Will had been here. The kid really packed a punch even though he was two years younger than me. It was obvious that the kid cared about Willa a lot - probably even was beginning to develop feelings for her. The two of them were planning to move in together and despite her father's protests, they were already shopping for apartments. It would be nice to have him around purely because he would be great muscle power, but having four over protective oafs would do nothing for us - and I wouldn't let Will get in the line of fire anyways.

"Andrew, don't tell me that you're thinking that I'm going to get hurt. There's nothing that could possibly happen to me - I'll be hacking from your safe room!" She says, a slight whine seeping into her tone.

It was my turn to narrow my eyes. "Really? Because the last time I agreed to let you help me with gang business, you snuck out onto the field and almost got yourself shot!" I said, scowling at the memory.

Her expression turns sheepish and a grin spreads onto my face as a lightbulb flashes above my head. "Actually, Willa...you can help us out. On one condition."

She brightens and I can feel Maloney and Lena sending me questioning looks. In my peripheral vision, I see Adam's mouth hitch up into a smirk.

"Call Oliver. Tell him to come. At least with him in the building I'll know that you'll stay here for sure."

Willa's mouth drops in disbelief as color floods into her face. "W - What? Wait, what? Call Ollie? No, Andrew - you know that he would never let me do something like this."

A grin spreads onto my face as I shrug, letting go of Lena's hand and casually resuming my dinner. Willa makes a noise, causing me to snicker. "F - fine. Fine! I'll call him."

Adam joins in with my snickering as Willa reaches into her hoodie to pull out her phone.

"Ollie?" She asks, her voice small. Willa looks up at Adam and glares at him, causing him to stop snickering right then. "I -"

I clear my throat and mouth that she put her phone on speakerphone. She narrows her eyes but puts the phone on speaker anyways and everyone on the table winces as Oliver's rough, deep voice echoed around the room.

"Why is it that I woke up from my nap with no explanation of where you went? And don't say that you left a note because 'brb' on a sticky note doesn't count, Willa!" Oliver says, almost growling.

"I'm with Andrew!" She snaps back, defensive. "And yes it is enough. It's enough to let you know that I definitely wasn't kidnapped and that I wasn't running away or anything - not that I would ever run away. That's dumb. Where would I get internet to hack into someone's server? Plus, I'm in the middle of hacking into Medicorp's servers and that's way too fun to just abandon -"

"Willa." Oliver says, his tone warning. "Why are you with your idiot cousin?"

I glower at the phone and Lena chuckles softly beside me. "I like this guy." She says, smiling at me. I try to keep the glower on my face but fail miserably at the sight of her smile.

"I went back to get my hoodie." Will replies simply.

"And why are you still there?"

"See, that's what I'm calling you about. Andy got into some trouble. Okay, well he didn't get into trouble. His girlfriend did - well, not really. She didn't really do anything but someone wants to kill her and they don't know who and I want to help but Andrew said that I can only do it if you come over so please, please -"

"No." Oliver says and I can tell that he's scowling just like you can tell when someone is smiling over the phone.

"But Ollie!" Willa says, pleading. "Please, Ollie? I swear I won't hit you on the head with the keyboard and sneak out again. Please?"

"No, Willa. You can get into serious trouble -"

"Stop treating me like a child, Ol! I can defend myself now! You know that!" Willa stands up abruptly and glances at all of us before her gaze falls on me as if asking for my permission to leave the room.

Lena turns to me, a smaller smile playing at her lips. "That's how you are with me, you know. Protective. Annoying. Patronizing. I don't know why you don't like him, especially because you guys seem so similar."

Adam snorts from his seat. "He doesn't like Oliver because the kid punched him in the face after he said some stupid shit about Willa. It's not a deeper reason like his personality or anything, it's because Andrew feels emasculated."

"You have to be some sort of masculine to feel emasculated." Maloney quips, a smirk on his lips.

I glare at the both of them and stand up. "You guys are idiots and because of those idiots comments, you both have to clear the table."

Maloney's eyebrows shoot up and he says, petulantly, I might add, "Well, you're not the boss of me." He crosses his arms across his chest and I half-expect him to stick out his lower lip.

"Really? Last time I checked, this is my home. I can kick you out if you piss me off enough." I joke.

But Lena doesn't take it as a joke and swiftly jabs me in my side. "Andrew." She hisses, turning to me frowning. "Just for that, you're going to help them clear the table too."

"You're not the boss -" I start, the words escaping my mouth until I realized that she very much was the boss of me. My head swivels and my eyes land on her face, which is dark, as if she had a storm cloud lingering over her features. I raise both of my hands in surrender and a smile makes its way onto my face. "Oops. I'm sorry, honey. I'll go clear the table."

As she walks off, Adam starts to chortle. "Honey?" He shrieks, laughing. "This is almost as bad as the time that you got drunk and tried to propose to me!" Maloney's eyebrows raise, almost disappearing into his hairline. A smirk appears on his lips and I groan.

"Adam. I thought you said we wouldn't talk about that!"

"Jeez, Wayne. You proposed to Adam? Everyone in the Heights always thought that the two of you guys had something more on the side but I never believed them." Maloney chokes out between his laughs.

I glower at the both of them but at this point, they must be used to my dirty looks and don't even flinch. I throw a napkin at Maloney, who promptly throws it at Adam, who starts whining. "Someone's mashed potatoes just got thrown at my face! That's gross, guys."

A grin spreads onto my face while I watch Maloney and Adam, who instantly start bickering. It was weird how only a couple months ago, I had wanted to murder Maloney with my bare hands. It was weird how a couple months ago, Lena and I weren't even close to admitting that we had feelings for each other. It was weird how suddenly, someone that was supposed to be my arch-enemy was bickering with my best friend and didn't have any intention of blowing him up.

It was weird, actually, how I knew that Maloney had no intentions of blowing any of us up. Strangely enough, in the past couple of days, I'd built enough trust and respect for Maloney that I knew that he wouldn't attack us like this.

Even though the four of us had come together under circumstances that were dangerous, dark and seriously fucked up, I found myself thinking that I wouldn't want to be friends with these idiots any other way.

Which sounds really sappy, but I guess it's true.

When the table is finally cleared, the three of us settle on the couch, Adam mindlessly flipping through the channels with Collin groaning everytime he skipped over a show that he wanted to watch.

"This is fucking weird." Adam says suddenly.

"I agree." I mutter, not having to even ask him what he was talking about.

"You know what's weird? How the two of you can read each other's minds. That's weird." Maloney grumbles, staring at the two of us. "What are you guys even talking about? What's weird? Bernie not being the psycho?"

"No, we're talking about the fact that the three of us are chilling on Andrew's sofa. That's what's weird." Adam chirps without making eye contact with Maloney.

Maloney is quiet for a little bit. "What's weird is that there's someone after Lena. What has she ever done to anyone? This can't be about her."

"It's not, dumbass." I growl. "It's about us. It's a grudge match. Someone is mad at the Waynes and they're taking it out on her. Does that plan ring a bell?"

"My bad, dude. I just figured, hey, maybe they're not after Lena. Maybe they're just fucking with someone. When I was still chasing after her, I didn't hear any buzz about her. Well, besides the buzz that I was making. No one was complaining about the Waynes, anyways." He says. "No one dares to complain about you idiots. They're all too afraid. You own the land that they live on." He adds on, grumbling.

"What's dumb is that we have no idea who could possibly want to do this to her. What's dumb is that none of us even know what's going on!" I spit out, agitated.

Willa comes out of the safe room, her eyes wide. "First, Ollie is going to be here in an hour. Second, I think I know who's after Lena. Okay, kind of. Not really."

CHAPTER 26

Lena's POV:

The guys are all immediately on Willa, yelling and questioning her as if the information would disappear if they didn't yell loud enough.

"What kind of statement is that? Kind of? Not really? Choose one." Andrew mutters, eyes narrowed.

"Stop being such a grouch. I have something - it's just speculation. I was looking at security tapes and - okay, mostly just social media centering in on the area around here and I saw interesting things. These guys - I doubt you even know who they are - they've been complaining about you. Online. I don't know if they'd go to the extreme of hiring those two meatheads but...the stuff is pretty inten -"

"Who?" Adam interrupts, eyebrows furrowed.

"Adam." Willa says, glaring at him. "Some guys - uh, the Kellers?"

"The Kellers?"

The guys fall silent for almost a minute before Collin and Adam both look up at each other. "The Kellers?" Collin says, his voice low. "Matthew and Royce Keller?"

Willa's eyebrow raised. "What, you know who they are?"

"Matt Keller tried to get into the building one night." Adam says, eyebrows furrowed.

"What? I never heard about -" Andrew says, clenching his jaw.

"I told you - almost 6 months ago, some guy tried to get into our floor using the window. He didn't try, actually. He got in." Adam mutters, sitting down. "The Kellers? What could they possibly have to do with any of this? They're -"

"Fucking annoying." Collin interrupts, eyebrows furrowed. "They're persistent little shits. Tried to get into the compound for some reason - and Royce Keller is a crazy sonofabitch."

"What did they do?" I ask cautiously, the tension so palpable that I didn't even want to move.

Collin glances at me and shrugs. "I don't know, just weird stuff. Royce attacked a lot of the other guys out of nowhere. They said he was screaming about equality and how nothing was fair in the Heights for people without gangs. I didn't think anything was wrong, everyone complains. He's a pest, honestly."

"They tried to get into the building - not the penthouse, the apartment. They were trying to break in through the fire escape and they tried it two times in a row. It was weird. I never understood why, I just remember telling you and you grunting." Adam says, eyebrows furrowed.

"They're annoying, but homicidal?" Collin asks, narrowing his eyes. "I'd recognize if they were homicidal and I'm pretty sure they're not."

Willa makes a noise in the back of her throat. "Who raised you morons? Since when were we allowed to underestimate the enemies? Just because they look harmless doesn't mean they are harmless."

"I wasn't raised by anyone, actually. My parents are dead." Collin deadpans.

Willa doesn't blink and instead fixes Collin with a dirty look. "Listen. I know you have a track record for being a lunatic, but don't underestimate me. I'm little but I can throw a mean right hook."

Collin snorts. "Yeah, okay."

"I -"

"Anything else, Will?"

Willa spears Adam with a dirty look and purses her lips. "Thanks for the interruption, Ah-dumb," she sticks her tongue out childishly and turns back to her laptop. "but that's really all I found. In reality, Lena doesn't seem to have many enemies or any at all, actually. I mean you guys do but that's normally, isn't it? I could only find the Kellers and besides that, I can't find anyone that might have the money to spend on Brett and Markus or whatever those morons are called."

"It's obviously someone. Someone is mad at us - all of us. Someone is holding a major grudge against us. Enough to pay two meatheads to try to kill Lena. It just doesn't add up. We're missing something important here." Andrew mutters, sitting back on the couch. "What if..."

Adam snorts, "Don't go there."

"But it makes sense!"

Adam fixes Andrew with a dark look as Collin, Willa and I turn to stare at the pair. "What are you guys talking about?" Collin asks, frowning.

"What if it is the Kellers? But what if we're missing someone else? The Kellers are too dumb to do this on their own - they need to have someone else. They need to have a mastermind."

Everyone in the room falls silent and Adam groans. "Don't tell me you're actually considering it? That's stupid - fuck, who would put all that energy into killing one person? For what?"

"Because they hate us. We fucked up somewhere and they're taking it out on Lena." Andrew says matter-of-factly. "Think about it. If they just burned the apartment or the penthouse, we wouldn't care. We could rebuild it. They can't reach any of our family - everyone is off doing something until this summer... Lena is my girlfriend and I didn't make that a secret. She's like a little sister to you, right, Adam? And she even means something to Maloney, who everyone in the Heights wants to kill."

"I'm not sure if I'm the luckiest girl in the world or not." I mutter dryly, sitting back on the couch.

"How does having three different people trying to kill you make you lucky?" Adam says, staring at me, eyebrows furrowed.

"Well, at least all three of you are hot."

"Ah, still isn't funny. Amazing." Adam sighs, dragging a hand down his face.

Willa snorts. "Well, whatever's happening? Or whoever's happening? We have to figure it out soon. She's in serious danger."

"Way to be Captain Obvious, Will."

"I -"

There's nothing more annoying than waking up to bickering. I can hear Adam and Collin out in the living room, screaming over probably something trivial, like who's getting breakfast or who's cooking breakfast. I moan, my eyes still shut.

"Stop that." Andrew rolls over, his arm now draped lazily on my waist.

"Stop what?"

"That. You're speaking. You're making noises."

I roll over and open my eyes, a smile curving lazily onto my face when Andrew pulls me closer to him. I snuggle into his chest, my nose pressed into the soft cotton of his t-shirt. "If only everyday could be like this."

"It could be, but someone's trying to kill you to get back at me and Collin." Andrew mutters, his arms tightening around me.

I chuckle and Andrew sighs. "When are you going to stop laughing at this? You can die, Lena. This is a serious thing."

"It's weird, that's all. I laugh because just a couple months ago, almost a year ago, actually, I was just some random girl whose biggest problem was a breakup with her boyfriend. Now, I'm best friends with two hot guys and I'm dating a rich gang member. It's a 180. It's almost funny how much things have changed." I say, snuggling deeper in Andrew's arms.

"Do you miss it?"

"Miss what?"

"Miss your old life. Do you miss Stephen?

I pull away from his chest, eyebrows furrowed. "Stephen? Do I miss Stephen? Andrew, what kind of question is that?"

"I just -"

"Goooooooooooood morning, lovebirds!" Adam yells, running into the room waving a spatula. "It's breakfast time! At first, fucking Collin wanted eggs and bacon but I wanted chocolate chip pancakes so we decided to cook both and have you guys judge so get up, get up!"

I turn around, narrowing my eyes at Adam, who's suspiciously upbeat.

"Adam...you ruined a moment."

"You're still young, Lena. You have plenty of time for moments with Andrew. Now get up, we need someone to decide -" I hear a door slam. "and possibly break up a fight. I think Oliver is here, Andrew."

I smile at Andrew, whose eyes are shut, lips pressed together in frustration. I raise a hand to his cheek and peck his lips. "We can talk about this later. Come on, I wanna meet Oliver and have breakfast." I say, sliding out of beg and tugging his hand at the same time.

When we sit down at the table, Adam and Collin are staring at us expectantly. I look down and realize they'd already set the plates. "What now?" I ask, picking up a fork.

"Eat mine first." Collin demands.

"Yeah, eat his first. Save the best for last." Adam says, a mischievous glint entering his eyes.

Willa sits silently at the end of a table next to a gigantic blonde guy whose arms are crossed over his chest, frowning at everyone.

"You're Oliver, I'm assuming?" I ask, trying for a smile.

Oliver narrows his eyes at me. "Yeah, and you're the reason why Will is taking part of some hare brained scheme, I'm assuming?"

I shrug. "If you put it that way, then yeah. But it's Willa's choice to take apart of this 'hare brained scheme'. She's more than capable of making her own decisions."

"I never said she wasn't. She's easily swayed -"

"I'm not a child." Willa spits out, cutting at her pancake angrily. "Stop treating me like one. I'm going to be fine. Andrew and Adam would protect me with their lives - and they always have."

"Oh yeah? Explain that one time -"

"It was one time, and it was my fault. I didn't give them any warning, I just wandered out into the line of fire!" Willa refutes.

After a couple minutes of fighting, Andrew cut in, annoyed. "Listen. I haven't been having a good morning and I honestly don't appreciate you morons fighting at the table. Shut the fuck up and let me eat my breakfast in peace."

"So." Willa says, rocking back and forth on her heels. "I did some digging last night after you and Lena decided to go cuddling, and I found some stuff."

"Helpful stuff?"

Willa ignores his question, "These are surveillance videos of Bernie talking to those two morons outside of some convenience store off of Canal Street downtown. I used facial recognition software to find them which took a shitload of time and -" She pauses. "Okay, none of you care."

"We have to talk to him. We have to find him. We -"

"Shut up, Andrew. We're not idiots." Oliver mutters.

"Oh, yeah? And since when did this turn into a group effort with you included?" Andrew retaliates, irritation clear in his voice.

"As long as Willa is involved, I'm involved." Oliver spits out, his lip curling up into a scowl.

"I see Bernie outside." Adam interjects before Andrew can start a fight with Oliver.

"What?"

"He's outside."

Everyone gathers around Adam, who's staring at a familiar figure right outside of the penthouse.

"What do we do?" I ask, my voice barely above a whisper.

"We said we were gonna talk to him, so we're gonna talk to him." Andrew replies, resolute.Willa moves and Oliver sucks in a breath. "No, you're going into the safe room. You promised that if I came and didn't drag your ass home, you'd listen to me and stay out of trouble. Get into the safe room."

Her eyebrows furrow and she opens her mouth to argue but I see Andrew shake his head at her and she backs down. Oliver, Collin, and Adam move towards the door, I see them pulling out guns from what I thought was the umbrella holder by the door.

"Why are they..."

"It's just a precaution." Andrew says, his tone dark.

"Wait - wait, promise you won't shoot him unless he makes a move to hurt you guys first." I blurt out, grasping Andrew's hands with mine. "Please."

He pulls his hands out of my grasp and presses a kiss to my forehead before turning and jogging out of the front door.

And, being the idiot that I am, I followed them out. I walked, knowing that if I caught up with Andrew he'd be angry with me. But by the time I was out at the front entrance with the rest of them, things had already heated up.

"...motive. I just got bored one day and wanted to wreak some havoc." I hear Bernie's voice, clearly taunting.

And with a snarl, "We trusted you." Andrew replied, but under the snarl I heard anger and hurt.

"Boredom can drive a man crazy."

"She didn't do anything to you!" Adam retorts, and I can imagine his jaw clenching and unclenching.

"I lied. I did have a motive. You're morons, you're idiot Waynes. You all have it all but still, you do such stupid things. You fuck around and do nothing to save the Heights. Yeah, you killed my fucking daughter. You left her there for dead. I got over that so many years ago, don't get me wrong. You know what I'm not over? How I got left on the streets to rot, just like everyone else. You live in luxury while I live in the cold, while I -"

I hear a click but I don't dare to lean forward to see who turned their safety off first.

"While I rot in the streets of this godforsaken place. You think you're so great but all you've done is fuck up my life. I just want to hurt you." I hear another gun cocking, movements and shuffling.

My blood freezes and I can actually feel the blood drain from my face. I'm stuck, and even if I wanted to move to help, I couldn't.

"Don't do this, Bernie. Lena trusted you. She spent so much time convincing us that you had nothing to do with -"

Bang.

One shot rang through and a gasp ripped through my throat. I pressed a fist to my mouth, my back pressing even harder into the pillar behind me. I was trying to disappear into the column. I didn't know who was talking. For once, I couldn't figure out whose voice it was. I hear a ton of moving and with a burst of confidence, I turn around and look at the scene unfolding before me.

Collin was on the floor, blood starting to pool around him. His hand laid shakily over a bloody wound on his stomach and I felt my own stomach drop. Collin was the one that had tried to keep the peace? His face is ashen and I see his eyes flicker up and meet mine. I can see the pain clear on his face, an emotion I never thought I'd see - an emotion I'd never seen. Even when he was shot in the leg and turned up at my house I remember seeing him completely neutral.

I don't see anyone else; Adam, Oliver and Andrew are nowhere to be found. Bernie seems to have vanished too. I step forward, my eyes dropping back onto Collin's still body but he shakes his head just barely and I stop.

And then another shot. And another. And another and another. Bullets are flying everywhere and I can hear shouts but I can't understand what they're saying. My ears are ringing and I fling myself back behind the pillar, sliding down and pulling my knees to my chest.

I hear an anguished cry and then a body dropping and I summon up more courage and lean forward, trying to see what happened. I see Bernie on the ground, staring right at me. His eyes are cold, completely different from what I'd grown used to seeing.

I stand up, my legs shaking and run out towards Collin, not bothering to see whether or not the other guys were okay.

"L...Lay..."

"Don't talk! Stop talking!" I demand, my hands shaking as I pulled his hands away from his wound. "You're going to be okay. You're going to be okay!" I say, knowing that I sounded more like I trying to convince myself than I was trying to convince him.

A small smile forms on his lips and he lifts his less bloodied hand to hold my shaking ones still. He shakes his head and closes his eyes, the smile still on his lips. "Thank you." He manages to whisper.

I feel my stomach drop and in that moment, all I can hear is my heartbeat pounding in my ear. I can't speak, can't scream for someone to call 911. All I can feel is his blood drying on my hands and his heart slowing beneath my hands. Tears leak out of my eyes and fall onto his body as he takes his last breath. He manages to squeeze my hands one last time...and then he's gone.

A sob tears threw my body and my entire body starts to shake. My chest is heaving and the tears are falling like torrents of rain. I feel warm arms trying to pull me up and a pair of hands trying to pry my hands away from Collin's.

I turn into the familiar chest and cry even harder.

Death hadn't seemed so real until now.

Epilogue

It'd been two years since everything had happened and we'd gone back to high school, finally, and all doubled up on classes to make up for all the schooldays we had missed. I graduated with a 3.8 GPA and Adam and Andrew graduated with a 3.6 and 3.7, respectively. We were all getting ready for college in the fall. Andrew was going into business to take over the company that his uncle had and Adam was going in as undeclared.

Bernie was put on trial and sentenced to life in prison for first degree attempted murder and Collin's murder. I never saw him again.

My parents came back from wherever they were a week after and still, to this day, have almost no idea about what happened.

We waved Oliver and Willa off, and they were bickering the entire drive out of the driveway.

After the gunfight, Oliver dialed 911 and cops and ambulances came. EMTs checked my vitals and asked me all sorts of questions that, by some miracle of God I was able to answer. Andrew and Adam explained the whole situation to the cops and Bernie was carted away on a stretcher and driven to the hospital while Collin was put into a body bag and driven to the morgue.

A part of me felt so glad that this was all over but another part of me, the dominant part, only felt loss.

Everything happened so fast, changed in a blink of an eye and only in that moment, sitting with a disgusting wool blanket over my shoulders did I realize that life was fleeting.

The turn out to Collin's funeral had been bleak. It was just Andrew, Adam and I and some random person that we knew was just there for the crackers and cheese. We stood around his casket and I could feel the sadness gnawing at me but there weren't any tears left to cry.

It was weird how things could change in the blink of an eye.

I didn't think I'd be involved in something like this a couple months ago. I never would have thought I'd be friends with some-one like Collin a month ago, and here we are at his funeral, all mourning over a lost friend - a lost family member.

Andrew, Adam and I sit on the end of the bridge at the park that I had picked up a drunken Andrew and agitated Adam from. It's silent except for the waves crashing gently onto the shore and crickets in the background.

"Did you ever think it would end like this?" I ask, the question slipping out of me before I could stop it. Andrew's hand tightens around mine and I lean into him, still grateful for his support.

"No. I never thought we'd all be best friends with someone we considered a homicidal maniac. Never thought we'd shelter someone who had spent so long trying to kill you. Definitely didn't think I'd graduate high school." Adam says, laughing slightly at the end.

I snorted. "Didn't think you'd graduate either."

Adam elbows me and Andrew laughs. "Nah, I didn't think we'd end up here. Pretty sure around this time two years ago I thought I'd be married to Lacey by now. Pretty sure I thought Adam woulda left by now. No, scratch that last part. Two years ago I thought I woulda killed Adam by now. Lucky moron is still alive."

I didn't think things would turn out the way they did, in all honesty. But sometimes, sometimes things happen. I started off as a girl crying over a bad break up and now I had two best friends and I was heading to college.

9 781933 121826